Kate Fortun

My faithful friend Sterling has informed me that someone is secretly buying up large blocks of shares of Fortune stock. It seems as if the stage is being set for a hostile takeover. I'm desperately afraid that we're going to lose everything!

But at least we'll always be a family, money or not. My only wish is that each of my children and grandchildren finds love and happiness. Something my grandson Michael has finally discovered. He'd always been mistrustful of women and love. I left him the ruby ring my dearly departed husband, Ben, gave to me as a symbol of true love. And now he's given the heirloom to his new fiancée. I couldn't be more pleased.

Though I worry about the hastiness of this engagement. I do hope he knows what he's doing....

A LETTER FROM THE AUTHOR

Dear Reader,

I found the FORTUNE'S CHILDREN series intriguing because it contained many elements that interest me. I love stories about families whose members are quite different from each other, who may or may not like and trust each other all the time but will rally together when threatened by outsiders.

A series with several generations and different branches of the family interacting with each other makes for an even more interesting read. I was happy to be given the opportunity to write such a story. There are lots of books about parent/child and sister/brother relationships, but in the FORTUNE'S CHILDREN series there are also aunts and uncles and cousins. Writing about those relationships added an extra dimension for me because I've seldom written about an entire extended family. It was territory I enjoyed exploring!

This series has the feel of a soap opera, with the many characters and situations interconnecting with each other. This was great fun for me, as I am an avid "soap" fan. I started watching the lineup of fifteen-minute shows with my grandmother way back when, and have been hooked ever since. I love the concept of continuing characters, with different ones taking turns on the "front burner" while the others make appearances or are referred to. I also enjoyed fitting Michael and Julia, my characters in *Stand-in Bride,* into the ongoing story while creating a specific one just for them.

I hope you will enjoy reading the FORTUNE'S CHILDREN series as much as I enjoyed my participation in it.

Barbara Boswell

BARBARA BOSWELL
Stand-in Bride

Published by Silhouette Books
America's Publisher of Contemporary Romance

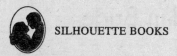 **SILHOUETTE BOOKS**

STAND-IN BRIDE

Copyright © 1996 by Harlequin Books S.A.

ISBN 0-373-38905-1

Special thanks and acknowledgment are given to Barbara Boswell
for her contribution to the Fortune's Children series.

This edition published by arrangement with Harlequin Books S.A.

® and TM are trademarks of Harlequin Books S.A., used under license.
Trademarks indicated with ® are registered in the United States Patent
and Trademark Office, the Canadian Trade Marks Office and in other
countries.

Visit Silhouette Books at www.eHarlequin.com

Printed in U.S.A.

BARBARA BOSWELL

loves writing about families. "I guess family has been a big influence on my writing," she says. "I particularly enjoy writing about how my characters' family relationships affect them."

When Barbara isn't writing and reading, she's spending time with her *own* family—her husband, three daughters and three cats, whom she concedes are the true bosses of their home! She has lived in Europe, but now makes her home in Pennsylvania. She collects miniatures and holiday ornaments, tries to avoid exercise and has somehow found the time to write over 20 category romances.

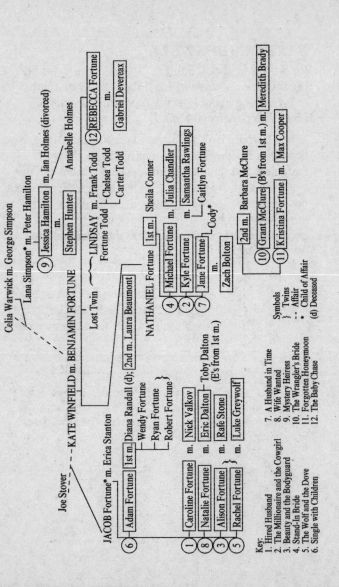

Joe Stover

Celia Warwick m. George Simpson

Lana Simpson* m. Peter Hamilton

(9) Jessica Hamilton m. Ian Holmes (divorced)
m.
Stephen Hunter

Annabelle Holmes

LINDSAY m. Frank Todd
Fortune Todd ─ Chelsea Todd
Carter Todd

(12) REBECCA Fortune
m.
Gabriel Devereax

KATE WINFIELD m. BENJAMIN FORTUNE

Lost Twin

NATHANIEL Fortune | 1st m. | Sheila Conner

(4) Michael Fortune | 1st m. | Julia Chandler
(2) Kyle Fortune m. Samantha Rawlings
(7) Jane Fortune ┐ Caitlyn Fortune
          └Cody*
      m.
Zach Bolton

2nd m. | Barbara McClure

(10) Grant McClure (B's from 1st m.) m. Meredith Brady
(11) Kristina Fortune m. Max Cooper

JACOB Fortune* m. Erica Stanton

| 1st m. | Diana Randall (d); | 2nd m. | Laura Beaumont

Wendy Fortune
Ryan Fortune ⎫ Twins
Robert Fortune ⎭

Toby Dalton
(E's from 1st m.)

Adam Fortune

(6) Adam Fortune

(1) Caroline Fortune m. Nick Valkov
(8) Natalie Fortune m. Eric Dalton
(3) Alison Fortune ⎫ m. Rafe Stone
(5) Rachel Fortune ⎭ m. Luke Greywolf

Symbols
⎫
⎭ Twins
-- Affair
* Child of Affair
(d) Deceased

Key:
1. Hired Husband
2. The Millionaire and the Cowgirl
3. Beauty and the Bodyguard
4. Stand-In Bride
5. The Wolf and the Dove
6. Single with Children
7. A Husband in Time
8. Wife Wanted
9. Mystery Heiress
10. The Wrangler's Bride
11. Forgotten Honeymoon
12. The Baby Chase

FORTUNE'S Children

Meet the Fortunes—three generations of a family with a legacy of wealth, influence and power. As they unite to face an unknown enemy, shocking family secrets are revealed...and passionate new romances are ignited.

MICHAEL FORTUNE: The Fortune Company executive doesn't want to settle down, but he needs help warding off his female admirers. So he proposes a no-strings-attached engagement to his faithful assistant....

JULIA CHANDLER: She can't believe it when her boss asks her to be his pretend fiancée! But what starts as a charade produces an unexpected Fortune heir....

MONICA MALONE: The glamorous movie star has ties to the Fortune clan that go way back. She's a woman scorned who will stop at nothing to get what she wants.

KATE FORTUNE: She has to find out who is out to sabotage her company...and destroy her family.

RACHEL "ROCKY" FORTUNE: Identical twin to beautiful Allie, Rocky is a tomboy whose adventurous spirit and inheritance from her grandmother will lead her to the wilderness of Wyoming....

LIZ JONES — CELEBRITY GOSSIP

Michael Fortune, named one of the "Ten Most Eligible Bachelors in the U.S.A." by *Fame* magazine, is engaged!

But I have my doubts about this pair. Who is Julia Chandler, anyway? She's not from any well-known society family that *I* ever heard of. She's just a plain-Jane mousy assistant who's probably a gold digger. But what I can't figure out is how she hoodwinked the savvy Michael Fortune.

My good friend Faith Carlisle from Channel 3 News interviewed the hastily engaged couple and told me that Michael was quite protective of his soon-to-be bride. She also claimed there was a strong attraction between the two.

But is this really a love match? Perhaps the conniving secretary is pregnant from an illicit after-hours encounter and is blackmailing him? Again, how could a woman like *that* ever hook the biggest catch in the U.S.?

My prediction: this marriage won't last long—if it ever really takes place.

One

It wasn't unusual for Kristina Fortune to make an impromptu visit to her half brother Michael's office, and Julia Chandler, Michael's executive assistant, greeted her with a warm smile. Julia occupied the smaller office adjoining Michael's luxurious corner suite.

"Julia, look at this!" Kristina stopped directly in front of Julia's desk and dropped a copy of *Fame* onto her desktop.

Julia glanced at the magazine cover. Bold block letters promised IN THIS ISSUE: THE TOP TEN MOST ELIGIBLE BACHELORS IN THE U.S.A.

"This is an advance copy. The issues don't officially hit the stands until tomorrow. Turn to page 15, Julia," Kristina ordered with an eager glee that immediately put Julia on guard. Kristina, a rising star in the advertising department, sometimes displayed enthusiasm for concepts and notions that caused headaches here in the product-development department.

"The predictable choices, I see," Julia remarked as she scanned the top-ten list, which began on page 15. She was somewhat relieved; predictability seldom caused departmental headaches. The bachelors included a former president's son, a millionaire talk-show host, a billionaire music-business mogul, a recently divorced United States senator, an actor who last year had been dubbed "the sexiest man alive" by the same magazine, a bestselling writer of legal thrillers, a superstar basketball player and...

"Michael Fortune!" Julia read number eight's name aloud and gasped.

"After the magazine hits the stands tomorrow, women all over the country will be lusting after my big brother. Mike will be a genuine sex object!" Kristina was exultant.

Julia felt an ominous stirring within her that kept growing stronger. She'd worked for Michael Fortune, the vice president of the Fortune Corporation's product-development department for fourteen months, plenty of time to know that he would absolutely hate his new status. It was the Fortune family business that was the abiding focus of Michael's life, not popularity with the opposite sex—though he was certainly sought after by women here in Minneapolis. After this magazine article hit the stands, Julia guessed he would be the object of a nationwide romantic pursuit.

"What do you think Mike will think of this?" Kristina asked, grinning.

Julia decided it would be prudent to keep her true opinion to herself. Who knew what part, if any, Kristina had played in this surefire fiasco? When it came to dealing with the Fortunes, Julia was always cautious. "This list isn't going to, um, thrill him," she hedged. To put it mildly! "I think he would've preferred to be named one of the top-ten most effective businessmen in the U.S.A.," she added carefully.

"Business! *Business!* That's all that Mike seems to care about!" Kristina suddenly grew agitated and began to stalk from Julia's desk to the windowless wall and then back again.

Another pacer, just like her brother Michael, Julia noted. All the Fortunes she'd met possessed a boundless, vital energy that seemed to require constant motion. She guessed their family get-togethers must be exhausting—all that high-spirited verve and drive and strong will emanating from each and every member of the clan. To a quiet, retiring person such as herself even imagining the scene was daunting.

"Mike is like Corporate RoboMan or something!" Kristina

ranted. "He's a workaholic, he has no feelings, he has no life! I swear, if you opened up his head, you'd find microchips. Nothing touches him, nobody can reach him."

She turned and pinned Julia with a laser stare. "Can you remember the last time you saw him react with even a shred of genuine human emotion?"

"Well, there was the time Anne Campell in the research lab brought her twins to Take-your-daughter-to-work Day and the kids decided to conduct their very own experiment with the latest test samples." The memory still made Julia chuckle, though she'd been careful to suppress her amusement after Michael had made it clear that he failed to see the humor in the situation. "Too bad their addition to the face powder turned skin a creepy, corpselike blue. Michael was livid about it. Doesn't that qualify as genuine human emotion?"

"But that's related to business so it doesn't count." Kristina dismissed the incident and turned her attention back to the magazine. "This is a good picture of Mike, isn't it, Julia? Even though he is my brother, I have to admit he looks really, really hot!"

Julia studied the picture of Michael in the magazine. It was a candid shot of him in well-worn blue jeans and a white cotton polo shirt bearing the Fortune company logo. The photo showed a compellingly virile man, whose muscular body would catch the eye of any female with a pulse. The strong features of his face—the well-defined jaw and square chin, the sharp blade of a nose and deep-set blue eyes arched by startlingly black brows, the hard sensual shape of his mouth—guaranteed him a second glance from any appreciative male-watchers.

And even reluctant ones. Julia was aware of her boss's masculine good looks, though she had never—nor would she ever!—let him know that she considered him an attractive man.

She well remembered her first meeting with Michael Fortune, on the day he'd hired her fourteen months ago after a brief interview. The sight of him had had a physical effect on her that she'd found unsettling. For the first several weeks of her employment, his presence had sent a rush of adrenaline surging through her. Her heart would race and her skin would feel flushed. She was acutely aware of his every gesture, his every move.

Fortunately, she had been successful in hiding her renegade responses from Michael and everyone else in the company. Friends she'd made on the job told her all about his previous assistants, who had fallen hopelessly in love with Michael Fortune and ended up either quitting or getting fired because they were unable to cope with his personal disinterest and his exacting professional demands.

Julia had no intention of joining that hapless number. She'd read countless articles on the futility of office romances and wasn't about to risk her job by indulging in a silly and hopeless infatuation with her boss.

Gradually, as the weeks wore on, her heart had stopped pounding when she saw Michael. In time, her body temperature was affected by the thermal conditions of the office rather than his presence.

She'd decided she was safely immune from his appeal. She was too sensible, too practical for such schoolgirl nonsense as having a crush on her boss, Julia assured herself.

An infatuation with Michael would've been as stupid as it was futile, for she knew he viewed her as something akin to office equipment. She was useful and efficient, like a fax machine, and more reliable than their copier, which was forever breaking down. His attitude toward her hardly fueled romantic fantasies, and Julia gratefully pronounced herself free of any.

"So how does it feel, working for one of the most eligible bachelors in the U.S.A., Julia?" Kristina demanded playfully. "You're single, and working with him day in and day out puts you on the inside track. Ever think of going after him?"

Julia laughed at that preposterous notion. She was under no illusions as to her status. Though the Julia Chandlers and the Michael Fortunes of the world might occupy the same space for a certain number of hours each day, they basically existed in parallel universes, never to converge outside the office. Julia was wise enough to accept that.

"Don't worry. Michael is safe from any advances from me."

"I wasn't worried, I—" Kristina began, but she was interrupted by the appearance of Michael Fortune himself.

He'd opened the connecting door between his office and Julia's and paused on the threshold. His blue eyes, alert and piercing, skimmed past Julia and fastened on his younger sister.

"Kristina, I thought I heard you raising your usual ruckus out here." He arched his dark brows, his voice a laconic drawl. "Let me guess—you're here to line up allies for another one of your outrageous ad campaigns? Scouting our advertising executives who, even as we speak, are reaching for their bottles of antacid, anticipating the upcoming battle?"

Kristina grinned. "I do have a fairly wild idea germinating, but I'm still working out the details. When I'm ready to present it, you'll be one of the first to know, because you agree with me that our ad execs are—"

"You were about to say cautious and conservative?" Michael interrupted.

"I was about to say retro and stodgy," Kristina countered. "How could they be anything else? They've been around since the Nixon administration. Their idea of something innovative is disco bingo."

"Spoken in the hyperbolic, back-stabbing style of a true ad executive. You fit right in that shark pool, Kristina. And I mean that in the most complimentary way." Michael's lips twitched. For him that passed as a smile.

Julia watched the byplay between the two, struck as always

by the differences between the siblings, something that went far beyond the six-year gap in their ages and their respective sexes.

Kristina was as open and outspoken as Michael was cool, closed and controlled. Though his family found him remote and enigmatic, over the past year Julia had come to regard him as an intensely private person, someone who did not feel the need to express his every thought or share his innermost feelings with one and all. An introvert herself, she thought she recognized some of the same qualities in Michael.

Not that he was quiet and shy, like she was. The notion of a shy, hesitant Michael Fortune was unfathomable. He exuded a confidence and sure sense of conviction that often bordered on arrogance.

He could be incredibly stubborn, too. Julia had seen him refuse to yield on an issue or stand, no matter how great the pressure—or who applied it. And though his gregarious family complained that he was aloof to the point of being a recluse, they'd never succeeded in converting him to their own exuberant brand of sociability.

"Actually, Julia and I were drooling over the hunks in this magazine." Laughing, Kristina grabbed the copy of *Fame* and thrust it into Michael's hands.

Before looking at the issue, Michael glanced quizzically at Julia. Color suffused her cheeks, and she quickly looked away when his eyes met hers.

Michael felt a stirring of sympathy for her. Clearly, Kristina was joking around and had incorporated poor Julia into the silliness, mortifying her.

He instantly exonerated his assistant, because he simply couldn't imagine Julia Chandler drooling over pictures of the pretty boys that Kristina would consider hunks.

Julia was always proper, circumspect and competent, qualities he especially valued because they'd been sorely lacking in the parade of assistants who had preceded her. He still held grim memories of the time before Julia had come to work for him.

He'd had to endure all those snide remarks and jokes about the ''revolving door'' on his assistant's office. There was gossip that he was impossible to work for and would never be able to keep an assistant longer than a few months. The people in the human-resources department were forever whining that his policy of changing personnel, which sometimes seemed to happen from week to week, made their record-keeping impossibly difficult.

His uncle Jake, the corporation's CEO, had actually suggested that Michael take a sensitivity-training workshop to put him in touch with the tender feelings of those hapless employees who couldn't live up to his workaholic standards.

Michael had been outraged. He didn't want an assistant who couldn't meet his demands, and he certainly didn't want to be in touch with their feelings! ''I'll sign up for that workshop when you do, Jake,'' he'd said to his uncle, whom he knew did a wicked parody of a sensitivity-training-session leader.

It had been a considerable relief when Julia Chandler— reliable, bright and efficient—arrived and put an end to the parade. That they worked so well together was still something of a wonder to him, when he paused to consider it.

Julia was quiet and unassuming, not the flashy type who sought male attention, and for that, Michael was profoundly grateful. Too many of his past assistants had imagined themselves in love with him and had dressed and acted provocatively to catch his attention, their minds focused on landing the boss instead of on their work. They'd never lasted more than a few weeks. A frazzled Michael, unable to get any productive work from them, had inevitably sent them on their way.

His eyes narrowed as he continued his thoughtful perusal of Julia Chandler. Her simple gray suit and her hairstyle were modest and professional. She had a smooth, ivory complexion that contrasted nicely with the darker color of her nut brown hair. And though Julia wasn't beautiful in the classic sense, her high cheekbones, firm little chin and large, intelligent gray eyes held an appeal all their own.

Not for him, of course, Michael was quick to assure himself. He was not interested in pursuing a relationship with the best and longest-lasting assistant he'd ever had. He wasn't interested in pursuing a relationship with any woman that extended beyond short-term safe sex with absolutely no strings attached. His work was the primary driving force in his life and he couldn't imagine anyone taking precedence over it.

"Go on, look at the magazine, Mike," Kristina ordered, jarring him from his reverie.

Michael frowned. "Why would I have any interest in looking at the well-oiled Neanderthals you've been drooling over?"

"Well-oiled Neanderthals, huh?" Kristina snickered. "Oh, I think you'll be very interested in seeing these guys, Mike. One in particular."

Julia tensed. It was like watching someone about to step in front of a speeding bus. She wanted to call out a warning, but her voice seemed to be frozen in her throat. She stood stock-still, watching as Michael cast a disdainful glance at the article.

She saw him gape in disbelief as he read the list of top-ten most eligible bachelors in the U.S.A., one of whom was him!

The magazine slipped from his fingers, and Julia knew it was a sign of how upset Michael really was. She'd never seen him drop so much as a pencil before. But the magazine hit the floor, its pages fluttering like the wings of a frantic bird.

"Who is responsible for this?"

Michael's voice was low, every syllable precise, his blue eyes like twin chips of ice. Though his expression remained impassive, Julia instantly recognized the signs of his fury. Her boss was the most controlled person she had ever met, never given to dramatic displays of temper, but she knew he was quite capable of rage.

She'd witnessed his wrath when something went awry within the Fortune Corporation, had seen his dark blue eyes turn cold with anger and had heard his sharp tone of voice, as unnerving as any blustery barrage.

Kristina, however, either didn't recognize or else chose to ignore his symptoms of anger. "It's so cool, isn't it, Mike? You'll be a household name along with—"

"I am insulted and infuriated at this atrocious invasion of privacy!" Michael's voice was low and deep. "Did you do it, Kristina? Is this another inappropriate idea of yours, one confusing advertising with publicity? Did you contact this magazine and—"

"I did not!" Kristina was offended.

"Then how did they get my name? And my picture?" demanded Michael. "Why would they put me on this stupid list unless somebody—*you*—engineered it?"

"The magazine editors picked you. I had nothing to do with it," Kristina exclaimed defensively. "It's your own fault you're one of the chosen, brother."

"I know that it's fashionable to blame the victim these days, but do you mind explaining why *I* am responsible for this—this…" Words failed him.

Julia was worried. She had never seen Michael driven to speechlessness in the entire time she'd known him.

"Just consider the facts, Mike," Kristina retorted, undaunted by her brother's fury. "You're twenty-nine years old and you're single, good-looking and rich. You're a member of a prominent family and you already hold an important position in the company. Plus, you're actually good at what you do, so you're probably going to succeed Uncle Jake as CEO sometime in the future. That makes you supereligible, and that's how you made the list."

Michael wasn't buying it. "What about that picture of me?" he demanded coldly. "Next you'll accuse me of sending it in myself."

"I don't know how they got your picture," Kristina said with a huff. "Maybe your mother sent it in, hoping that some heiress would hop a plane to Minneapolis and marry you, giving Mommie Dearest yet another crack at even more wealth. I certainly wouldn't put it past her. Your mother would do anything for money!"

Michael seemed to turn to stone, every muscle in his body tight, his eyes burning with dark fire. At six foot one, he towered over both women, and Julia shrank back, feeling suddenly, inordinately intimidated by his size and presence. Kristina, who was glowering at her brother, clearly did not.

When Michael spoke, his voice was eerily calm, his face a composed, expressionless mask. "I can't waste any more time on this nonsense—I have work to do. Julia, will you please escort my sister out of here?"

He turned and went inside his own office, closing the door behind him with careful, quiet finality.

Silence descended like a shroud for a few long moments. Finally, Kristina heaved an exasperated sigh. "Okay, so maybe I shouldn't have accused his mother. But to be perfectly honest, his mother is a greedy, vindictive witch! You've met Sheila, haven't you, Julia?"

Julia nodded reluctantly. Oh yes, she'd met Sheila, Nate Fortune's scheming, narcissistic first wife, the mother of Michael and his brother Kyle and sister Jane.

Nate, the younger brother of CEO Jake, was the lawyer in charge of contracts, patents, suits and other legal matters for the Fortune Corporation. Kristina was the product of Nate's second marriage to warm, down-to-earth Barbara, the polar opposite of Sheila.

Julia didn't care for Sheila Fortune, who had been sharp and condescending whenever she swept into the office. But being Michael's employee, Julia certainly wasn't about to join in trashing his mother.

Kristina didn't expect her to. She was perfectly content to trash her father's first wife on her own. "Truly, I don't know how my sister and brothers stood living with Sheila when they were growing up, even part of the time. My dad said Sheila deliberately got pregnant with Mike and Kyle and Jane to insure herself eternal child support, not to mention a cushy lifetime of alimony that—"

To Julia's immense relief, the telephone rang, cutting Kristina off in midtirade. While Julia answered the call, Kristina grabbed the magazine and left the office with a quick wave.

The rest of the morning was exceptionally busy, and Julia was in the midst of compiling copies of several targeted marketing surveys conducted by the company when Lynn, Margaret and Diana, assistants to other Fortune executives, arrived in her office.

"Time for lunch," Lynn announced. "We're debating between the Loon Café, where we can watch the yuppies eat while they talk on their cellular phones, or the mall. What's your pleasure?"

Julia visibly started. "I had no idea it was this late!"

"No wonder. You're buried under a ton of paperwork," Diana observed. "But even slaves have to eat, so climb out from under it and come with us."

The women made a point of lunching together at least once or twice a week, and Julia was always included. She hated to forgo their lunch date today, but these surveys were so time-consuming....

Michael chose that moment to enter her office. His expression could be interpreted as either questioning or accusing.

Julia chose to interpret it as questioning. "I was just thinking about going to lunch," she explained.

"Lunch?" Michael echoed, as if the concept were unfamiliar to him.

Julia saw her friends exchange glances. "I'll finish these surveys when I get back," she said, her decision made. She was not a slave and intended to prove it.

"Then I suppose I'll have to wait until after you get back to ask you to download these files." Michael placed a stack of diskettes on her desk. Without another word, he turned and went back into his office.

"Brr! The temperature always drops at least twenty-five degrees when he's in a room." Margaret pretended to shiver. "The man is an emotional refrigerator."

"Think of the career he could have in the frozen-food industry!" Diana said with a chuckle.

"He's sort of in a bad mood today." Julia came to Michael's defense. Having seen that eligible-bachelor list and guessing the uproar it was going to generate, she figured he was entitled to one. "He has a lot on his mind."

The four women left the office and started down the corridor toward the elevators.

"How do you tell his bad moods from his good ones?" Lynn queried. "Have you ever actually seen the man smile?"

"He is very reserved," Julia explained. "But when you get to know him well, he is really a nice guy." She was certain that was true, though she had yet to get to know him well.

"If you say so," Margaret said doubtfully. "Hey, I'm casting my vote for the mall. There's a fifty-percent-off sale at Lindstroms' starting today...."

It wasn't until later, when Julia was on her way home at the end of the day, that she had time to think about Kristina's uncensored comments on Sheila Fortune, the woman who'd married and bitterly divorced Michael's father.

Julia rode the bus to and from work because her job status did not include a parking place in the Fortune Building and the cost of all-day parking in town was prohibitive. But she didn't mind the bus rides. If she didn't have a book to read, she sat and gazed out the window, absorbed in thought. Today she did have a book—a thriller about a crime-solving coroner—but she laid it on her lap and let her mind drift to Michael Fortune.

Hearing those few basic facts about Sheila and Nate Fortune's rancorous marriage and divorce did explain Michael's uncompromising view of marriage, Julia mused.

He was adamantly against it. Julia had never heard anybody express such strong antimarriage views. And he certainly hadn't altered his perspective this past year, during which three members of his family had decided to marry.

He had distanced himself as much as possible from the events. Each time—when his cousin Caroline married Nick Valkov, when his brother Kyle married Samantha Rawlings and when Caroline's sister Allison married Rafe Stone—Michael had sent Julia to select a wedding gift.

"Buy whatever you think is appropriate. I certainly have no ideas and no interest in anything pertaining to marriage," he'd said, giving her carte blanche with his credit cards. He did not want to see or hear about what she'd bought for the happy couples.

Julia had hoped her selections were acceptable. The nice thank-you notes written to Michael by the brides had given her a warm glow. She sincerely hoped that all three couples would live the proverbial "happily ever after."

Michael did not share her optimism. Each time, before signing his name to the wedding cards she'd purchased with the gifts, he'd made a sound that was something between a sarcastic laugh and a growl.

"I guess if this is what they really want to do…" he'd said all three times, his tone disapproving. Julia had once heard someone make a similar statement in a similar tone when commenting on a family of acrobats who insisted on working without a safety net.

"Personally, I'd rather be dead than married," Michael had added all three times, while handing the cards back to her.

"Do you really believe it's better to be dead than wed?" Julia had paraphrased wryly the third time he'd expressed the sentiment.

"Better dead than wed," Michael repeated glibly. "Hmm, not bad. I think it has potential as a slogan. Maybe I'll run it by my cousin Caroline in marketing."

"Caroline would rather be wed," Julia murmured. "You bought her a pair of lovely, antique silver candlesticks and signed a wedding card for her a few months ago, remember?"

"I remember signing the card. I have no knowledge of the candlesticks, nor do I care to."

"Well, Caroline said that she loves them."

"Good. Since you're in sync with her tastes, I'll put you in charge of buying Baby Valkov its welcome-to-the-world gift when the time comes."

"I'd heard that Caroline was expecting a baby," Julia murmured.

Everyone in the company knew, because Caroline Fortune Valkov was visibly pregnant. From what Julia heard through the company grapevine, Fortune's vice president of marketing and her research-chemist husband were as blissfully happy as the card Michael had signed wished them to be.

"That seems to be the way it goes." Michael looked grim. "Get married and then have a kid, for all the wrong reasons. Of course, some people do it backward—get pregnant and then get married—but the part about the kid being conceived for all the wrong reasons still applies. Doubly so in the shot-gun-wedding cases."

Julia was nonplussed. They'd never had a discussion like this one. And while she had been uncomfortable discussing his family members, she was even more unsettled by his starkly pessimistic views regarding their future. "You don't believe your cousin and her husband are having a child be-

cause they love each other and want to create a family together?''

He'd given her an almost pitying glance, as if she'd just
confessed that, as a twenty-six-year-old, she still firmly believed in the existence of Santa Claus.

"Love has nothing to do with it, Julia. The kid could be
an accident, the result of a night of too much wine and an
overload of hormones. Or if the pregnancy was actually
planned, maybe Caroline believes a child will give Nick more
incentive to stay with her—and the Fortune Corporation, of
course. He is a valuable asset to the company, and Caroline
is too good a businesswoman not to realize it. As for Nick,
perhaps he sees a child as a way for him to stake a permanent
claim on the Fortune money."

"I think you're wrong," Julia said rather boldly. She'd
seen the couple together, and their love for each other was
obvious, even to an outsider like herself.

Michael shrugged. "Couples have been using children to
serve their own agendas from time immemorial, Julia."

"It's not always that way. Don't you think *anybody* has a
baby for the right reasons?" Julia had been unable to keep
herself from asking.

Michael had given that cynical laugh-growl and turned his
attention back to the papers on his desk, not bothering to
dignify such a naive question with an answer.

Having heard about Sheila Fortune, who according to Kristina had produced *three* children for monetary gain, Julia better understood Michael's scornful pessimism.

Understood, but did not accept. Julia believed in love and
marriage and the children who resulted from such a union.
She'd been one herself, and she intended someday to have a
loving union like the one her parents had shared. To have
children who were loved and wanted by two parents who
cherished each other.

She thought back to those wonderful days when her family

had been together—Mom and Dad, she and her younger sister, Joanna. A lump lodged in Julia's throat, and she blinked away the tears that suddenly filled her eyes.

The Chandler family's time together had been brief, making the happy memories particularly poignant and bittersweet. Her father's unexpected death from the complications of appendicitis had occurred when she was seventeen. Tragedy had struck again three years ago when a car accident claimed her mother's life and grievously injured poor Joanna.

Thinking of her younger sister rallied Julia, and she forcefully shook off the aura of gloom threatening to envelop her. Joanna was twenty years old now and in a superior rehabilitation center, working hard to overcome the effects of her devastating injuries from the crash.

Julia was filled with a quiet pride as she visualized her little sister fighting to overcome the odds stacked against her. With the help of a program tailored specifically for her recovery, consisting of grueling regimes of physical therapy, occupational therapy, speech therapy, music therapy and recreational therapy, Joanna never wasted time feeling sorry for herself.

And until Joanna was well again and able to live an independent life, Julia had put her own hopes and dreams on hold. Her job at the Fortune Corporation was all-important because her generous salary enabled her to pay Joanna's considerable expenses at the rehab center. Julia didn't protest about the long hours that workaholic Michael Fortune demanded because there was nothing and no one in her life as important as Joanna and their daily phone calls and weekend visits.

A happy marriage to a man who loved her as much as she loved him, and their much-wanted, much-loved children, had to wait. But when the time was finally right, Julia was certain she would find him. Or maybe he would find her.

Two

"Another bag of mail for the eligible bachelor!" Denny, the clerk from the mail room, sang out, heaving an industrial-size plastic sack into Julia's office. Three other sacks just like it took up most of the floor space. "There's more coming in. We had to clear this out to make room."

"Mr. Fortune will be thrilled to hear it," Julia murmured wryly.

"*Not!*" Denny chuckled, pleased with his own joke. "We heard he's furious about all this. But me and my buddies sure don't know why. If I had hundreds and hundreds of letters from hot babes craving my bod, you can believe I'd be in paradise!"

Julia glanced at the short, perspiring overweight young man, who was somewhere in his twenties and looked ten years older. There would never be hundreds of letters from hot babes craving his body. Maybe not even one.

"Mr. Fortune doesn't like the attention the magazine article has brought him," Julia explained tactfully.

For the past five days, ever since the magazine had hit the stands listing Michael Fortune as one of the top-ten most eligible bachelors in the U.S.A., she'd had versions of this same conversation with Denny whenever he arrived with another sack of mail.

Usually the mail clerk shuffled out immediately afterward, but this morning he seemed to be in a chatty mood. He lingered by her desk.

"We had to bring two more people into the mail room to

handle all this extra stuff." Denny stared at the bulging sacks with a proprietary air. "I was put in charge of them, since I've been in the department for five years. We call ourselves the 'Fortune bachelor team.'"

"Ah," said Julia. Were congratulations in order? She wasn't quite sure.

"Yep, we open every letter addressed to Mr. Fortune that don't have the special company code on it."

She nodded. To distinguish Michael's usual business correspondence from the mountain of letters inspired by the eligible-bachelor list, Julia had notified all his colleagues and associates nationally and worldwide to use a special code.

"We even open the letters marked Personal. Mr. Fortune said to *especially* open those ones." Denny leaned forward and lowered his voice to a conspiratorial whisper. "Those are usually the ones with the really good stuff in 'em."

Julia winced.

"You wouldn't believe what we've been finding, Miss Chandler!" Denny exclaimed exuberantly. "Women send Mr. Fortune panties with their phone numbers written on them! And we're not talking plain old underpants, either. These panties—"

"I hope you're donating any suitable items of clothing to charity," Julia interjected, before he could go into detail.

"Miss Chandler, no respectable charity would want them panties, I can tell you that," Denny said with alacrity. "And then there's the pictures being sent in! Wow!" His face reddened and he began to breathe heavily. "Mr. Fortune said we could have whatever is in the envelopes, so we divide up the pictures. Sometimes we trade 'em. Chuck actually bought one off of Jonesy for ten bucks! He offered me twenty for a really great one I got, but no way I'm selling!"

Julia's forced smile became even harder to maintain. She glanced at her watch, a time-honored cue of dismissal. "Uh-oh, I'm running late and have to—"

"But my favorites are the videos the women send in!" Denny did not pick up on her cue. He was not interested in being dismissed. "Picture this, Miss Chandler. Women wearing these real sexy getups or else lying naked on rugs or on beds with candles lighted and music playing while they tell Mr. Fortune how and what they're going to—"

"I really have to—to get this document to Mr. Fortune for his signature." Julia jumped to her feet, almost knocking over her desk chair. "It's extremely urgent."

"Well, tell Mr. Fortune we followed his orders. There are only letters in the bags. We took care of the other stuff for him." Smirking, Denny lumbered from the office.

The other stuff. Julia imagined Denny and his cronies slavering over their newfound panty, photo and video collections, and shuddered.

The door to Michael's office opened, and he stood on the threshold, grim faced. His dark blue eyes focused immediately on the latest sack of mail. "Oh, Lord, not more!"

"Denny wanted me to assure you that he and his crew have removed, uh, any accompanying paraphernalia, and that these sacks contain only letters."

"Only letters!" Michael echoed tightly. Exasperated, he ran his hand through his dark, thick hair, tousling it. "Do you have any idea of the content of those letters?"

"A fairly good idea," Julia admitted. She felt a totally unexpected, strange and disconcerting impulse to smooth his hair back into place, and she clasped her hands in her lap, as if to physically prevent herself from acting upon it. "From Denny. He's extremely enthusiastic about your bachelor-list mail."

Michael groaned. "This is a nightmare!"

He entered her office and began to pace. It wasn't easy, since the big mail sacks took up most of the room. Nevertheless, Michael wound restlessly among them.

"Ever since that damnable magazine hit the stands, I

haven't had a moment's peace. I'm hounded unmercifully day and night by women. I've had to get an unlisted phone number. I have to sneak out of my apartment at odd hours and go skulking in and out of the building like a criminal on the run. I don't dare go to a restaurant or a store or—or anywhere. Women come up to me and tell me the most incredibly intimate things, like their bra size or what they'll do if I—''

He broke off abruptly, a dark red flush staining his neck. Julia was both amazed and amused. Was Michael Fortune *blushing?*

"I guess it's a good thing Denny and his pals have taken custody of the pictures and videos your, er, fans have sent,'' she murmured. "According to Denny, who's become something of an expert in the field, they're way beyond an *R* rating.''

"Don't be flippant, Julia!'' Michael reprimanded sternly. "You have only to think about what has happened in the last five days to recognize what an upheaval that list has caused, not only to me personally but to the company!''

"There was definitely an upheaval when the company's entire computer system had a seizure because all the voice-mail boxes were overloaded with messages for you,'' Julia agreed.

"The whole system was down for hours on three separate days!'' Michael was beside himself. "How can we possibly conduct business under those conditions? It's a catastrophe!''

"It certainly isn't business as usual,'' Julia affirmed mildly.

Michael's eyes glowed like blue flames. "When I told Kristina that having my name on that list constituted an atrocious invasion of privacy, I had no idea how bad it would actually be. The phones and fax machines are jammed with messages from women demanding to meet me. Every radio and TV station in Minneapolis and St. Paul calls at least once a day to schedule an interview with me. The newspapers—both in and out of state—want pictures and interviews, and those syndicated TV tabloid shows have actually sent people to try to get me to consent to appear on their programs. And then there are the talk shows who want to get the ten of us from that wretched list into their studios with an entire audience comprised of single women!''

"That could get ugly," Julia said dryly. "I have visions of the ten of you being torn limb from limb by your overly enthusiastic prospective brides."

"It's not a far-fetched scene. After living through this, I can well believe that there are hundreds of women out there crazy enough to do anything to snare a man!"

"If it's any consolation, I'm sure the other nine eligible bachelors are being harassed, too."

"It isn't any consolation at all!" Michael growled. "The situation is intolerable. I can't live this way. Bad enough that *I* can hardly focus on my work with all the distractions and interruptions, but the entire company has been disrupted by this—this army of zealous women who—" Abruptly, he stopped talking, stopped walking and turned to face her. "I just don't get it, Julia. Why are they doing this?"

"The magazine said the ten eligible-bachelor picks were the 'Prince Charmings of the '90s'," Julia said thoughtfully. "I guess they tapped into all the fairy-tale magic that surrounds—"

"Fairy-tale magic!" Michael gave a derisive snort. "Prince Charming! Give me a break! What woman in her right mind wants to be a sniveling simp like Cinderella?"

"I agree the Prince Charming concept is outdated, and I've always thought Cinderella was passive to the point of being dysfunctional." Julia grinned. "But these letter writers aren't passive, they're assertive, and they probably find the prospect of being Mrs. Michael Fortune—"

"There is never going to be a Mrs. Michael Fortune," Michael promised fiercely. "But even if I did have the slightest inclination to marry, I would never choose a wife by drawing a letter out of a sack. What sane man would? So why do these women bombard us with mail?''

"Hope springs eternal, I guess.''

"There is hope and there is delusion, Julia. These letters fall firmly into the latter category.''

"Well, all those women who wrote in can't be delusional, so maybe it's, uh, ambition that is motivating them,'' Julia suggested gamely.

"I'm quite familiar with that particular *ambition*.'' Michael's lips twisted in a cynical grimace. "This entire debacle simply proves what I've always known—that women are obsessed with money and will do just about anything to get it.''

"That's a very depressing point of view, not to mention a vast over-generalization,'' Julia said, in defense of every member of the female sex who was not a money-grubbing fortune hunter. Or Fortune hunter.

"Sure.'' He laughed coldly. "Whatever, Julia.''

He leaned against the wall and folded his arms in front of his chest. "Did you hear that my mother was the one who sent in that picture of me? She admitted it and didn't even apologize for doing it. The magazine contacted her, told her about the article, and she express-mailed the photo the next day. Charged the mailing expenses to my dad, of course.''

Julia nodded. She'd heard. She also knew that Nate Fortune had refused to pay and had sent the bill back to Sheila, prompting a visit by her to company headquarters.

Julia knew all about it because Sheila and Nate Fortune had had a screaming match in the corridor of the legal department. Everybody who worked there had heard every word, and news of the scene quickly spread throughout the company.

"Kristina was also right about my mother's reason for sending my picture into the magazine.'' Michael stared broodingly at the floor. "Mother actually said she hoped that the daughter of a 'sinfully rich billionaire' would become aware of my existence and contact me.''

His piercing blue eyes met Julia's, and she shifted uneasily under his gaze. He seemed to be waiting for her to comment.

"I don't know very much about the daughters of sinfully rich billionaires." She chose her words carefully, determined to be tactful. "But I don't think choosing a husband from a magazine list is, uh, quite their style."

"As if *that* would deter Mother! She also delivered her standard lecture on the importance of acquiring one's own immense personal fortune, by whatever means possible. I've been hearing that one since I was in kindergarten." He gave Julia a hard stare. "Did your mother talk to you like that?"

"When I was in kindergarten, my mother and I talked about my dolls and the Easter Bunny and things like that. I can't remember any advice about financial planning for the future."

"What? No counsel on how to land a rich husband? No advice on ways to hold out against a prenuptial agreement or on the number of carats requisite in the diamond engagement ring to be purchased by the sucker on the hook? I thought all mothers indoctrinated their daughters about the necessity of marrying into wealth, from the time they were in the cradle."

"Did your mother have discussions like that with your sister?" Julia asked curiously.

"Of course. For all the good it did. Poor idealistic Janie! She was determined to find true love without money and only succeeded in getting abandoned by the father of her child when he learned she was pregnant. I don't know what upset our mother more—the fact that Jane slept with a man who wasn't wealthy enough to be sued for a seven-figure child-support settlement or the fact that Sheila was going to be a grandmother. She still finds it difficult to admit her grandmother status."

"But Cody is such an adorable little boy," Julia murmured. She'd seen pictures of Jane's six-year-old son.

"And my brother Kyle's little girl, Caitlyn, is an adorable

child, too. That doesn't mean Mother wants to be Cody's and Caitlyn's—or anybody's—grandmother.''

"Sheila Fortune isn't exactly my idea of a grandmother," Julia admitted quietly.

"She isn't anyone's idea of a grandmother, hers included. However, she does believe in carrying out what she calls her 'maternal duty,' and that included sending a picture of me to the magazine. Naturally, there is always an element of self-interest in Sheila's maternal actions. For example, if that list happened to net me an heiress, I'm certain Mother would arrive at my door, demanding her cut.''

Julia's lips quirked. "Sort of a finder's fee."

"Exactly." Michael actually smiled—for a split second or two. Then he sighed heavily. "I just want all of this to be over. I'm sick and tired of feeling trapped. I want my privacy back. I want my life back!''

"The magazine comes out weekly, and a new issue will be on the stands in a couple of days," Julia commented, her voice soothing. "I think you can expect the level of interest to drop then.''

"I hope you're right," Michael muttered, stepping deftly around a bulging sack. "Call maintainence and have them dispose of all these bags immediately. And instruct the mail room to stop using this office as a dumping ground. From now on, any superfluous correspondence addressed to me is to be taken directly to the garbage." He retreated into his office, slamming the door behind him.

He'd begun slamming doors three days ago. Julia sank back in her chair, oddly unsettled by the long personal conversation she'd had with her boss.

It was apparent that this bachelors-list business was really taking its toll on him. The door-slamming, the personal revelations, even the brief flashes of dark humor—all were cracks in Michael's previously impenetrable armor of control.

She thought of Denny and his cronies in the mail room,

enjoying a vicarious thrill at the overwhelming attention that Michael found repugnant. A psychologist could have a field day analyzing the situation.

Maybe someday when she was a psychologist—Julia always thought *when,* never *if*—she would write a paper entitled "One Man's Curse, Another Man's Blessing," exploring the topic in detail.

Someday. Julia allowed herself to daydream about the future for just a few moments—a future in which Joanna would be completely recovered. Though the doctors at the rehab center were cautious about Joanna's prospective ability to attend college, Julia liked to picture her sister as a future student at the University of Minnesota, right here in town at the Twin Cities campus. Julia had earned her own undergraduate degree in psychology there and...had completed one year of graduate school, the first steps toward her goal of becoming a clinical psychologist and working with troubled children and adolescents. A goal Julia intended to achieve. Someday.

But she never lingered very long in the fantasy world of the future. She'd learned that it was far safer to live in the present than to dream of tomorrow. As a survivor of sudden devastating losses, she was well aware that everything could change in an instant, painfully and irrevocably altering one's life in the most profound and unimaginable ways.

Her thoughts swung back to the past, and she silently thanked her mother for insisting that she take some courses at the local business school during her summer breaks from college. It had been hard at the time, working a forty-hour week to earn her next year's tuition money while taking business courses. But it had been Julia's office skills, not her degree in psychology, that had enabled her to land well-paying jobs, first at the Olson, Anderson & Lake Consulting Firm and now here at the Fortune Corporation.

The telephone rang, and Julia quickly answered it. Somehow an enterprising reporter had managed to slip through the receptionist's call-screening and reach the desk of Michael Fortune's executive assistant. She asked some intrusive and highly intimate questions about Michael's sex life and responded to Julia's terse "no comment" with snickers and not-so-sly innuendos.

Julia's cheeks turned a ruby shade of red. "I repeat, no comment!" she said sternly and slammed down the phone. The action was oddly satisfying. No wonder Michael had taken to slamming doors.

Julia shared an apartment with three other young women— Jen, Debby and Kia, all students at the West Bank segment of the University of Minnesota, just west of the Mississippi River.

Kia, a graduate student in social work, shared a room with Julia; they'd lived together for the past two years. Jen and Debby, both drama majors in their senior year, had moved into the apartment in August and occupied the other bedroom. All four used the common areas—kitchen and living room.

Lamentably, there was only one bathroom. During her rare flights of fancy, Julia visualized having a bathroom that was hers alone. It seemed like the ultimate luxury.

The apartment was no worse and a lot better than many of the rental units available to upper-level students who didn't live in university-owned dorms. The building wasn't too old and the rent wasn't too high. Split four ways, it was downright cheap for Julia, which was exactly what she wanted.

And needed. Almost all of her salary went to pay Joanna's expenses at the rehabilitation center. Though Medicaid had paid for Joanna's eleven-month hospitalization, coverage stopped when she was discharged from the hospital.

Had Joanna gone to a nursing home, the government would have picked up the tab, but Julia didn't consider it, not even for a moment. She'd spent the long months after her sister's accident researching facilities, and the rehabilitation hospital on the outskirts of town was superior in every way. There Joanna could receive the intensive specialized therapy she required to eventually lead an independent, productive life.

The alternative—the nursing home—provided custodial care only. Julia viewed placing Joanna there as giving up hope, of resigning her little sister to a life of institutional dependency.

So Julia had sold the Chandler family's house, used the money to fund Joanna at the rehab center and had moved back into cheaper living quarters in the university section of the city.

Though she was only twenty-six, sometimes she felt decades older than her student neighbors. "Greek Week," when the fraternities and sororities took over the neighborhood, had certainly lost its charm for her, especially when drunken serenades and contests went on till dawn and she had to get up for work by six.

But both the apartment and the neighborhood were quiet when Julia arrived home a few minutes before eight-thirty. She didn't know where her roommates were. The four seldom socialized together, although Julia and Kia occasionally ran or biked together in the evenings or on weekends when their schedules coincided. There were a number of suitable trails and paths around the many lakes and criss-crossing parks throughout the city.

Julia gazed longingly out the window into the darkness, wishing Kia were around now. Julia could use a brisk run to work off the frustrations of the long day.

For a few minutes, she stood by the window and debated whether or not to go out alone. The weather was warm for early October, perfect for an evening run, but the darkness concerned her. What woman anywhere wasn't aware of the dangers of being out alone at night?

But tonight she felt confined and resented the restrictions. Tonight she wanted to be free of both risks and precautions.

Two years ago she'd taken a self-defense class at the Y, and the neighborhood was considered safe, she rationalized. There were people around at all hours, especially since she lived so near the theater district, home of an incredible number of productions staged by the university drama department.

Julia vaguely recalled Jen and Debby mentioning a play they were both working in, Jen as an actress and Debby as a "techie" behind the scenes. A light satire, they'd said, and it sounded entertaining. Julia made a mental note to ask them about the dates and times of the show.

She would go see it, if she ever got out of the office in time to make the first act. The way things were going now, she had her doubts. Just thinking about the long and dreadful day at work stressed her all over again.

The events played through her mind like a tape in a VCR. She only wished she could fast-forward certain nerve-jangling scenes. Like when the voice-mail system had crashed *again* due to an overload of lovelorn messages to Michael Fortune. The mishap had been followed by an angry visit from Jake Fortune himself.

Unfortunately, Michael had been in a meeting and unavailable, so Julia had been the hapless recipient of Jake's fury. In a steely, formidable tone, Fortune's boss-of-bosses had ordered her to pass along his vituperative message to Michael, even making her repeat it back to him word for word, to prove she'd gotten it right!

Her palms had been sweating after that encounter. It was bad enough to get chewed out by the CEO of the entire corporation, but to be expected to spread the vitriol to her boss was ulcer inducing. Julia had *not* delivered Jake's message to Michael, and she'd spent the rest of the day worrying that her crime of omission would be detected by Jake Fortune. To her great relief, he hadn't checked back to find out if she had or hadn't followed his orders.

The day hadn't improved as morning dragged into afternoon. The voice-mail system took longer than usual to fix, and by the time it was running smoothly, and an exasperated group of buyers from department stores around the country were able to contact the Fortune Corporation about new orders, everybody's tempers were frayed.

Next came word that a vital shipment of ingredients from overseas had been delayed at the docks in New York, which meant an even longer wait on the production line. That meant dealing with frustrated supervisors in production who were not pleased with the ensuing delays, as well as relaying the bad news to stores that would not be receiving their Fortune products when expected.

Julia had placed the calls for Michael and received a number of tongue-lashings in true shoot-the-messenger fashion. She could only imagine the wrath they would have expended on Michael.

Finally, Kristina had arrived to complain about her latest fight with the head honchos in advertising, whom she claimed lacked vision and guts and were hopeless prudes in the bargain. Julia had ushered her into Michael's office and hadn't been privy to Kristina's latest campaign to "definitively capture the youth market," but from the raised voices radiating from Michael's office and Kristina's stormy exit, she'd guessed the meeting had not gone well.

Neither had the flurry of calls Julia then had to place to the advertising department. Cast in the hapless-messenger role once again, she had been snarled and snapped at by world-class snappers and snarlers.

And, of course, she could say nothing back to any of them. That wasn't in her job description. She had to grit her teeth and swallow any retort, however appropriate. Her jaws ached from all that gritting.

Julia decided she definitely was going to run. She was wired and edgy, filled with tension that needed to be discharged. In the mood she was in, God help any potential attacker if he dared to attack *her!*

Shedding her prim office wear, she pulled on a pair of bright gold running shorts and a purple-and-gold University of Minnesota T-shirt, laced up her running shoes and stepped out into the balmy October night. A slight breeze rustled through the branches of the trees. She ran along the sidewalk, moving to the street whenever she encountered pedestrians. Fallen leaves, the first of many more to come, crackled under her feet. Their brilliant red, orange and yellow hues were already beginning to fade as they lay drying on the ground.

She had run a full mile before the tensions of the day began to slowly drain from her. She turned onto a well-lit path that followed the river and glanced at the dark, swiftly-flowing waters.

Julia found herself wondering if Michael was unwinding right now and if so, where and how. She knew he sometimes used the gym in the downtown City Club, and he'd been known to enjoy beating his brother Kyle at racquetball.

But Kyle wasn't living in Minneapolis anymore, he was at his ranch in Wyoming with his wife and daughter, so there would be no more friendly games on the racquetball court to help alleviate Michael's stress. And the City Club gym closed at eight o'clock.

Of course, there were other ways to alleviate tension, other kinds of physical activity that didn't involve leaving the bedroom. Julia felt heat suffuse her skin and knew it wasn't completely due to the exertion of running.

She didn't want to think of Michael and sex, but it was hard not to, considering the fact that hundreds of women had been innundating him with offers of sex all week long.

And he had spurned them all.

It wasn't that he was bent on leading a life of celibacy. Julia knew very well that her boss had women companions from time to time. She ought to know; she was the one who made the dinner and theater reservations in the city and the travel arrangements when the couple took the occasional get-away weekend. She was the one who ordered the flowers to be sent—always roses; Michael was not cheap when it came to florist bills. She was also the one who either put through or refused to put through calls from his lady friend of the moment, depending on the instructions of Michael Fortune himself.

During her tenure as his faithful assistant, Julia had learned quite a bit about the ABC's of courtship, Michael Fortune style:

A. Michael favored what he called "serial monogamy." He dated only one woman at a time and expected his chosen candidate to limit herself strictly to him during that period.

B. None of his relationships seemed to last very long. Julia attributed that to his strong antimarriage bias. An involvement with no chance of becoming permanent, or even serious, was doomed to be self-limiting and short-term.

C. Once Michael decided to end the relationship, it was truly over, no matter how his current partner might feel about the matter. If the woman happened to be the one to call it quits, he accepted her decision without ever trying to change her mind. He just didn't care enough to bother.

Once, one of his exes, bitter over "being dumped just before I was going to dump him," had given Julia an earful. "Michael Fortune has to be the one in control," the woman had griped, while Julia maintained a discreet silence. "He demands that the power he holds as an executive in his office be extended to his personal life, and that makes him a lousy candidate for a romance. I'm sure it's better to work for him than to be in love with him.''

Julia wholeheartedly agreed. Michael was a considerate, even thoughtful boss, but as a lover... She didn't pursue that line of thought, steering clear of the dangers of an impossible romantic fantasy.

All those eager women in hot pursuit of Michael should've done the same, but they couldn't have known that being placed on the magazine's ''most eligible'' list would render him totally *in*eligible to them. Michael would never consent to being sought after. He had to be the one in charge of a relationship, which meant beginning it himself. He was the proud hunter, not the hunted.

As she ran, Julia passed a number of other joggers and several strolling couples as well. A great many people had opted for outdoor exercise tonight. When she saw a tall, very familiar masculine form running along the path toward her, she blinked in astonishment.

It couldn't be! Her imagination was playing tricks on her.

She'd spent so many hours working with him and so many of her off-duty hours thinking about him that now she was conjuring up images of Michael Fortune.

Except that the dark-haired man in the blue running shorts and white T-shirt who was approaching her was no figment of her imagination.

It was Michael Fortune himself, and he looked as startled to see Julia as she was to see him.

Three

"Julia?" Michael stared at her as they met on the path.

He could hardly believe his eyes. This young woman, whose face was glowing with perspiration and whose clothes were damp with sweat, seemed the antithesis of the always impeccable, unruffled Julia Chandler whom he worked with day in and day out.

He had never seen the office Julia with a hair out of place, but right now strands of her brown hair were escaping from the confines of her usually tight French braid. She quickly, self-consciously, brushed them back with her hand.

His eyes followed her gesture, and he was suddenly struck by the sight of her small, perfectly shaped ears. Earrings in the shape of small golden balls pierced the dainty flesh of her earlobes.

Michael stared, more than a little disconcerted by his inability to tear his eyes away from her. After all, it wasn't as if he'd never seen her ears before. Julia wore her hair in that braided style almost every day. But he had never noticed the pink, shell-shaped perfection of her ears. And if asked, he wouldn't have known whether or not her lobes were pierced or if she ever wore earrings.

Nor did he have any prior recollection of how slender and graceful the curve of her neck was. Now, suddenly, he couldn't stop looking at it.

Julia touched the side of her neck in a decidedly nervous gesture.

Michael frowned. Her anxiety was understandable; he was

staring at her with the avidity of a hungry vampire! What on earth was the matter with him tonight?

He decided to blame that cursed list. Lately he blamed *everything* on the stresses of being hounded by all those avaricious Mrs. Mike Fortune wanna-bes.

"Hello, Michael." Julia smiled uncertainly. Her pulse rate, accelerated by her running, continued to beat just as rapidly though she was standing still.

She recognized the encounter as a singularly odd and awkward one. Until now, she and her boss had never seen each other anywhere but their workplace. The protocol there was familiar and well-defined, but it didn't seem to apply out here on the moonlit trail.

Their apparel tonight was stunningly different from their office clothes, too. In the fourteen months they'd worked together, she had never seen Michael in such decidedly *brief* attire.

The short sleeves of his T-shirt emphasized bare muscled arms that had always been concealed by his crisply starched shirts and custom-tailored suit jackets. Her eyes darted to a pair of hard, muscular thighs that had never been revealed beneath the trousers of his conservative suits.

Julia quickly averted her gaze. Her mouth felt dry. She wished she had brought along her portable water bottle, but until this very moment, she hadn't given a thought to being thirsty.

"You're out here running?" Michael said at last, as the silence stretched uncomfortably between them. He instantly mocked himself for his inanely obvious observation. No, she wasn't out here *running*, on the *running* trail in *running* clothes, sweating from the exertion of *running*. She was waiting for a bus!

He felt like a fool, and it was not a pleasant sensation for a man who seldom made a mistake in any area. He wouldn't blame Julia if she zinged him with a caustic response. Kristina

would undoubtedly look at him, roll her eyes and say,
"Duh!"

Being Julia, his diplomatic assistant, she merely smiled that
pleasant, detached smile of hers and replied politely, "Yes.
After today, I felt like I really needed the exercise to un-
wind."

"Believe me, I know exactly how you feel!" Michael said,
his relief heartfelt. The ice was broken. Julia's remark had
placed them back in their familiar Fortune Corporation roles.

By tacit agreement, they resumed their run, side by side
and at a more leisurely pace. They discussed the horrors of
the day, even managed a bit of gallows humor about the mis-
fortunes at Fortune.

Julia actually found herself confessing that Jake Fortune
had visited her office to vent his frustration about the voice-
mail mess, though she refrained from repeating his irate message or even mentioning the fury he'd expressed toward his
nephew and toward herself.

But Michael guessed. "Poor Julia. You got caught in the
blitzkrieg meant for me, didn't you? I hope you didn't take it
personally."

"Oh no," Julia assured him. "I would never take being
called an idiotic sycophant personally."

"He called you that?" Michael felt anger flare through him.
"No matter how angry Jake was at me, there was no reason
for him to verbally abuse you."

"He was upset. I understood," Julia said quickly.

She was on shaky ground here, discussing the CEO with
her boss! The last place she wanted to be was in the crossfire
of a Fortune-to-Fortune battle. She never should've mentioned
Jake Fortune at all, but running with Michael under the rel-
ative cover of darkness had provided the illusion of confiden-
tiality and companionability. Somehow the words had slipped
out, as if she were talking to a friend from work instead of
Michael Fortune, her employer.

She strove to rectify the situation. "In fact, until now, I'd forgotten all about that conversation with Mr. Fortune."

"Now why don't I believe you?" Michael arched his dark brows. "I know from experience that my uncle's verbal jabs have a way of searing your brain like a brand, at least for a while. And if Jake called *you* an idiotic sycophant simply because you work for me, I can imagine the choice words he had to say about me. Are you going to tell me?"

She shook her head. "You don't want to hear."

"You're right, I don't." Michael stared ahead at the starry expanse of the sky. "I'm not condoning his actions, but Uncle Jake has been under a tremendous amount of pressure since my grandmother's death. Not only does he have to deal with losing his mother, but as you know, the reorganization at the company has caused stock values to fall. Jake feels responsible, and unfortunately, my father is more than willing to let him shoulder the blame alone."

Julia nodded her understanding. Everybody who worked for the company knew that Nate Fortune was fiercely competitive with his older brother, Jake, and that the brothers' relationship had long been strained as a result. Sadly, their mother's death had driven them further apart, rather than bringing them closer in mourning.

The sudden death of Kate Fortune, the seventy-one-year-old matriarch, had impacted sharply on everybody connected to either the Fortune family or the company. In the public arena, Kate's unexpected death and the subsequent reorganization of the company had caused stock prices to tip alarmingly, and privately, the Fortunes were devastated by their loss.

Julia had learned some of the details from newspapers, some from employee gossip and a few from the various Fortunes who passed through her office on their way to Michael's.

She knew that Kate had been flying one of the family

planes solo in Brazil when it crashed and burned in the rain forest. The charred remains of the wreckage had yielded one body, naturally presumed to be the pilot, Kate Fortune.

As someone intimately acquainted with the stunning grief resulting from sudden death, Julia understood exactly how the members of the Fortune family must've felt upon hearing that terrible news. How they still must be feeling as they struggled to reconcile themselves to life without Kate.

"I had the pleasure of meeting your grandmother several times when she came to your office," Julia said quietly. "She was a delightful person, so warm and witty and dynamic. And what a memory she had! I think she knew the names of everybody who worked for the company, and she always had time to say something nice to us."

"That was my grandmother, all right." Michael smiled in reminiscence. "I, uh, I got the card you sent right after she…was lost. I appreciated the note you wrote, but I don't think I ever thanked you for it."

"I didn't expect you to, I just wanted to tell you how much I admired her," Julia murmured. "You must miss her terribly."

"I don't let myself dwell on it," Michael said curtly, uncomfortable at the turn their conversation had taken. "Keeping busy is the best antidote for…" He cleared his throat and shrugged. "For…" He couldn't bring himself to say the word.

"Grief." Julia supplied it for him. Her heart swelled with sympathy. "Yes, work does help."

She wasn't about to add that talking about the lost loved one helped even more. Obviously, Michael's style of mourning forbade such an open display of emotion. "I guess working has helped everybody in your family cope," she added softly.

"That's true. But unfortunately for my uncle Jake, he is

currently facing another crisis that has nothing to do with losing Grandmother.''

Though Michael was rarely this forthcoming, it was a relief to talk about things that had been roiling in his mind for weeks. He felt secure in confiding in Julia. She had a proven track record of loyalty to the company and to the Fortunes.

''I've heard from my cousins that Jake's marriage to Erica is on shaky ground. Their girls, Caroline and Natalie and the twins, are worried sick about their parents. Apparently, Jake's schedule and his demands are finally taking their toll on Erica, and to make matters worse, she is suffering from a major case of the empty-nest syndrome.''

''Many women have a difficult time adjusting when their children grow up and leave home,'' Julia said sympathetically.

''Not my mother. She was only too happy to have *her* nest all to herself. But Erica is feeling her years without them. Plus she's spouting all this midlife-crisis stuff about not fulfilling her career ambitions, blaming Uncle Jake for her decision to drop out of college to marry him and stay home to raise children. Like he put a loaded gun to her head and made her do it!'' Michael's disparaging laugh made it very clear whose side he was on in this particular Fortune war.

''Has your aunt Erica ever considered going back to college?'' Julia's psychologist leanings made it impossible for her not to offer help. ''Lots of people return to complete their education these days. I've read about grandparents in their seventies going for their degrees.''

''Maybe you should give Erica this pep talk,'' Michael suggested drolly. ''She's fifty-two, old and fading by her standards, but still full of zest by yours.''

Julia visualized Erica Fortune, who'd always struck her as the quintessential expensively kept, country-club-executive wife. Erica was an elegant blond beauty whose classic looks were ageless. She was married to one of the wealthiest men in the state. She was a mother and grandmother, with strong and healthy progeny.

"It's hard to imagine a woman with so much not being happy," Julia murmured.

Michael's lips curved into a sardonic smile. "Surely you've heard the famous maxim, 'money doesn't buy happiness'? Not to mention that other old chesnut, 'there's more to life than money.' Of course, all that is heresy to my mother, who staunchly holds the opposing view."

"There are maxims and chesnuts for that viewpoint, too. How about 'money isn't everything, but it sure is far ahead of whatever is in second place'?" Julia cast him a quick, bright smile.

Michael felt queerly disoriented, as if he'd been cast out of time, out of place. For one dizzying moment, he scarcely recognized the young woman at his side. He was accustomed to the calmly bland, impassive mask Julia wore at the office. But when her face was alight and lively, as it was now, she was stunningly pretty!

As if of their own volition, his eyes traveled over her, taking in the sight of her small, firmly rounded breasts bobbing softly as she ran. He realized for the first time that her office clothes were not only loose fitting, they were a downright disguise, hiding a very shapely figure. Nor did those modest, below-the-knee skirts and sensible shoes she wore to work encourage anyone to glance at her legs.

Tonight, Michael's gaze fixated on them, as if making up for lost time. She was only of average height, about five foot four, but her legs were long and sleek and very well shaped. He stared at the bare smooth skin of her thighs and heat flooded him.

Sweat beaded his forehead and his pulses pounded. He fell several paces behind her, but that tactical retreat only gave him a clear view of the shapely curves of her buttocks. Gulping for air, he began to conjugate Spanish verbs in his head as a very necessary diversion.

When Julia realized he'd stopped running, she paused and turned, looking back at him. By that time, Michael had his unexpected and thoroughly unwelcome lusty impulses under control.

"Leg cramp," he explained briskly, catching up to her. Well, it wasn't too far off.

For a while, they ran side by side in a not uncomfortable silence.

Then he said, "Julia?"

"Yes?"

"I apologize for what my uncle said to you today. After Uncle Jake lets off steam, he puts the incident behind him. I hope you can forget it, too."

"I won't give it another thought," Julia promised. "You seem to get along with your uncle most of the time," she added hesitantly. She hoped she didn't seem presumptuous, making observations about Fortune family dynamics.

"I've always gotten along okay with Uncle Jake, even though he blows up at me from time to time." Michael shrugged. "He can be demanding and controlling, but I know where he's coming from." He smiled wryly. "I think I'm coming from the same place."

His flash of self-awareness surprised Julia. She tried and failed to suppress a grin.

Michael noticed. "So you agree that Jake and I are cut from the same cloth, hmm?"

"Let's just say it doesn't stretch the bounds of reality to imagine you using the term 'idiotic sycophant,'" she dared to say.

"I'd never use it to describe you."

"But it just might fit one of Jake's assistants?" Julia suggested, sliding him a wry, sidelong glance.

"You know, it just might."

They both laughed. She had a nice laugh, Michael noted. Warm and real. Not one of those phony shrieks or high-pitched trills. He'd always liked her laugh, though they didn't do much laughing at the office. Lately, even smiles were scarce.

"Uh-oh," Julia exclaimed.

She saw the group of young women heading toward them at the same time Michael did. The girls were in their late teens or very early twenties and were staggeringly drunk. They were singing and laughing loudly as they careened along the path...and then they spied Michael.

He tensed as one of them shrieked, "Oh, my God, it's him! One of the top-ten bachelors, the one that lives right here in Minneapolis!"

The girl's companions joined in the squealing. The scene stirred memories of the newsreels Julia had seen of the Beatles' arrival in New York back in 1964. She glanced at Michael, who was staring at his admirers, utterly appalled.

Her protective instincts were instantly roused. Perhaps some self-preservatory instincts, too. She didn't want to be caught in the midst of a wild and amatory throng.

She'd read that highly effective people were supposed to be proactive instead of waiting around to react. Well, here was a chance to prove how effective she could be. Julia walked right up to the girls in what she hoped was a highly proactive manner.

"Do you really think he looks like that guy in the magazine?" she asked the girl who'd first identified Michael. Before she could answer, Julia turned quickly to Michael and called out, "Denny, they think you look like Michael Fortune! Can you believe it?"

Michael stared in confusion.

"That's my brother Denny," Julia went on blithely. "He works in the mail room at the Fortune Corporation."

''The mail room?'' one of the girls repeated, her voice ringing with disappointment. ''He's not *the* Mike Fortune?''

Julia laughed. ''He delivers *the* Mike Fortune's mail. Is that close enough?''

''I don't think he looks anything like Mike Fortune,'' another girl declared with a disdainful sniff. ''Mike Fortune looks like a millionaire. This guy—'' she nodded disparagingly in Michael's direction ''—looks like he works in a mail room. You can tell.''

''Denny's job pays benefits, health and dental,'' Julia said. ''And he's eligible, too. He doesn't have a girlfriend.'' She gave them a hopeful look, inviting one of them to volunteer for the position.

That was all it took. The girls weren't drunk enough not to realize that a guy whose sister was on the prowl for a girlfriend for him did not meet their standards.

''Tell your brother to take out an ad in the personals,'' one of them said, as they giggled among themselves. ''Maybe he'll luck out there.''

''We're holding out for Mike Fortune,'' said another. ''Or a Mike Fortune type.''

''I think he really does kind of look like Mike Fortune,'' Julia called after them, as they hurried on their way. She'd managed to sound credibly forlorn, as the sister of a perennially dateless Denny might.

''He only looks like Mike Fortune if you're drunk out of your mind, like Wendy is,'' one of the girls shouted back.

''Wendy also thought the pizza-delivery guy looks like Tom Cruise,'' exclaimed another, and they all laughed raucously.

The girls disappeared around a bend, leaving Julia and Michael alone.

''*Denny?*'' Michael tried to look stern, but he couldn't quite pull it off.

''It was the first name that popped into my head,'' Julia

confessed. "And then, somehow you became Denny." She dissolved in laughter. "You had that glazed look in your eye and your mouth was hanging open. I wouldn't have been surprised if you started babbling about getting your jollies from opening mail from all of Mike Fortune's female admirers."

"My *jollies?*" he repeated incredulously. Suddenly, he couldn't stop the laughter that bubbled within him.

They were both too breathless from laughing to run, so they walked along the path, making bad jokes. "I know Mike Fortune, Mike Fortune is a boss of mine and *you* are no Mike Fortune," Julia paraphrased. "You are a faux Denny."

"I think I'd rather be a faux Denny than an idiotic sycophant," countered Michael. "Although if Uncle Jake were to see us carrying on like this, he'd write us both off as giddy nitwits."

"No one could ever accuse you of being either giddy or a nitwit," Julia assured him.

"I suppose not." Michael frowned thoughtfully, turning serious once more. "I can't even be accused of smiling, according to my stepmother, Barbara. She told me to lighten up, that lately she could count on one hand the number of times I've smiled."

"There hasn't been much to smile about at the Fortune Corporation this past year," Julia murmured.

"No, there hasn't. We've had a series of incidents ranging from calamitous to catastrophic." A grim and somber Michael proceeded to list them. "There was that fire set in the laboratory by an intruder who was never caught, and Grandmother Kate's plane crash. Then my cousin Allison was stalked by some nut."

"At least that calamity had a happy ending," Julia replied. "Allison married her bodyguard, Rafe."

"Marriage. A happy ending." Michael arched his brows in that superior, sardonic way of his. "I suppose you would view it that way."

Julia refrained from pointing out that according to his "better dead than wed" sentiments, *his* view of a happy ending was a permanent trip to the cemetery.

"Meanwhile, the company's stock values keep dropping." Michael heaved a worried sigh. "And of course, there's that latest mysterious break-in at the lab. Whoever was responsible caused some deliberate destruction that's resulted in further setbacks in the development of the special youth formula."

Julia nodded knowingly. She was aware that the company had been working on the youth formula for years, and that Kate Fortune had made her fatal flight to Brazil to procure a rare vital ingredient for it. All told, it was beginning to look as though the Fortune family, blessed for so long with the very best life had to offer, had somehow become cursed instead.

"And on top of everything else," Michael continued, "I was named one of the top-ten most eligible bachelors in the U.S.A., prompting an avalanche of unwanted attention."

"And the unprecedented abuse of the voice-mail system," Julia added.

She sounded serious and sympathetic, but Michael caught the gleam in her gray eyes. "I can tell you don't think the bachelor list belongs in my account of family troubles, but it's been a severe inconvenience, Julia," he said defensively.

"Oh, I know. I've been fending off your eager admirers by phone and by fax, too."

He had the uncomfortable feeling that she was patronizing him. "Tonight, right here on this path, I was almost mobbed," Michael reminded her. He was determined that Julia understand the full extent of his plight. "If those girls hadn't been drinking, they never would've bought your Denny ruse."

"Probably not."

"I'm getting desperate, Julia. I can't take this continual harassment. I came out here to run tonight because I felt like a hostage trapped in my own apartment. I couldn't face the stack of mail there—oh yes, I get mail at home as well as at work, and at home I don't have Denny and his gang to dispose of it for me.''

He started to run again, and Julia picked up her pace to keep up with him.

''There were women hanging around the lobby of my apartment building when I left,'' he continued grimly. ''I had to sneak out wearing a jumpsuit and cap I borrowed from Al's Auto Parts. Al and his sons have been servicing the company cars for years and were very understanding when I explained my need for a disguise.''

''A mechanic's jumpsuit and hat is a good disguise. Do you have a fake mustache and glasses to go with it?''

Her expression was so demure and her tone so sincere that he couldn't tell if she was teasing him or not. Since he didn't view Julia as the teasing type, he decided to answer her seriously. ''Believe me, I've considered buying them. If this mayhem keeps up, I may have to.''

''Maybe you should consider buying a wig, too. How about a long, blond, California-beach-boy style, like Kato Kaelin? Nobody would know you then.''

''Now I know you're being glib.'' Michael studied her intently. ''You're very good at subtext, Julia—saying one thing while conveying something else altogether. I never knew that until tonight. Have you been mocking me for the past year while I remained oblivious?''

''Of course not! We idiotic sycophants are too stupid and too smarmy for subtext.''

Michael laughed. He was enjoying himself, he realized with some surprise. It had been so long, he'd almost forgotten what it felt like.

They reached a lighted parking lot. ''My car is here,'' Michael said, pointing to his vintage, candy-apple red Corvette.

"I was on my way back to it when I met you. I insist on driving you home."

She accepted his offer with a polite, "Thank you."

"I'll refrain from delivering a lecture about the dangers to a woman out alone at night," he said lightly.

The words were no sooner out of his mouth when Michael realized that he *wanted* to deliver that lecture. The idea of Julia falling prey to some criminal on the prowl sickened him. "But you really shouldn't go out alone after dark, Julia. You took a foolish risk in doing so tonight."

"I took a self-defense class a couple years ago," she explained. "I don't like having to curtail my freedom, so I decided to make sure I can protect myself."

"Isn't the first principle of self-defense to avoid placing yourself in a dangerous situation?" Michael frowned. "Your class has given you a false sense of confidence, Julia. Promise that you won't go running alone at night again."

"Mmm," Julia murmured noncommittally, putting her hand in back of her and crossing her fingers, undoing her vague promise even as she gave it. After all, it wasn't Michael's business where she spent her off-work hours.

They were standing under the light, and he gazed down at her flushed cheeks, at the brown hair that had escaped from its braid to frame her face. She looked small and soft and very feminine.

He cleared his throat. "Would you like to go somewhere for a drink or something to eat?" he asked impulsively, surprising himself. He rarely acted on impulse.

"Looking like this?" Julia glanced down at her sweaty clothes and ran her hand through her tousled hair. "I'd scare away the other customers."

"You wouldn't, but I certainly might. Why don't we make use of the drive-through window at one of the places along the boulevard? That way we wouldn't have to leave the car.

We could sit in the parking lot and have a sandwich and a cup of coffee or a soda or something.''

Julia understood that he was going through the motions of being polite, but there was really no need. ''It's kind of you to offer, but I have to get home.'' She glanced at her watch, startled by the time. ''In fact, I have to go right away.''

It was almost time for her nightly telephone call to Joanna. And tonight it was important that she call a bit early, because Joanna watched a program on television in the lounge with a group of other young patients. The weekly program had become a regular social event, with popcorn, soft drinks and candy shared among them.

Julia was thrilled that her little sister had gained the interest and the ability to socialize. And to be able to comprehend and concentrate on a plot was a major accomplishment for Joanna. For a year and a half after the accident, the girl's attention span had been as short as a toddler's. She'd barely been able to follow the fast-paced, visually stimulating programs designed for preschoolers.

But now... A small smile curved Julia's lips. Joanna had a circle of friends and enjoyed age-appropriate shows. She was showing improvement every single day.

''You'll have to give me directions to your place,'' Michael said as he walked her to his car. He wondered why she had to rush home—or if the real reason for her hasty departure was because she was eager to escape from his presence.

Michael Fortune, currently being pursued by hundreds of women who claimed to be willing to do just about anything with him or for him, could not even persuade Julia Chandler to drink a soda with him in the parking lot of a fast-food restaurant. The irony was not lost on him.

His lips twisted in a grim smile. Wasn't there a verse about a prophet not being valued in his own land? Or words to that effect. It seemed that the same principle applied to the appeal of an eligible bachelor boss in his assistant's eyes. Julia spent hours in his company at work. Who could blame her for wanting to steer clear of him in her off hours?

Still, the notion rankled, and the fact that it did bothered him even more. Withdrawing into a moody silence, Michael steered his car through the steady stream of traffic, turning on the radio to a station broadcasting a Minnesota Twins baseball game. The game was meaningless, since neither team had a chance of making it to the play-offs this year, and the Twins and their opponent were merely filling time with lackluster performances.

Neither Julia nor Michael spoke, except when she told him where to turn. When he pulled up in front of her three-story frame apartment building, she opened the car door before he had braked to a full stop.

"Thanks for the ride," she called, jumping out and slamming the door behind her.

Her abrupt departure was jarring. Irritating, too. Michael watched her dash into the building. He wondered which apartment she lived in. It occurred to him that he didn't know if she lived alone or with someone…or if that someone was a man. Julia never talked about her personal life at work, at least not with him. He'd never bothered to ask her anything about her life outside the office, and she had never volunteered any information.

Michael drove to his own apartment, a penthouse in a futuristic new building downtown, not far from the Fortune Building. His jumpsuit disguise was in the back seat, and he groaned at the thought of having to put it on again. Luckily, his admirers had given up for the night, and the entrance to the building was clear.

He hurried inside, punching in the code to disengage the security system of the private elevator, then riding it to the top of the building. The elevator doors opened onto a small vestibule directly in front of the door to the penthouse. To the left stood a wall of windows that provided a spectacular view of the Twin Cities skyline.

Michael didn't pause to glance at it.

Four

The new issue of *Fame* finally hit the stands, and the top-ten most eligible bachelors in the U.S.A. were last week's news. The syndicated TV tabloids and talk shows stopped calling, as did the out-of-state newspapers. The number of letters began to drop off. Denny informed Julia that one of the new hires on the "Fortune bachelor team" had been let go, but the other had been asked to stay on in the mail room, as he'd proven himself to be both efficient and accurate on the job.

Though the national media had lost interest, locally Michael was still very much a celebrity in demand. Since his new home phone number was unlisted and he used an answering machine to screen his calls, he was safe from the telephone overtures of his admirers, at least while in his apartment. He continued to be plagued by amorous phone calls at work, but fortunately, the voice-mail system was able to handle the reduced number of them.

However, the Twin Cities media kept up their requests for interviews. They were well aware of local interest in the area's own homegrown bachelor and knew that information about him would capture the attention of the all-important 18-to-34-year-old female market share.

"Just *one* interview with Mike and we'll back off," promised Faith Carlisle, among the most persistent reporters on the "local beat" at Channel 3 News. Somehow Faith consistently managed to elude the Fortune Corporation's receptionists, secretaries and voice-mail system, and though her calls never made it through to Michael, she talked to Julia at least once every day.

Julia was amazed by Faith's proficiency. And one could only admire the newswoman's tenacity. Faith Carlisle said she would never give up until she'd landed her interview with Mike Fortune, and so far, she hadn't.

"You're wearing me down," Julia confessed when Faith's second call of the day came through. "I actually told Michael that I thought it would be a good idea if he met with you."

"And what did he say?" Faith pressed eagerly.

"He said no." Julia sighed. "Sorry. I tried."

"Doesn't he know that by being elusive, he is increasing his appeal?" Faith was frustrated. "Think Jacqueline Onassis. Everybody wanted to interview her because she was the one interview nobody could ever get. Well, Mike Fortune is playing by those rules."

"I don't think he's playing by any rules. He just wants to be left alone."

"It's not going to happen, Julia. Say, how is the voice-mail system over there? Any problems with it lately?"

"No, thank heavens." Julia remembered Jake Fortune's fiery visit the last time the system had crashed. She shivered. "The number of calls have dropped off. I think interest in Michael Fortune is finally starting to fade."

"Don't be too sure of that, honey," Faith said, hanging up.

Julia thought nothing more of the conversation until later that day. Not until the voice-mail system abruptly and unexpectedly became so overloaded with messages for Michael Fortune that it short-circuited. Again! Worse, the company's entire computer system shut down along with it, like a sympathetic unionist supporting a fellow laborer's strike.

Michael paced his office, infuriated and distraught. Julia leaned against the wall, her arms folded, staring anxiously at the pearl gray carpet.

"Faith Carlisle is responsible, I'm sure of it," she murmured. "She made a threat, but I didn't recognize it as a threat at the time. I'm positive she orchestrated this call-in campaign, just to show she could do it. And she'll keep on doing it until you give her an interview, Michael."

"Never!" Michael pounded his fist with his hand. "I will never knuckle under to blackmailing media sabotage. We'll sue, we'll—"

"Dammit, Michael, I've had all I'm going to take!" Jake Fortune's roar could be heard through closed doors along the entire length of the corridor.

Julia froze. She could hear the CEO's footsteps thundering along the carpeted hall from the elevator banks to his nephew's office. The enraged giant from "Jack and the Beanstalk" instantly leapt to mind; she wouldn't have been surprised to hear Jake Fortune promising to "grind their bones to make his bread." Michael's bones and hers, his idiotic sycophant.

She raised wide, apprehensive eyes to Michael. "We could lock ourselves in your closet," she whispered. "Maybe he'll think we aren't here." She wasn't sure if she was kidding or not. A safe haven away from Jake Fortune's threatening onslaught held great appeal.

"Feel free." Michael gestured toward the closet door. "But I'm certainly not going to hide from my uncle. I'm not afraid of him."

They heard Jake enter Julia's office. She eyed the closet longingly. Maybe Michael wasn't afraid of his raging uncle, but she was. Out of sight, out of mind seemed a sound policy in this situation.

But it was too late. The door to Michael's office was flung open and Jake Fortune stormed inside.

"Are you aware of the disruption your imbecilic groupies have caused this company?" Jake launched immediately into his tirade. Which went on and on and on.

Michael was respectful at first, but Jake continued to rage, and the scope of his anger seemed unlimited. Soon Michael gave up all attempts at apology or civility and launched a counteroffensive of his own. Blame was cast, aspersions hurled. They were family, and they had ammunition that extended back for years.

Julia stood plastered against the wall, too unnerved to move, watching and listening to the two men verbally annihilate each other. Each seemed to hold the other accountable for everything that was wrong in the company and in the family. She wouldn't have been surprised if they started in on global culpability, blaming the other for famines and floods and for destabilizing foreign governments.

Her temples began to throb. She'd never had a migraine headache before, but if she was going to have her first one, this would be the time and place for it.

And just when she thought things couldn't possibly get worse, Nate Fortune arrived, his expression dark as a thundercloud.

"Word has it that you're threatening my son, Jake." Nate leapt into the fray without waiting for an invitation.

Julia guessed what had happened. One of the alarmed employees in product development, overhearing Jake Fortune threaten their boss with extinction, had taken the self-protective step of getting word to Nate, Michael's dad.

Her stomach gave a sickening lurch. Now a turf war was about to break out, and she was stuck right here as an unwilling witness.

"Thanks to your son's obsessive fan club the entire company has been disrupted, not to mention the costs of getting the damn computer system up again." Jake glowered at his brother. "And this isn't the first time it's happened. I was understanding, I was patient, that first time. The second time, too. Even the third time, I was the model of restraint. But it's happened five times! *Five times!* As CEO, I have a responsibility to our employees and our shareholders, and that means ending this sort of insanity!''

''It's not my son's fault that women find him irresistible,'' Nate said.

Michael winced. ''Dad, please. Uncle Jake and I can work this out on our own.''

''What kind of a father would I be if I stood by and let my brother bully you?'' Nate demanded. ''I saw the way he treated his own son. Poor Adam, the kid was literally driven away by the pressure Jake put on him. Well, I won't allow my boy to be subjected to that sort of treatment.''

Jake paled at the mention of his only son. His estranged son.

''Dad, this has nothing to do with Adam. And just for the record, Adam is no longer a kid and I'm not a boy,'' Michael said firmly. ''Indirectly at least, I am responsible for the overload on the computer system. Since that stupid article came out, I've been a liability to the company, and as CEO Uncle Jake has every right to be furious over what's been happening.''

''I have every right to fire you!'' snapped Jake.

''Just try it!'' Nate took a menacing step toward his older brother. ''You dare to fire my boy and I'll—''

''You'll what?'' Jake interrupted, his tone and stance challenging. His fingers flexed into fists.

Julia watched in horror as Nate Fortune followed his brother's lead. The two brothers seemed quite willing to pulverize each other, right here and now. She quickly lowered her eyes, unable to watch the carnage.

''You two aren't really going to duke it out, are you?'' Michael asked incredulously.

''Stay out of this, Mike,'' ordered Jake.

''This has been a long time coming,'' Nate said through gritted teeth.

But before either brother could make a move, a tall, slim

young woman with a thick mane of long, curly auburn hair entered the office and immediately went to stand between the men.

"You two look like a pair of angry hyenas! Now please do us all a favor and break it up this minute." Rebecca Fortune, Jake and Nate's youngest sister, stood between them, placing a graceful hand on each man's chest. Her expression was a mixture of sadness and chagrin.

Julia felt weak-kneed with relief. She'd never been so glad to see anybody in her life! Had Rebecca not arrived when she did, Julia was certain that Nate and Jake would have come to blows. Add Michael to the volatile mix and it was anyone's guess what might've ensued. It was Julia's own guess that she would've ended up calling 911 and hoping the rescue team arrived in time.

"This doesn't concern you, Rebecca," Jake growled at his sister, but Julia noticed that his hands were no longer balled into fists.

Neither were Nate's. "Jake is throwing his weight around." He addressed his sister, ignoring his brother. "Treating my boy in the same arrogant, tyrannical manner that he treated his own son. He drove Adam away from the company and now he's trying to do the same to my Mike. By God, I won't stand for it."

"Dad, I'm twenty-nine, not nine years old, and nobody is trying to drive me away from anything." Michael was exasperated. "I appreciate your concern, but please, go on back to the legal department and—and sue somebody or something."

"So you're aligning yourself with your uncle, are you?" Nate glared balefully from Michael to Jake. "Toadying up to Jake because he's the chief executive officer while I'm merely the general counsel and vice president? Oh, you're your mother's son, all right, Michael. You're as manipulating and self-serving as she is!"

He stormed out of the office.

"Michael is nothing like that grasping witch, Sheila!" Jake went charging after his brother. "It's high time that you appreciate your son for the man that he is! Mike works his tail off for this company, and he doesn't have a manipulating or self-serving bone in his body. What kind of a father are you to malign your own son that way? No wonder poor Kyle had to move all the way to Wyoming to finally become his own man. You undercut both your sons every chance you get!"

The brothers' quarrel continued down the corridor to the bank of elevators, where they each took a separate one to different floors.

Rebecca, Michael and Julia were left in Michael's office. "I love to come to company headquarters and visit my family," Rebecca said dryly. "They're such a congenial group."

"You have impeccable timing, Aunt Becky," Michael said, smiling at his aunt. It amused him to call her that because at thirty-three, she was only four years older than he was. She was one of his favorite relatives and always had been, from the time they were children.

"I came to have lunch with Kristina and got the word that there was a big showdown here in your office, Mike." Rebecca shook her head. "To come up here and see Jake and Nate ready to scrap like a couple of hotheaded teenagers is downright depressing. Mother would be appalled."

"No, she wouldn't," said Michael. "She was too used to Jake and Nate's clashes to be appalled by them."

"And here is Julia! Poor thing, you look like you've been accidently trapped in a den of grizzly bears." Rebecca smiled warmly at her. "Are we going to have to peel you off that wall?"

Managing a shaky smile, Julia slowly moved away from the security of the wall. She was flattered that Rebecca remembered her name, for they'd only met twice before. Michael's mother, Sheila, had met her son's assistant at least a half-dozen times and still had no idea that she had a name.

"It's wonderful to see you again, Miss Fortune," Julia said deferentially. Rebecca was a mystery writer, and Julia had read all her books and enjoyed them immensely. She was a little awed by the author's presence.

"Please, call me Rebecca. Or even Aunt Becky will do." Rebecca grinned. "Anything but Miss Fortune, which is just too eponymous. Should I ask what the latest brouhaha between my brothers was all about?"

Michael proceeded to fill her in. "And of course, neither one can resist taking potshots at each other as fathers," he finished with a sigh. "Dad loves to twist the knife about Adam refusing to work for the company, and Uncle Jake can't resist the opportunity to needle Dad about Kyle's screw-ups."

"Except Kyle is no longer screwing up," Rebecca interjected loyally. "He is happily married, he is a father and he's making a success of the ranch Mom left him."

"Uncle Jake noted that in his updated version," Michael said. "His new argument now seems to be that Kyle had to get far away from Dad's pernicious presence in order to stop being a screw-up. Slightly different but, overall, still an effective slam."

"The alliances shift so fast," Julia blurted out.

She'd felt as if she had been gyrating in a kaleidoscope while listening to the Fortunes argue. She still felt that way. One minute Jake had been berating Michael, the next he was defending him against Nate, who'd suddenly turned against his son after being adamantly protective of him only moments before.

Life in the quiet Chandler family had not prepared her for a volatile tribe like the Fortunes, who said awful things to each other, yet turned fiercely loyal the very next instant. Julia thought of her parents and her sister and their time together. They'd been a family who liked each other, who were nice to each other. An unheard of concept for the Fortunes? It seemed to be, at least for some of them.

"I know what you mean." Rebecca sighed. "And I think I'd better have a talk with Jake and Nate—separately, of course," she added, after catching Julia's look of alarm. "I don't think either of them is ready to sit down at the peace table yet. Mike, if you see Kristina, tell her I'll take a rain check on lunch."

Rebecca left the office, her long, crinkled voile skirt swirling around her ankles.

"Rebecca is a calming, neutral presence. She'll manage to get Dad and Uncle Jake to cool off and back off. A temporary peace, that is, until the next round," Michael added dispiritedly.

If Rebecca could achieve detente between the two warring Fortune brothers, she deserved the Nobel Peace Prize, Julia thought. But she kept her observation to herself.

Kristina arrived moments later, just as Julia was leaving Michael's office for her own. "You don't have to go, Julia. In fact, I'd like you to stay," Kristina said tersely. "I'm feeling homicidal and I don't trust myself to be alone with my brother."

"Am I supposed to serve as a witness or as a restraint?" Julia attempted a little joke, hoping to change Kristina's scowl to a smile. It didn't work and she tensed, bracing herself for the next skirmish in the Fortune wars.

"What's the problem, Kristina?" Michael asked wearily.

"I just want you to know that I lost three pages of dialogue I was working on for my newest ad idea when the damn computer crashed again!" Kristina announced, glaring at her brother. *"Three pages! Gone!"*

Michael was in no mood to sympathize or apologize. "Haven't you ever heard of saving after every page?"

"The way things are going around here, I'm going to have

to save after every word!'' Kristina snapped. "Honestly, Mike, I'm so sick of all this!''

"Oh, well, I'm enjoying it,'' Michael countered caustically. "Computers crashing, relatives raging, days disrupted! What could be more fun?''

Kristina looked ready to punch him. Since there was little chance that Rebecca would reappear to halt the bloodshed, Julia felt obligated to step in.

"Your aunt Rebecca said she would take a rain check on lunch, Kristina,'' she said with commendable perkiness, hoping to divert the hostile pair. "Have you eaten at the Black Forest Inn? They have the most delicious desserts there.''

Michael and Kristina eyed her as if she'd taken leave of her senses.

"Uh, maybe I'll just go back to my desk,'' Julia suggested.

"No, stay here, Julia,'' ordered Kristina. "Since my brother is being such a smart-ass, I'd rather deal with you. I heard that Mike's admirers jammed the voice-mail system *again* and caused the computer to seize again! What gives? I thought this bachelor mess was winding down.''

"It is!'' Michael insisted. He lowered his eyes. "Almost,'' he added, looking glum.

"It would be over by now except for Faith Carlisle,'' Julia interjected.

"The reporter on Channel 3? The one who looks like she could turn you to stone with that beady-eyed stare of hers?'' Kristina made a face like a gargoyle.

"That's the one,'' Michael said dourly. He explained the Faith Carlisle situation to Kristina, with some assistance from Julia.

"Well, I agree with Julia,'' said Kristina. "You're going to have to give the woman her interview or she'll continue to plague you, Mike. Which means she'll continue to plague all of us.''

"Absolutely not! I will not give into that—that telecommunications terrorist." Michael was adamant.

"But what if Faith Carlisle manages to jam the system every day?" Julia felt herself panicking at the thought. "Your father and your uncle will end up killing each other by the end of the week." She cast an apprehensive glance at Kristina, who looked ready to commit some mayhem herself.

"There has to be a way out of this!" exclaimed Kristina. "We can't spend every day worrying that the computer could crash at any given moment."

"Well, an interview with Faith Carlisle would be like throwing a lighted match into a container of gasoline," predicted Michael. "It would only generate additional calls and letters. The last thing we need is more attention about my eligible status."

"Wait! Hold on! I'm getting an idea!" Kristina cried suddenly. "A fabulous idea!"

She eased herself onto the edge of Michael's desk and began to swing her legs back and forth. "Mike, you'll give an exclusive interview to Faith Carlisle, but not the one she's expecting. This interview will solve the problem of your eligibility and get your admirers out of your hair and out of the voice-mail system, too. If that's what you really want," she added slyly.

"Of course, it's what I want! You can't possibly think I enjoy being hunted down like a—a trophy elk, do you? And I hate the computer disruption at least as much as Uncle Jake and you do. I'd do anything to stop it!"

"Then why not announce your engagement?" Kristina suggested. "Call Faith and tell her you want to give her an exclusive interview, and use the opportunity to announce to all of Minneapolis and St. Paul that you are no longer available. Voilà! You're a free man. Free of Faith and free of your pursuers."

"That's the stupidest idea I've ever heard, and in this department, I've heard plenty," Michael said impatiently. "You're missing the whole point, Kristina. I don't want to get engaged and I sure as hell don't want to get married."

"It's true," Julia seconded. "He'd rather be dead than wed. That means he would probably prefer to be terminally ill than engaged," she added.

Kristina laughed. "*You're* the one missing the point, Michael. The engagement wouldn't be real. You'd have an ersatz fiancée, one who would be going along with the charade until this whole eligible-bachelor nonsense is finally laid to rest. Think about it, Mike. Faith Carlisle would broadcast the word to all Twin Cities singles that you are no longer eligible. You'd get your peace and your privacy back, and the company would be safe from the ardent enthusiasm of all those Mike Fortune–hunting women."

Michael automatically opened his mouth to protest, then closed it as he reconsidered his younger sister's idea. "Theoretically, it could work," he admitted. "But in reality it doesn't stand a chance."

"Why not?" demanded Kristina.

"Because where am I going to get this ersatz fiancée who'll go along with the charade? The engagement will have to appear legitimate for Faith Carlisle to buy the story."

"Faith Carlisle will sniff out a bogus engagement in a second," Julia said. "She's already proven how resourceful she is."

"Then we'll have to make this engagement appear very real, won't we?" Kristina exclaimed, already caught up in the scheme. "This fiancée will have to be someone we trust implicitly. Someone who knows what is at stake and who is wholeheartedly committed to going along with the plan. And she will have to seem like a logical choice for you, Mike. Someone who has been in your life all along but has remained discreetly in the background during all the hoopla."

Michael met his sister's eyes. She held his gaze, conveying a silent message.

"I've always thought of you as one of the sharpest knives in the drawer, Mike," Kristina said playfully. "Am I going to have to spell it out for you?"

Michael's neck reddened. "Kristina, I really think we should—"

"*J-U-L-I-A.*" Kristina sang out the letters.

"—Finalize the details before we tell her," Michael finished, the flush spreading to his cheeks.

Julia, who had been trying to think which one of Michael's previous amours would be suitable as the ersatz fiancée in a bogus engagement, was caught entirely off guard when Kristina spelled her name. She stared at one, then the other, her face a study of confusion.

"Congratulations, Julia," Kristina exclaimed. "You're it, I mean you're *her.* Mike's brand-new fausse fiancée."

Julia gaped at them, aghast. *"Me?"*

"Will you do it, Julia?" As usual, when Michael made a request, it sounded like a command—which, of course, it was.

That was fine when it came to office matters, but commanding her to pretend to be engaged to him was something else entirely.

"You can't be serious!" Julia knew she sounded desperate. She saw Michael and Kristina exchange glances, and she wanted to flee from the office. Their feuding was over and they were about to join forces—against her!

"Oh, we're very serious," Kristina assured her. "You're the ideal candidate, Julia. You meet all the requirements."

"Except for the most important one, and that's credibility!" Julia started to slowly back away from the pair of Fortunes. "Nobody will ever believe that Michael is engaged to me. We've never been seen together outside of this office. Why, we've never even walked to the water cooler or eaten lunch together, not even once!"

She kept inching away, until her back touched the wall, impeding further movement. She flattened herself against it, staring from Michael to Kristina. They didn't really expect her to go along with their demented plan, did they?

"I'm afraid she has made a valid point on the problem of credibility." Michael was frowning. "Let's examine the facts objectively. If Julia and I had been having a personal relationship serious enough to culminate in an engagement, we would have been seen together by somebody at least *once*. And once is all it takes. You know how efficient the company grapevine is."

"It's amazingly efficient," Julia seconded. "Remember last month when Drew Markeson in accounting asked out the new paralegal?"

Michael nodded, grimacing. "The words were no sooner out of his mouth than the news began to circulate through the entire corporation. Even Jake knew about their date!"

"If we were, uh, a couple, we would have been a hot topic of gossip for a long time," Julia added earnestly.

"Ah, but suppose the two of you have taken care to be extra discreet?" Kristina suggested. She absently began to twist several strands of her long, light blond hair as she spoke. "Just turn your argument around, Mike. The reason you and Julia have never been seen together is because you both *know* how efficient the grapevine is. You've deliberately kept your relationship a secret because you didn't want to be scrutinized and gossiped about. And it seems you've been spectacularly successful. Nobody in the company has a clue that you've fallen madly in love."

"Including the two of us," Julia mumbled darkly.

Kristina was undeterred. "Which brings us to the current chapter in your secret romance. You two were finally ready to go public and announce your engagement when the magazine placed Mike on that embarrassing most eligible list."

Mike sat at his desk, picked up his pen and jotted something down. "Actually, that story does have a credible ring, Kristina. And the more I think about it, the more certain I am that this plan is viable."

He gazed thoughtfully at the paper in front of him. "Julia and I are not flamboyant types. It would be characteristic of us to decide to maintain our privacy instead of exposing ourselves as a couple. It would also be logical to decide to wait until the eligible-list madness died down before we went public with the relationship."

Julia stared at him. It was as if he were in a product-development brainstorming session. Except the product being developed in this case was their bogus engagement! The thought of indulging in such a pretense with Michael Fortune sent anxious shivers coursing through her.

Her gaze was riveted to his hand, holding the pen. His fingers were long and well shaped, masculine and strong and—

"It'll never work!" she blurted out. Her voice sounded nervous and shaky, even to her own ears. "I've talked to Faith Carlisle every day, remember? She'll know we just made this whole thing up on the spur of the moment!"

"How?" Michael demanded. He was getting into the plan, Julia could tell. His blue eyes always glinted in that particular way when he was putting together a report or pursuing a project that interested him. "Faith Carlisle is merely a reporter, she's not omniscient, Julia. And in our version of the story, you have been very skillful at keeping her at bay. Not even her news-hound instincts detected an involvement between you and me. Carlisle will respect you for outsmarting her. Plus, she'll be flattered that we chose her to interview us."

"And in that interview you will publicly announce your engagement and end all this eligible-bachelor harassment," Kristina finished. "May I be the first to congratulate you two? You do make a lovely couple."

"I'll never be able to pull it off!" Julia was almost wailing.

"It's no use, Michael. You'll have to find someone else to be your bogus fiancée."

She felt both pairs of eyes upon her, studying her intently, and her cheeks flushed scarlet. "If you'll excuse me, I really do have some things at my desk that—"

"This is an interesting twist, Mike." Kristina's face creased with laughter. "You've been inundated with letters and phone calls and videos from hundreds of women, all eager for an intimate relationship with you, but your very own assistant feels incapable of even pretending to have one with you. What does that signify, I wonder?"

"I wonder," Michael said grimly.

"It doesn't signify anything," Julia assured them.

She felt as if she were one of those acrobats walking on the high wire without a net. This was her *boss* she was offending by her refusal, she reminded herself. She'd better try to smooth things over before she ended up in the unemployment line. "I'm just not a very good liar. In fact, I—I'm a terrible one. If I tried to tell Faith Carlisle or my friends or anybody that I was engaged to Michael Fortune, they'd laugh in my face."

"Why?" asked Kristina. "I don't find it hard to believe that my brother would fall in love with you."

"It's as bizarre as a story from the 'X-Files,'" Julia countered. "Furthermore, anyone who knows Michael knows his views on marriage. He'd rather be dead. So why would he ever get engaged to anyone, especially someone like me?"

"He was soured on marriage until you came along and changed his marital death wish, Julia." Kristina verbally trumped her.

"Yeah. Now I want to get married and live happily ever after," Michael interjected sarcastically.

"And have children for all the wrong reasons, too, I suppose," Julia added. She didn't bother to hide her resentment. Michael Fortune's disrespect for marriage and his belief that children couldn't possibly be the products of a mutual abiding love, concepts she cherished, irritated her beyond measure. "How are you supposed to play the part of a man contemplating marriage when you can't even mention the word without sneering?"

"Good point," said Kristina. "You've got to lose the bad attitude, Mike. Practice looking tenderly at your fiancée. Put a wistful note in your voice when you talk about finally meeting the right woman. Sound bemused when you mention how wrong you've been about marriage and be joyfully confident when you talk about your future with the woman you love."

"He'll never be able to pull that off!" Julia declared.

Her assertion, so fervid, so certain, annoyed Michael. "I can and will do whatever is necessary for the welfare of the Fortune Corporation, and if that includes playing a certain role, even the role of besotted fiancé, I will play it to the hilt. Don't ever underestimate my willpower and my devotion to this company, Julia."

He stood up and began to walk toward her. Julia drew a deep, shuddering breath. She much preferred him behind his desk, with the wide expanse of mahogany and half the office between them.

He was wearing one of his custom-tailored suits, this one a lightweight gray wool with a thin blue pinstripe running through it. Julia blinked. Somehow, in the edgy state she was in, her mind had taken to playing tricks on her. Somehow another image of him had become superimposed on top of the one she was seeing.

Mentally stripping him of his conservative suit, she saw his body in those brief running shorts and T-shirt that he'd been wearing on the running trail. In her mind's eye, she saw the powerful thighs, dusted with dark, wiry hair. She saw his strong arms and broad shoulders, the muscular wall of his chest flexing beneath the cotton T.

Her body tightened with alarm. At least, she thought it was

alarm. The peculiar feelings stirring within her were ones she couldn't easily categorize, and the closer Michael Fortune came to her, the more tumultuous she felt inside.

Julia swallowed hard. "I would never underestimate your devotion to the company." She wished her voice sounded more like a ringing endorsement and less like a squeak. "But you're not the only one playing a part in this—this psychodrama. You and your sister have cast me in it, too, and it—it's going to be terribly awkward to try to pretend to my friends that I'm engaged to a Fortune."

She tried to visualize telling Lynn, Margaret and Diana over lunch that she was engaged to Michael Fortune. Or breaking the news to her roommates. Julia flinched at the imaginary scenes. "I just can't do it."

"Awkward," Michael repeated laconically. "Is there anyone in particular that would find our pretense of an engagement too *awkward* to handle? To be more specific, I am talking about a man, Julia." His blue eyes were cool and assessing. "Is there a man in your life who would object to your participation in this venture?"

Julia considered the question. A simple yes would get her off the hook. She could invent a weight-lifting, steroid-chugging, trigger-tempered boyfriend who would go ballistic if she were to pretend to be engaged to another man.

"Keep in mind that you've already confessed that you are a terrible liar," Michael said in the silky tones she'd heard him use when summoning an employee into his office to deliver an unsatisfactory performance review. "And it follows, of course, that I would be extremely wary of having an assistant who blatantly lies to me. I couldn't work with someone I can't trust to tell the truth."

Julia picked up his unsubtle message. He intended to check her story, and if there was no objecting boyfriend, she would be terminated from the Fortune Company. She thought of Joanna, depending on her.

No, losing her job was not an option. Julia would do whatever it took to stay gainfully employed. She heaved a small sigh. ''There isn't any particular man in my life who would object,'' she confessed.

Currently, there was no man in her life at all, and the choice was hers. She felt light years removed from the world of dating. The getting-to-know-you questions, the smiles while feigning interest in someone or something you had no interest in…all the time and effort of beginning and maintaining a relationship took far more energy than she had to give at this point in time.

''I see,'' Michael said, his expression impassive. *There was no special boyfriend!* ''Well, good.'' He felt relief surge through him. ''That removes the one major stumbling block. A jealous lover is the only complication that could've wrecked the bogus-engagement plan.''

Which was why he felt this strange elation, of course. ''I think we should proceed as soon as possible. Julia, call Faith Carlisle and set up the interview for the day after tomorrow.''

Five

Julia shifted uneasily from one foot to the other. She felt as if she were standing on the top ledge of a skyscraper and the phone call to Faith Carlisle would send her plummeting to the ground.

Kristina was aware of her discomfiture. "Mike, no one could ever underestimate your devotion to the company, but let's not overestimate Julia's." She crossed the office to stand by Julia's side. "Let's look at this situation from her point of view. There is really nothing in this entire plan for Julia but deception and inconvenience."

Michael frowned. Julia's reluctance to play her part in the pretend engagement irked him. He wasn't taking her refusal personally, of course, he assured himself. But he was goal oriented, and this mock engagement was the means to his goal—the end of being plagued by women hoping to snare him. The end of the Fortune Corporation's daily routine being disrupted by people like Faith Carlisle, who manipulated those hopeful Fortune-hunters into action.

His eyes slid over Julia, whose modest beige suit and dull, buttoned-to-the-neck white blouse successfully hid all her feminine attributes. Executive secretary Dolores Vernon, who'd worked for the company since the dawn of time, wore styles and colors similar to Julia's, he noted. And those thick-heeled pumps Julia wore looked almost orthopedic.

Not even a grandmother would've been caught wearing those staid, sensible shoes. *Especially* not his stylish Grandmother Kate, whose tastes had been as timelessly elegant as she was herself. He quickly blocked the pain evoked by the thought of his late grandmother. And put his admittedly irrational irritation with Julia's wardrobe out of his mind as well.

"Julia is an employee of this company," he said loftily. "It is in her best interest that business proceed as smoothly as possible. Isn't that enough for her?"

Julia nodded vigorously, while Kristina shook her head.

"Mike, this mock-engagement is going to require time in addition to your regular office hours," Kristina explained. "Once the engagement is announced, you'll have to make some effort for it to appear real. You two will have to be seen together in public, going places and doing things a normal engaged couple would do."

"Suppose we're a normal engaged couple who prefer to keep to ourselves?" Michael drawled.

Julia felt heat suffuse her, from the top of her head to her toes. For a moment, she wondered what it would be like to be engaged—really engaged—to Michael Fortune, to spend evenings alone with him…

She lifted her eyes to his, only to find him studying her intently. She quickly looked away.

"Michael, face facts," Kristina said firmly. "If you want this mock-engagement idea to work, you'll have to convince people that you are no longer eligible, that you really are engaged to Julia. That means going out—to parties, to dinner, to the theater. Not every night, of course. Nobody would expect you to suddenly become a social extrovert, but it's only natural that you and your fiancée would go *somewhere,* once in a while!"

"I suppose you're right," Michael conceded, heaving a sigh. "Julia, make dinner reservations this week. And get theater tickets."

"Shall I send myself some roses?" Julia asked politely.

"Sounds like you know the drill." Kristina chortled. "Dinner, theater tickets and roses are standard fare for week one of a Mike Fortune courtship. But we're getting off the subject, which is that this engagement business is going to require overtime on Julia's part. Fiancée duties are *not* in her present job description, and it's only fair that she be paid for her time.''

Michael watched Julia's face while she reconsidered the engagement, not as a favor to him but as a moneymaker for her. His lips twisted into a cynical smile. He should have presented it that way from the start. What woman could resist the seductive lure of cold hard cash? How could he, Sheila Fortune's son, have forgotten even for a moment that any woman could be bought if the price was right? Even quiet, demure Julia Chandler.

Julia cast a sidelong glance at him, saw his coldly sardonic expression and knew exactly what he was thinking: that the offer of money would wipe away any doubts, apprehension or concerns she might have about playing the role of his fiancée.

Wouldn't he be shocked if she were to make the grand gesture of refusing any overtime pay? Of telling him that her current salary would cover the extra social duties? Such an unexpected action would surely blow to smithereens his all-women-are-greedy-and-willing-to-do-anything-for-a-buck theory! Julia's mouth curved in a secret smile. It would be satisfying indeed to challenge his ingrained attitudes about women and money.

But before she could make her offer, Michael spoke up. ''Kristina is right. We'll follow the union schedule for overtime pay. Is that all right with you, Julia? And I would like to sweeten the deal by throwing in a bonus. How about...'' He paused to deliberately build suspense, his blue eyes cold and calculating. He was curious. What price would Julia consider worthy of her?

"Fifty thousand dollars," he said coolly, and watched Julia's jaw drop.

"That's a high-priced sweetener, Mike," Kristina said incredulously.

"Don't worry, it won't come out of company funds." Michael feigned boredom, as if the subject at hand were a tiresome nuisance to be disposed of as quickly as possible. "I'll pay the bonus personally, since Julia is doing me a personal favor."

Julia watched him, saw the mockery on his face, heard each word dripping with contempt. Michael was playing his own game, which was all about women and money, and the moment she accepted his offer, he would declare himself the winner.

And she *had* to accept. There was no way that she could afford the luxury of turning down his offer. If she didn't have Joanna to consider, perhaps she would enjoy throwing his bonus "sweetener" back in his face, but their circumstances made such a grand gesture as unattainable to her as a lilac Rolls Royce.

Joanna needed at least one more year of the intensive, interrelated therapies at the rehab center. Furthermore, as her condition improved, additional opportunities became available to her. The center sponsored outings and trips that offered invaluable experiences to recovering patients who were striving to get back to the outside world and be a part of it, who needed a break from the protective and sometimes boring cocoon of the center. These "field trips" all cost extra.

Julia knew the overtime payments and the bonus would be money well spent on Joanna. She knew she was going to accept Michael's offer. It would be selfish of her not to.

"I take it we have a deal?" Michael's tone was a chilling combination of triumph and scorn. "I'll direct Sterling Foster to draw up an agreement. You'll receive half the bonus upon signing, and the second half after this farce has been played out. That will be when we break off our engagement, due to—shall we say—irreconcilable differences?''

Julia knew he thought less of her since she'd proven to him that she could be ''bought.'' For a split second, she considered telling him about Joanna, then dismissed the idea almost instantly. She refused to use her little sister to ingratiate herself with Michael Fortune. Michael's cynicism was his problem, not hers. Still, she resented his unspoken indictment—that she was avaricious and unscrupulous, for sale for fifty thousand dollars.

Or less. Julia's cheeks burned. She would've accepted whatever sum he offered as a bonus. She didn't have the choice of turning down money for Joanna out of a misplaced sense of pride.

''We have a deal,'' Julia affirmed. ''Thank you for the generous bonus,'' she added quietly.

''I'm sure you'll earn every penny of it, Julia. Pretending to be engaged to this guy is going to require an Academy Award performance,'' Kristina interjected jovially in an attempt to break the tension that vibrated almost tangibly between her older brother and his assistant.

''You get what you pay for,'' Michael said, with a smile that wasn't really one at all, but more like a wolf baring its fangs. ''Are you sure fifty thousand is enough, Julia? You're holding all the aces here, you know. You could blow the entire scheme by telling Faith Carlisle everything. If you make further demands, what recourse do I have but to meet them?''

Julia bristled. He was goading her, challenging her to challenge him. She guessed that over the years he had witnessed countless matches of the gimme-more-money, try-and-get-it game between his perennially feuding parents.

Understanding the psychology behind his actions didn't make them any less insulting. ''I accept the conditions you offered,'' she said coolly, refusing to be drawn into the game.

''Good! Now let's get to work on the plan,'' Kristina said,

gazing thoughtfully from one to the other. "We have to keep this a secret. Nobody but the three of us can know that the engagement is bogus. If a lot of people are in on a secret, it doesn't stay secret very long."

"I'm going to tell Sterling," Michael insisted. "I want a lawyer to draw up a legal agreement, and while I don't trust my father not to give away the secret—I can hear him shouting it at my mother during one of their inevitable games of one-upmanship—I do trust Sterling implicitly."

"So do I." Kristina turned to Julia, in a deliberate move to include her in the discussion. "All of us do. Sterling Foster is more than our family's personal lawyer, he's an unofficial member of the family. He's a bit of a curmudgeon sometimes, but he's a charming one."

Julia smiled slightly. Having met Sterling Foster briefly, she was familiar with his crusty exterior. However, she had never experienced his alleged charm. She doubted that he would bother to expend any of it on her.

While Michael and Kristina set about planning the details of the bogus engagement, Julia listened with a growing air of detachment. She felt like a pawn on the Fortune chessboard, a piece to be used in their game. So she tuned them out and concentrated on Joanna instead, on the security that the bonus would provide.

That same aura of unreality enveloped her again the next day during the meeting with Michael and Sterling Foster, which had been scheduled for six-thirty, after everyone who worked in the product-development department had gone home.

The three of them gathered in the conference room down the hall from Michael's office. Sterling Foster, aged sixty-something, was a tall and commanding figure with a thick shock of white hair and piercing blue eyes, a dignified man who radiated intelligence and power.

The lawyer withdrew a sheaf of papers from his briefcase

and placed one stack in front of Julia. "You'll want to read this through and then sign in the three places I've marked with a blue *X*," the attorney said brusquely.

"I don't have to read it," Julia said, eyeing the typed pages. She was hungry and she wanted to go home, not hang around here reading what had to be an excruciatingly boring document the length of the Constitution. "Just tell me where the *X*'s are and I'll sign."

"And give you grounds to sue us for inadequate legal representation?" Michael scoffed. "What kind of fools do you take us for, Julia?"

Julia restrained the almost irresistible urge to reply. While firmly holding her tongue in check, she happened to glance at the attorney. He studied her for a moment, then a small smile curved his mouth. "I would advise not answering that, Miss Chandler. It's called 'pleading the Fifth'."

"That would be the Fifth Amendment," Michael added, so obviously patronizing that Sterling Foster rolled his eyes heavenward.

Michael had been like that all day, Julia noted irritably. When he wasn't snapping at her, he was making snide innuendos, maligning her intelligence, her competence, her values. And all afternoon, she'd deflected him by pretending she didn't comprehend any of it. Never had she been so thick, so impassive and bland. She didn't know how Michael could tolerate it; she'd been getting on her own nerves for hours!

"The Fifth Amendment? Really?" Julia asked with credible ingenuousness. She would not give Michael Fortune the satisfaction of ruffling her implacable composure. "I thought Mr. Foster was referring to the Fifth Commandment. Thank you for explaining it to me."

Sterling Foster guffawed. Michael frowned. Julia stared into space, looking as vacuous as she dared.

"I'll go over the agreement with you, Miss Chandler," Sterling offered.

For whatever reasons, Julia could tell the attorney had thawed a bit toward her. She was relieved that he was willing to spare her from having to read the entire tedious document, instead offering her a summary of each page. Michael paced the conference room for awhile, then left Julia and Sterling alone.

"I went over this with Mike last night," the attorney remarked as Michael made his exit. "Can't blame him for not wanting to hear it twice. Too boring."

Julia didn't disagree.

"It's certainly thorough," she murmured, when they finally finished the last page.

According to the iron-clad agreement, she would get the money agreed upon: union-scale overtime during those times her presence as a fiancée was required, plus the bonus. But she was not eligible for one penny more. If she tried to extort any extra money, she would be fined, and the fines would come out of her final bonus check. If she were ever to break the secrecy and reveal that the engagement was bogus, she would forfeit all the money she had earned, to be repaid with double interest, retroactively.

Michael stuck his head in the door, saw they were finished reviewing the document, and rejoined them.

"Well, what do you think?" he asked, giving Julia a hard stare.

"Every possible contingency is covered," she said, rather awestruck by the exhaustive scope of the agreement.

"I've handled simpler divorces," Sterling admitted. "But after his experience with Delilah DeSilva, I guess Mike doesn't want to take any chances." The older man's brows knitted together and he frowned at Michael. "Although your lack of faith and trust in women is disheartening, to say the least, Mike. After talking to Miss Chandler, I can tell she is different from your mother and Delilah. You've spent the last year working with her. Why haven't you figured out that she's not like them?''

If Sterling expected an answer from Michael, he didn't get one. An uncomfortable silence descended.

"Who is Delilah DeSilva?" Julia broke the silence to ask. She was too curious to let the reference pass.

"That doesn't concern you," Michael said curtly.

"Of course it does, if she's supposed to be your fiancée," Sterling countered. "Since Delilah is part of your, er, romantic history, someone will surely refer to her, Mike. Knowing your family, somebody won't be able to resist making at least one Delilah joke. Julia has to know the story. If you were really engaged, you would have told her, and since you're striving for realism…" His voice trailed off and he shrugged.

"All right," Michael said tightly. He turned in Julia's direction, but didn't look at her as he spoke. "I was very briefly engaged to a woman named Delilah DeSilva. It is ancient history, relevant to nothing, but since Sterling thinks you should know—there, you've been told."

"I hope nobody expects me to pass a quiz about that particular subject," Julia said dryly. "I'll flunk for sure."

"Delilah was gorgeous, but she had a bank vault in place of a heart. That woman had dollar signs in her eyes—I swear you actually could see them flashing!" Sterling exclaimed reminiscently. "Poor Mike, he was only twenty-one, a college senior, when he met her, and she was five years older. He was so young, a sitting duck for a woman like Delilah, and she made sure she bewitched him."

"Sterling, will you kindly shut up?" Michael growled. "I'm sure Julia is not interested. Let's wrap this up so we can all go home."

Julia was fascinated. And though only a short time ago she'd been eager to leave and appease her hunger pangs, her appetite now took a back seat to her curiosity.

"You were actually engaged to a twenty-six-year-old

woman when you were only twenty-one?'' she asked incredulously.

She thought of the twenty-one-year-old frat boys she knew
from the predominantly student neighborhood. The idea of
someone her age being engaged to one of them was truly
incomprehensible. They seemed like such kids to her, rather
boring ones, who bragged about how much beer they drank
and whose response to any remark was inevitably, ''Cool!''

''It was an extremely short engagement, lasting slightly
over a month,'' Michael replied in icy, clipped tones. ''We'd
met a few weeks before that. The relationship was a debacle
from beginning to end, but at least it was only a nine-and-a-
half-week debacle.''

''Which cost you plenty,'' Sterling reminded him. He
turned to Julia. ''After Mike became aware of…hmm, how
shall I put this?…Delilah's true character, and broke the engagement, she threw the mother of all scenes. Claimed he'd
made promises that she was damn well going to collect upon.
Made all kinds of threats. I advised Mike to pay her off—for
services rendered, so to speak—and drew up the settlement
myself. Delilah got a lump sum when she signed, and then
she took off.'' He tapped his teeth with his Mont Blanc pen.
''Wonder how many other hapless suckers she's had her
claws into since then?''

''Do you think her weapon of choice is still bewitching
twenty-one-year-olds?'' Julia mused aloud.

''I don't know,'' replied Sterling. ''She was so patently
transparent that only a very young man would buy her act, if
you get my drift.''

Julia nodded. ''But her name is definitely a tip-off. Delilah.
After all, that was the bad girl in the Bible story.''

''Well, Ms. DeSilva definitely lived up to her name,'' said
Sterling. ''Or down to it, as the case may be.''

''She could have been named Gold Digger and I wouldn't
have caught on, not at that particular time,'' Michael said

grimly. "Not only was I too young, I was also too stupid and naive and trusting. I was desperately eager to believe that all women weren't acquisitive and obsessed with money."

"Like his mother is," Sterling added.

"So you chose a patently transparent fortune hunter who was way too old for you." Julia studied Michael for a long moment. This was textbook psychology, the stuff of her earliest courses. "I think it was the other way around, Michael. You wanted to prove that all women were *exactly* like your mother, so you chose a woman who would verify your beliefs. Unconsciously, of course," she added.

Michael groaned. "No psychobabble, please! For future reference, I find armchair psychology tedious and offensive."

Julia was stung. Armchair psychology, indeed! "I have a degree in psychology and one year of grad school in the field of counseling."

"Even worse. A little knowledge is a dangerous thing."

"Mike is touchy when it comes to the subject of Delilah," Sterling confided. "Who can blame him? She made a prize chump out of him, and that is annoying at any age. Now, about the ring..."

"What ring?" Julia was confused. There had been no mention of a ring in the long legal contract she had signed.

Sterling pulled out another sheaf of papers from his briefcase.

Julia slumped in her chair. "I guess that's a contract dealing with the ring?" The Versailles Treaty ending World War I couldn't have been this complicated.

Sterling nodded. "Yes, it is. Mike, do you have the ring with you?"

"It's locked in my desk. I'll get it." Michael left the conference room.

"It's not that Mike is paranoid about being financially fleeced by a woman," Sterling murmured, rather apologetically. "He's just extremely cautious. And suspicious. And distrustful."

"How about paranoid?" Julia smiled wryly. "But it doesn't matter, I understand." She leaned forward in her chair. "Mr. Foster, I have a legal matter of my own that I need to discuss with you. May I retain your services? You can take your fee from the bonus I'm to be paid."

Sterling drew back in consternation. "If it is in regards to this engagement business, I can't represent both you and Michael. That is a conflict of interest."

"This won't be a conflict. All I want is for you to put the money in trust for my sister's expenses," Julia hastened to explain. "In case something should happen to me, I want the bonus to be paid directly to the rehab center where she is a patient. I don't know any other lawyer to ask, and since you know why I'm getting the money, you are the natural choice."

For the first time since she'd met him, the attorney appeared perplexed. Julia quickly filled him in on Joanna's situation, wanting to get the story told and the lawyer's consent before Michael returned.

Sterling's expression was grave by the time she'd finished. "I'll handle the transfer of funds, gratis," he said. "But I think you should tell Michael about your sister and the responsibilities you've assumed these past years. Believe me, he doesn't have a clue."

"I know. He thinks I'm a money-hungry piranha, greedy for all the cash I can get. And when you come right down to it, I am accepting an outrageous amount of money for my part in this charade. I guess that actually does make me a money-hungry piranha, doesn't it?"

"It most certainly does not!" spluttered Sterling. "Michael shouldn't be so damn judgmental. He needs to learn that women's motives impact their actions for better as well as for worse, that most women are not users, but have integrity and compassion. I would like nothing better than to have you be the one to teach him.''

"No.'' Julia lifted her chin, too proud and too stubborn to use her family tragedy to seek Michael's approval. Or to teach him anything. ''There is no reason for Michael to know about Joanna. And I'm not going to tell her about him, either. It would only confuse her. TV viewing is monitored at the hospital, and I'll ask the staff not to mention the engagement to her.''

"You can't tell the hospital staff the engagement is bogus,'' Sterling cautioned.

"I know. My lawyer has duly informed me of all the penalties if I dare to break the vow of secrecy.'' Julia smiled at Sterling.

"I wish Mike knew the real you,'' Sterling muttered, shuffling the papers. He seemed genuinely disturbed. ''I wish he weren't so *paranoid* about women and money. These airtight contracts, tailored to include the most preposterous conditions, are downright insulting. I thought so last night when I drew this up, and now that we've talked, I feel I should apologize. Mike ought to know that you are not a Sheila or a Delilah clone, but a selfless young woman who—''

"If you're my attorney, you have to keep what I told you in confidence, don't you?'' Julia persisted. ''I need you to keep Joanna a secret, Mr. Foster.''

"Of course, I'll keep your secret, but I wish I didn't have to, Julia.'' Sterling sighed. ''Won't you reconsider and—''

He stopped speaking when Michael strode into the room, carrying a small velvet box.

"Here's the ring.'' Michael placed the box on the table in front of Julia.

When she didn't touch it, he reached over and snapped open the lid to display the exquisite, antique ruby ring inside. ''My grandmother left me this ring, presumably to give to the woman I marry. I thought it was wasted on me because I have no intention of ever marrying, and I certainly can't wear it myself.'' He smiled without mirth. "The whole family knows that Grandmother left me this ring to give to my future bride, so they will be expecting to see you wearing it, Julia. Try it on. We'll have it sized for you."

Julia's fingers were trembling slightly when she removed the ring from its velvet bed. She slipped it onto the ring finger of her left hand. It fit perfectly.

"Look at that!" Sterling exhaled an audible breath. "It's as if that ring were made especially for her."

"I'm sure it's a standard size and her fingers are of average size, so naturally, it fits," Michael said coolly. He stared at the heirloom ring on his fausse fiancée's finger. "Sterling, the agreement, please."

He sounded like a maestro cuing the orchestra, Julia thought, as she eyed the thick agreement. She guessed that it would take at least fifteen minutes to slog through Sterling's abbreviated edition.

"Can't wait to delve into that," she murmured. Her empty stomach growled in protest.

The gist of the second contract was that Julia was aware that the ring was Michael's exclusive property, that she agreed to return it after the breakup of the mock-engagement and would not make any claims on it. If she were to attempt to keep the ring or demand financial compensation, she would be fined the whole amount of the final bonus check. She would also have to repay whatever money she'd been given during the phony engagement, at double interest, retroactively.

Julia sucked in her cheeks as she signed the contract in three different places.

"Fines and paybacks with double interest. Retroactive penalties. That's classic Nate-and-Sheila," Sterling grumbled, as he watched her sign. "To be honest, it spooked me to hear

Michael demand such terms himself, but it's what he grew up hearing and seeing.''

"Dysfunction is often passed down from one generation to the next," Julia murmured, remembering some typical case studies.

Michael cleared his throat. "I don't appreciate you two discussing me like I'm not here."

What he really didn't appreciate was the unexpected camaraderie that had developed between Julia and Sterling. He felt left out, which was ridiculous. Knowing it but feeling it anyway only heightened his foul mood.

"I wanted this contract to be irrevocable because I don't want any questions regarding the ring's ownership after this—this foolish game is played out," he said, glaring at his assistant, then his attorney. "My grandmother wanted this ring to remain in the family, and I eventually intend to give it to one of my sisters. Perhaps I'll pass it along to the first one to have a daughter, with the stipulation that the baby girl is to inherit it herself later on. That way, the ring will remain in the Fortune family, just as Grandmother Kate would've wanted."

"You missed the point entirely, Michael. Kate wanted you to give this ring to the woman you married," Sterling said impatiently. "She very much hoped that you would find a woman you loved and trusted enough to wed. Don't think she wasn't aware of your negative attitudes about love and marriage. That is why this ring was her symbolic gift to you. Keeping the heirloom in the family wasn't one of her concerns."

"Well, it's one of mine," retorted Michael.

"Furthermore, if your grandmother wanted Jane or Kristina to have the ring, she'd have left it to one of them," Sterling said through clenched teeth. "This ring is meant for your much-loved bride, and possibly your own daughter, later on."

Julia stared at the hard, tightly drawn line of Michael's mouth and thought of his grandmother, the late Kate Fortune.

The woman must have been an extraordinary optimist to have entertained hopes that her grandson Michael would one day have a much-loved bride. The chances for total world peace seemed more likely.

Michael seemed to think so, too. "Some of Grandmother's specifically chosen gifts were well meaning, but missed their mark. Like leaving this ring to me." He shrugged. "But some of her choices were right on target. Kyle's inheriting the ranch in Wyoming, for example. He finally found a purpose and a goal out there."

"What Kyle found there was the love he's been searching for his entire life," Sterling injected sharply. "Which is what your grandmother wants for you."

"I had no idea you had such a romantic streak, Sterling." Michael flashed a dark, cynical smile. "Perhaps that's why you and Julia have become such instant soul mates. She believes in the power of a redemptive, restorative love, too, don't you, Julia?"

Julia smiled sweetly. "And if that's not possible, group therapy is an option." Her eyes met Sterling Foster's. "If everything is signed and legal, I'd like to go home now." The attorney nodded his head.

She pulled the ring off her finger and put it back into the box. "I'll only wear this ring when I'm in your presence, Michael. I don't want to be charged for any accidental damage or loss."

Rising to her feet, she snatched her purse from the table and quickly exited.

"God forbid she should forfeit a precious penny of her money," Michael said caustically.

"If only you were as smart as you think you are." Sterling snorted. "This has turned into an unholy mess, and your grandmother is not going to be pleased."

Michael noticed the attorney's lapse, referring to his grandmother in the present tense. It was one he'd made himself for weeks after her death. He knew how close Sterling and Grand-mother Kate had been, especially after Grandfather Ben's death. He felt a twinge of compassion for Sterling's personal loss.

Michael picked up the ring box and stared at the ruby ring bequeathed to him by his grandmother...in the hope that he would find his true love and give it to her. Who would have thought that his grandmother, so shrewd and tough in busi-ness, was capable of such a silly, wishful gesture? His lips twisted in a grimace.

"The phony engagement isn't an unholy mess, Sterling. With these contracts, I'm in complete control, and Julia is intelligent enough to realize that."

Sterling stuffed the contracts back into his briefcase. "Mi-chael, you're a damn fool," he growled as he stomped out of the conference room.

Six

"Did Julia tell you the reason why I agreed to talk to you?" Michael demanded as Faith Carlisle and the cameraman accompanying her carried a videocamera, additional equipment for it and a box filled with supplies into his apartment.

"She said that you two are engaged and want me to break the story." Faith Carlisle eyed him speculatively. She was fortyish, with a helmet of blond hair that looked as if it could withstand gale-force winds.

"That's right. We're going to put an end to this eligibility nonsense once and for all."

"Is that the real reason why you decided to announce your engagement to your assistant?" Faith asked shrewdly.

Michael stared at her in horror. This interview was going to be even worse than he'd imagined. He had spent less than thirty seconds in the newswoman's presence and had almost blown the entire scheme!

"No, of course not!" he snapped. "That is insulting to Julia and to me! We're getting engaged for all the usual reasons—which we will discuss when this interview officially begins."

Faith and the cameraman, Ken, went about setting up the video equipment and arranging their supplies. Michael watched them in silence as five minutes dragged by, stretching interminably to six, seven, eight minutes.

"I don't know what's keeping Julia," he said at last as he began to pace the floor of the living room.

There was a wide expanse of floor to pace—twelve-hundred square feet—and he covered all of it from corner to corner, while Faith Carlisle and the cameraman stared at him, bemused.

"It's not like her to be late," Michael muttered, glancing at his watch. He didn't see the numbers. He was too agitated to focus on them.

"She's not late," Faith assured him. "We arrived early. Not intentionally," she added quickly. "We usually run late, but this time we happened to be ahead of schedule. I didn't realize it would be so...upsetting for you."

"When I make an appointment for a certain hour, I expect it to commence at that hour." Michael gritted his teeth. "Not earlier, not later, but at that precise time!"

"Sorry for the inconvenience." Faith did not sound sorry, she sounded annoyed. "Do you want us to leave and come back in ten minutes? That will be the *precise hour* set for our interview." She caught the cameraman's eye. He shrugged.

Michael considered ushering the two invaders into the hall for the next ten minutes, then reluctantly decided against it. "You can stay here," he said grudgingly. "I'll be in my study."

He left the two in the living room, Faith's muttered, "What a control freak!" echoing in his ears.

Control freak? Michael stiffened. He silently conceded that he did have a tendency to be controlling, but this situation—the interview, the bogus engagement—was enough to drive even a mellow soul into a frenzy.

Julia had set up the interview with Faith Carlisle for this evening, but it was Kristina who'd suggested that it be held here in his apartment rather than at the office, which he would've preferred.

"If you set the interview in the office, I just know you'll be stuck in your boss-and-assistant roles," Kristina had declared. ''Maybe in another setting you'll manage to seem like lovers.''

Michael had conceded the point, but the implication hadn't really registered with him until Faith's untimely appearance. He and Julia Chandler had to act like lovers while that intrusive, aggressive blond barracuda looked on, assessing their performance! He pulled his handkerchief from his pocket and mopped his brow. Would they be able to pull it off?

The news team's arrival twenty minutes before the appointed time was nothing less than a waking nightmare. Now he and Julia wouldn't have a chance to plan their mutual performance. She would show up and they'd have to do the interview cold, with no preparation.

There had been no time for a rehearsal or discussion of any sort at work today. He had been booked solid in meetings from the moment he arrived at the office until he departed, an hour after Julia did.

Michael reached into the pocket of his suit jacket and removed the ring box. He would have to slip the ring on Julia's finger as she was entering the apartment, away from Faith Carlisle's eagle eyesight. The newswoman would not understand why a brand-new fiancée wasn't wearing her engagement ring all the time.

Anger flared through him. Why couldn't Julia have kept the ring with her? Her insistence that she wear it only in his presence to avoid being fined for damage or loss was ridiculous! If he'd been worried about that particular possibility, he would have had Sterling mention it in the contract. But he hadn't been worried because he knew how competent and careful Julia was. In the fourteen months they'd worked together she hadn't broken or misplaced a single thing, not even a paper clip.

The doorbell rang, and he shot from his study like the legendary speeding bullet. ''It's Julia,'' he announced, and the sound of his own relief echoed in his ears.

"She doesn't have a key?" Faith asked, her tone deceptively casual.

But Michael wasn't deceived. Faith Carlisle was already suspicious of this arrangement, looking for clues to verify her hunch. He forced himself to calm down and carefully consider the circumstances. If he were engaged, would he have given his fiancée a key to his apartment? It was hard to fathom, but chances are he would have.

"Julia lost her key." Michael congratulated himself on his brilliant improvisation. "We're having a new one made for her."

"Right," Faith said snidely to Ken the cameraman. "More likely he confiscated it because she violated his *precise hour* law."

Thanks to his exceptionally acute Fortune ears, Michael heard every word. He felt a queasy foreboding. The interview hadn't even begun, and already Faith Carlisle was hostile toward him.

He swung the door open. Julia stood on the threshold.

"Hi, honey!" She hurled herself at him, throwing her arms around his neck. Michael was so taken aback that he stood stiff and tense, his arms at his side.

"Real demonstrative type, isn't he?" Faith Carlisle snickered to the cameraman.

"I saw the Channel 3 news van in front of the building," Julia whispered in Michael's ear. "I knew they were here. Pretend to hug me."

How did one pretend to hug? Michael wasn't sure, but his arms encircled Julia tightly and he proceeded to hug her for real. He felt the rounded softness of her breasts pressing against his chest, and the spicy scent of her perfume filled his nostrils.

He vaguely recognized it as one from the Fortune line, but his mind was reeling too wildly for him to recall what it was. An unheard of lapse, because as vice president of product development, Michael knew the names, colors and scents of each and every product that Fortune produced as well as he knew his own name.

But if someone had asked him his name at this particular moment, he might not have been able to come up with the answer. Julia's arms were locked tightly around him and he found it entirely natural to bury his lips against the soft, slender curve of her neck. He closed his eyes as a swift surge of sheer desire swept through him with tidal-wave force.

She was so soft and feminine, and she felt wonderful in his arms. A roar of blood pounded in his veins, deafening him. Slowly, he began to move his hands up and down her back, stroking, caressing. Unable to stop himself, he slid one hand over the firm curve of her bottom. His body quickened with tension, his muscles tightening.

Abruptly, she pulled away from him, leaving him standing alone, his arms empty, his body hard and aching.

"Faith!" Julia exclaimed in delight, as if seeing the newswoman was a dream come true for her. Dazedly, Michael watched her cross the room to the long, wide, gray sectional sofa, where Faith and the cameraman had risen to their feet.

"I feel as if we're already old friends, we've talked so often on the phone," Julia said gaily. She glanced from the news team to the oversize coffee table, where several large books of modern art were strategically arranged.

Julia guessed that the interior decorator had placed them there and Michael hadn't touched them since. She knew he had no interest in art. His only real interest was the Fortune Corporation.

"Has Michael offered you anything to drink?" she asked, playing the role of hostess. She'd never been a fiancée before, but she assumed hostessing duties went with the territory.

"No. We made the mistake of arriving twenty minutes early," Faith said pointedly. "What he would like to offer us is a quick jump off the balcony."

"Uh-oh." Julia glanced from Faith to Michael. "I'm sorry I wasn't here."

"So am I," Faith seconded. "Then again, if you'd been here, you probably would have covered for him, and Ken and I wouldn't have seen what a time-oriented obsessive Michael Fortune really is."

"All successful corporate executives are time-oriented obsessives to some degree," Julia said quickly. "I'm sure anyone who has a successful media career is obsessively time oriented, too, including you, Faith."

"I suppose you have a point," Faith conceded rather grudgingly.

"Would you like something to drink?" Julia interjected. "Coffee or..." She turned to Michael. "What else do we have to offer Faith and..." She smiled questioningly at the cameraman.

"Ken," he said, offering his hand.

Julia took it. "Ken," she repeated, beaming.

Michael watched the scene, goggle-eyed. The unexpected physical contact with Julia and his response to her nearness had thrown him off-balance, and now the sight of her rendered him speechless.

The pretty, poised young woman chatting with those two media vipers was nothing like the quiet, calm, staidly attired Julia he knew from the office. His blue eyes widened as they traveled over her.

She was wearing a short black-white-and-red-plaid pleated skirt that swung around her legs, accentuating the shapely length of them. And her stretchy black shirt softly conformed to the outline of her breasts and waist, displaying curves that her starchy office blouses never did. Her shoes were strappy and sexy, and he swallowed hard as his gaze settled once more on her legs. He was not a man given to fantasizing, but he could certainly conjure up fantasies about her legs, strong and silky smooth, raised high in the air or wrapped tightly around his waist....

Sensual heat struck him with the force of a lightning bolt. He couldn't move; he couldn't breathe. And he couldn't formulate an answer to her question because he'd forgotten what she had asked.

"Something cold?" Julia prompted. "Ice tea or soda or something?"

Michael continued to stare at her. Her hair was different, too. Instead of the tight French braid, it swung soft and loose in a shiny bob that framed her face and nearly reached her shoulders.

"Let's skip the refreshments and get started," Faith said, casting a sharp-eyed glance from Julia to Michael. "As an opening shot, Ken will pan the room, starting with the windows—great view of the city, by the way—then to the fireplace—stone, impressive—and then focus in on the two of you sitting on the sofa. If Michael will join us over here?"

Julia held her breath. Michael was still standing by the door, as if frozen in a catatonic state. Why didn't he say something? She had been trying to be hospitable, and he had simply stood there and stared at her and Faith and Ken as if they were aliens who'd been dropped from a space ship into the middle of his living room.

"I suppose it's now or never," Michael muttered.

Julia watched him as he walked toward them. He was wearing his executive power suit, the navy blue pinstripe he'd worn to the office today, with a snowy white shirt and silk tie. He looked tall and strong, successful and powerful—and completely unapproachable.

Julia's eyes darted from Michael to Faith, and she stifled a sigh of dismay. There was no way that Faith Carlisle, let alone the Twin Cities TV viewing audience, was ever going to buy this act. A man like Michael Fortune was a man out of reach of the Julia Chandlers of the world. He was too good-looking, too sophisticated, too rich and too well connected to be attracted to a nobody like her. An unexpected gloom swamped her.

"I admit to being a bit disconcerted by this interview," Michael said, seating himself beside Julia while the videocamera rolled. "If I have been—a bit brusque, I apologize."

He took Julia's hand in his, linking their fingers.

Julia stiffened. When she'd flung herself into his arms at the door, she had been too distracted by the part she was playing to be aware of any physical effects. But as she sat here beside him, the feel of his big hand enveloping hers sent a frisson of heat shooting through her. She felt the strength of his fingers wrapped around hers, the pad of his thumb pressed against her palm. Her heart turned a wild somersault in her chest and she forgot to breathe.

Michael was too aware of her not to be unaware of her reaction. She looked panicky, ready to bolt! And Faith Carlisle reminded him of a lazy cat about to take a swipe at its cornered prey.

Well, he was nobody's prey, and he was not about to be bested by any manipulative media queen. The Fortune pride, always formidable, bolstered his resolve. He and Julia were going to pull off this deception!

Julia had made an admirable start. Now he had to do his part.

"Julia and I are very private people." Michael inched closer to his fausse fiancée. "Talking about ourselves—especially to a stranger with a camera rolling—doesn't come easily or naturally to either of us." He lifted Julia's hand to his mouth and brushed her knuckles with his lips. "Does it, darling?"

Get in character and stay in character. Julia thought of Jen's acting advice, taken from her drama courses. Earlier this evening, Julia had asked her flatmate some questions on acting techniques, without revealing that she wanted to make use of them within a few short hours.

"An actor has to give herself to the role, and that means thinking, living and breathing the character," Jen had declared rather dramatically. "The actor leaves her own self behind and becomes the character."

It made sense in a way, Julia decided. She hadn't felt these terrible feelings of inadequacy when she'd first entered the apartment, literally thrusting herself into Michael's arms—and into her role of fiancée. It was only when she'd slipped back to being ordinary, everyday Julia that doubt and anxiety had assailed her. It was time to leave her own self behind and become the character—Michael Fortune's fiancée.

Any woman who managed to get *him* to propose would possess monumental self-confidence. Julia took a deep breath and willed herself to become that woman. To get in character and stay in character, until that sublime moment when Channel 3 News left the apartment.

Following Michael's lead, Julia lifted his hand and rubbed it against her cheek. "We prefer each other's company to anyone else's, and we cherish our time alone together," she cooed softly.

She recalled reading a similar statement made by a newly wed celebrity in a magazine interview. It was generic enough to work for anybody.

Faith looked bored. Perhaps she'd read the same quote? "Why don't you tell me how you two met?"

Julia and Michael looked at each other.

"Would you like to tell the story, Julia?"

"Oh, no, you do it, Michael. You tell it so much better than I do." Julia gave him a smile as adoring as that of any wife of a political candidate on the campaign trail.

"Well, as you know, Julia works for me," Michael began. He'd hoped that Julia would opt to tell the tale. She certainly was being paid enough to dream up a beginning for them.

"We met when I interviewed her for the job. The interview went well, her qualifications were good and I hired her on the spot. We grew, uh, closer as the months went on, and as a result we decided to get engaged."

"And that's it?" Faith was clearly disappointed with the prosaic rendition.

Julia wished that Michael had had the benefit of Jen's acting pointers. He had not left his own self behind to become the character of a man madly in love with his new fiancée. She decided she had better take center stage and do a bit of necessary embellishing.

"Michael is giving you the abridged version," Julia said, flashing a smile that she hoped was sufficiently dazzling. A woman in love would definitely have a dazzling smile. "I'll be honest with you, Faith. For me, it was love at first sight. The moment I met Michael I knew he was the man I'd been waiting for my entire life. And when he hired me, I was certain it was fate. That we were destined to be together." She snuggled closer to Michael and gazed at him raptly.

Michael was staggered. She really had beautiful eyes; he had never been close enough to her to fully appreciate them. They were an intriguing shade of gray, with just the slightest bluish hue, and were framed by thick, dark lashes.

"But it wasn't love at first sight for Mike?" asked Faith.

"No," Julia replied. One could only suspend disbelief to a certain point, and she didn't want to push beyond it. Michael Fortune would not fall in love with Julia Chandler at first sight, not even in one of Rebecca's tales of romantic suspense.

"Yes," Michael said at the same time.

"No or yes? Which is it?" Faith demanded.

Julia and Michael looked at each other.

"Yes, I fell in love with her at first sight, but I didn't let her know," said Michael. He wished Julia didn't look so blatantly disbelieving. Faith was sure to notice. "I'm admitting it for the first time tonight,'' he added, hoping to cover for his fausse fiancée's incredulity.

"How sweet!" Julia faked a sigh. "But it's not true."

Michael was laying it on too thick, she thought worriedly. It was almost predictable that quiet Julia Chandler would fall in love with her handsome, dashing boss the moment she laid eyes on him. However, it was totally incongruous that he would take one look at her and lose his head. Some element of credibility had to be maintained in this bogus love story.

"Michael's recollection of our first meeting falls under the category of retrospective falsification," Julia explained, relying on Psych terminology to bail them out of this ticklish situation. "That means you remember past incidents colored by what has occurred since then. He really didn't fall in love with me until—until we'd known each other for months."

"There is nothing retro-falsely..." Michael gave his head a shake. She was going to undo them with her psycho-glossary. "Julia, I ought to know when I fell in love, and it was at first sight," he insisted. He was frustrated. Why couldn't she simply go along with his story? "I can even remember what you were wearing. A beige suit, a white blouse and a pair of very sensible, very practical pumps. Your hair was pulled back in that French-braid style I hate so much."

Of course, he didn't remember what she'd been wearing that particular day. He scarcely remembered interviewing her for the job, because at that point he'd done so many interviews with potential assistants they tended to blur together. But it was easy to fake a memory. He'd simply described Julia's daily uninteresting office attire.

"You hate my hair in a French braid?" Julia sat up straight. Was he serious or had he suddenly become a world-class actor? He certainly sounded believable.

"I always have," Michael affirmed. "I like it when you wear it down."

With one smooth movement, he slipped his arm around her waist and pulled her closer to him. This time they were so close their thighs were pressing, their shoulders rubbing. Julia squirmed uneasily, but he kept his arm anchored securely around her.

She felt the warmth of his body heat and the strength in his long fingers as he casually caressed the hollow of her waist. She was flushed and flustered.

"The braid is a very easy, practical hairstyle to maintain in the office," Julia murmured defensively.

Faith was amused. "Mike, are you telling us that you fell in love with Julia at first sight even though her clothes and her hairstyle were hardly sexual weapons?"

"That's right. I think I fell in love with her because she *wasn't* trying to sexually bewitch me with flashy, sexy clothes and a luxurious mane of hair forever being tossed and twirled. I'd seen too much of that in the past. From the very first day, it was clear that Julia took her job seriously, that she was in the office to work, not to try to—to enchant me."

"And yet, ultimately, you were enchanted by her," Faith said thoughtfully. "So much that you asked her to marry you."

"Yes." Michael nodded his head. It was an incredibly plausible story, he decided, feeling the same excitement he felt when a new product exceeded expectations. And Faith believed it, he could tell.

"So when it came to women, your attitude was pretty much 'been there, done that, seen it'?" continued Faith. "Until Julia came along, a sort of office Cinderella with a wardrobe to match and—"

"Oh, please! What woman in her right mind wants to be Cinderella these days?" Julia interrupted, remembering the conversation she'd had with Michael on that very subject. "The Prince Charming concept is so outdated, it borders on the dysfunctional," she added for good measure.

"So you don't view me as either princely or charming?" Michael parried lightly. "I'm crushed."

"Well, you don't view me as a bewitching enchantress, and I've tried so hard to be." Her gray eyes were warm, inviting him to share the secret joke.

Michael did, laughing at the very premise of Julia Chandler as a bewitching enchantress. "You wouldn't have lasted fourteen days in the office in that role, let alone fourteen months." A surge of affection for her, as sudden as it was unexpected, rushed through him. With his left arm still locked around her, he reached for her hand and laid it on his thigh, covering it with his palm.

Julia felt the muscular wall of his chest against her back, breathed in the subtle male scent of Fortune's sandalwood aftershave and for a moment was thrown into a morass of sensual confusion.

Was this a dream? The aura of unreality seemed so hazy and surreal. But the feel of his hard thigh under her fingers, the rise and fall of his chest in sync with her own breathing were very real indeed. She was surrounded by Michael, all of her senses aware of his virile masculinity.

Was she getting too much into her character? Julia wondered nervously. It was one thing to put on a believable act, but to begin to physically feel the things that the character would be feeling was crossing the line. This honeyed warmth suffusing her limbs, the fluttering of her pulses and jittery breathlessness would be appropriate for Michael Fortune's real-life fiancée, but not for Julia Chandler, employee, who was being paid union-scale overtime for sitting here on the sofa with him.

She badly needed a break to recover her scrambled wits.

"I'm awfully thirsty. If you'll excuse me for a minute, I'll go get a glass of water." Julia wriggled away from Michael and rose swiftly to her feet. Hopefully, a drink of cold water would douse her internal heat as effectively as that old recommended panacea, the cold shower. "Would anybody else like anything?"

Michael glanced from Faith and Ken and the videocam to Julia, who was already heading out of the room. "I'll help you prepare some refreshments for our guests, sweetheart," he called, and went rushing after her.

He caught up with her as she walked into the dining room. It was quite small in comparison to the mammoth living room. A black, lacquered, Oriental-style table with six matching chairs almost filled the room. Julia stared absently at the stylized jade tree serving as a centerpiece. Her eyes flicked to an elaborate birdcage that dominated one corner of the small room, and she quickly looked away.

"You didn't have to come with me," she murmured. "I can find the kitchen. I'm assuming it's adjacent to this dining room."

"It is," Michael agreed. "But there was no way I was going to be stuck alone again with Channel 3's team of sharks. They were smelling blood—mine—before you arrived. Here, come this way...."

He guided her into the kitchen. Julia glanced around with wide, curious eyes. The kitchen was done in blue-and-white gingham and oak, and though the appliances were gleaming and modern, the decor of the room was unmistakably country or Americana or whatever the current term for that particular style was these days. And whatever it was being called, it clashed violently with the Oriental motif in the next room, which in turn clashed with the modern minimalist look of the living room.

"What's the matter?" Michael demanded. "You look as awestruck as little Dorothy when she landed in Oz."

"I was just admiring your eclectic room-by-room decor," Julia said politely.

"Say no more." Michael heaved a sigh. "I rarely have company here, so I forget the impact this place has on people.

You're very tactful in describing it as eclectic. Schizophrenic is probably more apt—and I have my mother to thank.''

"I didn't know your mother was an interior decorator."

"She isn't. But she's been through a number of friends who are. The friendships lasted about as long as it took for each one to decorate a room. Then it was 'off with the old, on with the new.' Since I refused to keep buying new stuff each time the decorator changed, I ended up with this mess.''

"I wouldn't call it a mess,'' Julia murmured tactfully. "It's...interesting.''

"Kristina said my apartment reminds her of a theme park.'' Michael grimaced wryly. "But thank you for not asking why I allowed my mother to become involved in the first place.''

Julia wasn't about to ask such a loaded question.

So Michael told her. "Mom is a first-class manipulator. She can switch from sweet to desperate to vicious so fast you expect to see her head doing one-hundred-eighty-degree spins. So when she decided she wanted to use her decorator friends to redo my apartment, I decided it was easier to stay out of her way and just let her do what she wanted. I lived in a hotel room during the months she was occupied with this place, and it was great. She was out of my hair—in fact, she stayed out of everybody's hair for the duration. Once the project was finally done, Kyle and Janie begged me to move to another place and turn Mom and the decorators loose again, so we could enjoy some additional months of peace.''

Julia managed a polite laugh, but she was visibly uncomfortable. "I'll get my water now. If you'll show me where you keep the glasses?''

"Mother bashing is not your sport, even if the mother is the notorious Sheila Fortune?''

She nodded. "Something like that.''

"You've never mentioned your folks,'' Michael observed, realizing it for the first time. "You know all about my entire family, but I don't know a thing about yours. In fact, I don't know anything at all about your life outside the office, except that you run the river trail and once took a self-defense course that you believe has rendered you invulnerable.''

As Michael showed no inclination to get her a glass, Julia proceeded to open several cabinets until she found one. She filled it with water and took a few long gulps.

"If Faith asks, I should know something about your family—and more about you," Michael pressed. He realized that he was actually curious about her. Had he ever met a woman who talked so little about herself?

"There's not much to tell." Julia stared at the polished wood floor. "My parents are both dead and I have a sister. Someday I hope to become a psychologist and work in a clinic counseling children and adolescents. Meanwhile, I work for the Fortune Corporation."

"I see." Michael was disconcerted. "You are very young to be alone in the world."

"I'm twenty-six, an adult," Julia countered quietly. "And I'm not alone, I have my sister. She lives in the outskirts of Minneapolis."

Michael, who always had been surrounded by—and sometimes felt suffocated by—his sprawling extended family, could barely comprehend her solitary state. "I'm sorry for your loss," he murmured. "When did—"

"Thank you for your sympathy," Julia interrupted with polite finality.

Michael took the not-so-subtle hint. No further questions were welcome.

They stared at each other for a long, uneasy moment.

"In your situation, you were wise to think of your financial status," he said at last. As a conversation filler, money always worked. "Perhaps you ought to ask Sterling for help in investing your bonus. He seems to possess an uncanny knack when it comes to the stock market."

Julia smiled. "I'm surprised you aren't urging me to invest every penny in Fortune stock."

"An excellent idea. The shares are lower than they've ever been, and while that is a nightmare for us, it's a bonanza for the potential investor. Buy cheap and then settle back and watch the values go through the roof—and they will," he added with steely Fortune determination. "The company is going to bounce back from—"

"Are you two still here or did you take off? Where are you?" Faith Carlisle's voice seemed to reverberate throughout the penthouse. It was the booming tone she used for Channel 3's *Film at Eleven* promos.

And it sent Julia into a panic. "Faith is looking for us!" she exclaimed in a frantic whisper. "It sounds like she's heading toward the dining room."

"'Something wicked this way comes,'" Michael quoted grimly.

"What are we going to do? We don't have any refreshments prepared."

"I don't have any to prepare, because I didn't buy any. I didn't consider this interview a social occasion."

"But you said you were coming to the kitchen to help me prepare some refreshments." Julia stared at him anxiously. "How can we explain why we've been in here all this time without—"

"We won't offer an explanation. I have a better idea."

There was a glint in his blue eyes that Julia knew well. She'd seen it when a Fortune product won its market share over a competitor's product; she'd seen it when he was prepared to go head-to-head with his father or his uncle over an issue that they opposed and he favored.

It was his winner-take-all, no-apologies expression. Julia had no doubts he would be wearing that same expression, his blue eyes glinting with challenge and victory, when he was installed as CEO of the Fortune Corporation at some future date.

Oh yes, he clearly had a winning plan in mind, but Julia was clueless as to what it might be.

"We'll let them find us together, behaving as any newly engaged couple would." Michael smiled wolfishly. "We're about to convince Faith and her camcorder-toting sidekick that we're so caught up in each other we forgot all about them. Ready?"

Michael moved toward her, his swift, sudden approach catching Julia completely off guard. She stumbled a few steps backward, until her hips touched the edge of the counter.

He stepped forward and placed his arms on either side of her, laying his palms on the counter, trapping her between it and his body. Automatically, her head jerked upward. He was towering over her, close, but not quite touching his body to hers. His size and strength, his warmth and his scent filled her senses, dizzying her.

"Michael, I—" She broke off, her lips parting as she gulped for air.

Her thoughts splintered as his mouth came down and covered hers.

Seven

For a split second, Julia was too startled to move. *Her boss was kissing her!* She was far too stunned to respond. Surely Michael didn't expect her to. After all, this kiss was as much a hoax as their engagement.

Faith Carlisle's voice grew louder. Julia felt Michael's arms encircle her, pulling her closer.

"She's coming," he urged, whispering against her lips. "And you're stiffer than a mannequin. You can fake it better than this, can't you?"

"I—I guess so," Julia managed to stammer.

She drew back her head a little and looked into his deep blue eyes. The focused intensity she saw there was oddly reassuring because it was so familiar. Michael was always intensely focused when it came to anything pertaining to his family's company.

I can and will do whatever is necessary for the welfare of the Fortune Corporation, and if that includes playing a certain role, even the role of besotted fiancé, I will play it to the hilt. The vow he'd made echoed in her mind.

This embrace was merely part of him playing the role of besotted fiancé. And Michael did have a point, Julia conceded. If Faith found them kissing, they wouldn't have to explain the lack of refreshments. A small point, perhaps, but the less subterfuge the better, especially since they were up to their proverbial necks in it.

"Put your arms around me," Michael whispered. "Let's pull one over on that media hotshot."

This was all about hoodwinking Faith, Julia kept reminding herself. About ending Michael's eligibility woes for the sake of the company. She had signed a contract—one that seemed as long and legally binding as a Supreme Court decision—to play the part of Michael's loving fiancée.

"Well, here goes." Julia gulped and slipped her arms around his neck. The action brought her firmly against his hard, solid body. She raised her face to his.

"You look utterly appalled," Michael murmured. Strangely enough, he found her reticence appealing, even charming. It was both a novelty and a relief to be with a woman who didn't want anything from him except what they had contracted. "Relax. It'll be over before you know it," he added, his voice light with humor, his lips touching hers as he spoke.

The kiss began tentatively, his mouth brushing gently over hers, then lingering longer and increasing the pressure. His hands roamed the length of her back, smoothing the soft, stretchy black top against her skin. He liked the feel of the material under his fingers, and he especially liked the way her breasts were crushed against his chest as he pressed her closer and closer to him.

Julia's fingers stroked his neck, running through the soft thickness of his hair at the nape. Touching him wasn't as unnerving as she'd feared. After all, at this particular point in time Michael was not her boss, he was merely a fellow actor. They were playing a scene, one that included a pair of villains named Faith and Ken. It definitely helped to keep that in mind.

Their lips touched and clung and broke apart, then went through the cycle all over again. It was an enticing, unthreatening series of little kisses, and Julia's confidence grew. She could play this role.

Michael lifted his mouth slightly from hers. "Hear anything?" His breath was warm against her cheek as his fingers followed the fine, straight line of her spine, kneading lightly.

"No. Do you think the dastardly duo has given up and left?" Reflexively, Julia arched into him. His caressing fingers felt so good, paradoxically relaxing and stimulating.

"We should be so lucky." Michael's mouth brushed hers. "More likely, they're robbing me blind. Carrying stuff out of here and stowing it in the Channel 3 van to sell to a fence."

Julia stifled the urge to giggle. "If they are, I hope they take that hideous green birdcage in the corner of the dining room—*and* the fake birds that are in it."

"No self-respecting fence would accept that object d'art–gallery reject," Michael murmured. "I was hoping you hadn't seen it, since you didn't mention it at the time."

"It's impossible to miss." Her eyes danced. "But I was determined to be tactful."

"You should be rewarded for your tact. Your take-home prize is the birdcage, complete with fake birds."

"Oh, please, not that!" Julia feigned horror. "As garish as the birdcage is, those fake birds are even worse. They look like the work of a deranged taxidermist. Do you think the whole thing was the decorator's revenge for being fired after only doing one room?"

"I've often wondered that myself."

Michael stared down at her. Her cheeks were flushed, her mouth soft and moist, her gray eyes bright. The feel of her warm, curvy body was sending jolts of sensual heat through him. He couldn't seem to keep his hands off her, couldn't keep them still, either.

It was as if his mind and body had split, and his physical, sexual self took control, sending his cool, intellectualizing alter ego into oblivion. His hands slid over the curve of her hips, then to her derriere. He cupped her firmly, lifting her harder and higher against him.

Julia felt his hard arousal against the softest, most vulnerable part of her and uttered a startled cry, which was instantly silenced by the warm pressure of his mouth. Her lips parted automatically under his and his tongue penetrated her mouth, probing and rubbing in seductive rhythm. Something inside her went weak and soft, and suddenly, thrillingly, Julia felt her body catch fire.

Her senses reeling, she slipped her tongue into his mouth to tease him into an erotic little duel. The kiss grew deeper and hotter and hungrier. Another kiss followed, longer and wilder, and then another and another until it was impossible to distinguish a beginning or an end. Lips, tongues, kisses melded and merged as the flames of desire blazed between them.

A low rumble came from the back of Michael's throat, a primitive mating sound that triggered a fierce feminine response from deep within her. She glided her hands over the taut muscles of his shoulders, familiarizing herself with the feel of his body, of his strength, wanting to learn more.

Julia writhed sensuously against him, a passionate need burning and building within her. It was an urgency she had never before experienced, and it drove her every move. Instinctively, her thighs encircled one of his, heightening the intimacy of their already intimate position. A thick, syrupy warmth surged through her and pooled deep in her abdomen. Her legs felt shaky and weak, and she had to cling to Michael for support.

Her mind was hazy. Lost in a sensual daze, she succumbed to the desire swirling through her. She wished they weren't in the brightly lit kitchen; she wished they weren't standing up. It would be heavenly to be able to lie down with him in the quiet darkness of—

"Aha! Here you are!" Faith Carlisle declared triumphantly.

Michael and Julia sprang apart, like a pair of guilty teens caught necking in school by the principal.

Standing beside Faith, Ken was still videotaping.

"Turn that thing off," Michael ordered testily, but the cameraman didn't until he got an affirming nod from Faith.

Julia clutched the edge of the counter, her heart thundering in her ears, her legs rubbery. She didn't trust herself to look at Michael, so she stared blindly at Faith, who was studying the two of them with real interest.

"Don't worry, we won't show any footage of you two groping each other," Faith promised cheerfully. "Just a little kissing. After all, this is for the five-thirty broadcast, the soft-news segment, and we don't want to shock the senior citizens and kiddies who might be watching."

"We weren't groping each other," Michael growled. "We—we're…" His voice trailed off. What could he possibly say? That his whole body was shaking in reaction to the passionate encounter with Julia? That the kiss that had begun as a sham to con Faith Carlisle had turned into something else altogether?

He cast a quick, covert glance at his assistant and felt a surge of panic mixed with resentment. He had taken Julia Chandler in his arms and kissed her, and suddenly every nerve in his body had short-circuited. There had been nothing feigned in the passion that flared between them. The urgency that had shattered his control was still rippling through him, and was very real indeed.

When was the last time he'd kissed a woman and lost his head? Mental alarm bells seemed to go off, sending his mind racing back to the bad old days of Delilah DeSilva. But he had been so young then, and Delilah had been a skilled seductress.

Michael frowned. Now he was fully mature and too cynical and experienced to believe that a kiss meant anything special. Kissing did not lead to out-of-control sexual fireworks; that kind of self-serving rationalization was the province of the immature and irresponsible, of which he was neither. He was the master of his passion—passion did not master him!

None of which explained his explosive response to Julia during that sexy little interlude set up to deceive Faith Carlisle. Confusion and frustration ripped through him. *I do not want Julia,* he told himself sternly, though his body was still throbbing with evidence that proved otherwise. He could not want her; he refused to want her. Therefore, he would not. The Fortune willpower was mighty, and he had inherited more than his share. His will would prevail!

"Take your time, gather your thoughts." Faith smirked. "Ken and I don't mind waiting."

Since Michael was standing mute and solemn, Julia realized it was up to her to handle the news team.

"We're terribly sorry, Faith." Her voice was husky and thick, and she cleared her throat, blushing. "We, uh, sort of got—distracted and—"

"We noticed, honey," Faith said. "Listen, forget about the coffee or whatever. We can wrap this up after just a few more questions. Ready?"

Julia nodded her head and glanced questioningly at Michael. He shrugged.

"When is the wedding?" Faith asked, as Ken began to tape again.

Julia looked at Michael, who was staring into space, clearly not paying the slightest attention to the conversation going on around him.

"The wedding," she repeated, when it became obvious that Michael had no intention of answering. "We haven't set a definite date yet." She moved closer to Michael and subtly nudged his foot with the narrow high heel of her shoe, hoping to catch his attention. "We're just going to enjoy being engaged for a while, aren't we, Michael?"

Being close to her had an aphrodisiac effect upon him. Michael's mind became clouded again as his body pulsed with the hunger he couldn't deny. His mighty Fortune willpower faltered, then gave up the ghost. Acting on sheer impulse, he wrapped his arms around Julia's waist and pulled her back against him. It felt so very right, as if she belonged there. He nuzzled her neck, savoring the sweetness of the moment, ignoring Faith and the videocamera recording them.

"Aren't we, Michael?" Julia repeated, a bit louder.

He had no idea what she was talking about. "Whatever you say, sweetie."

Julia felt the hard ridge of his arousal pressing against the cleft of her buttocks. She inhaled sharply, fighting the sensation to sink back against him. This game of theirs was getting a little out of hand. She had to set things back on track.

She forced herself to look into the camera and address Faith Carlisle. "In that case, I say the wedding will be in June. I know it's corny and traditional, but I've always wanted to be a June bride."

"That will give you plenty of time to make arrangements for the wedding," Faith said approvingly. "Care to share any of your plans with us?"

Julia was suddenly seized by a most uncharacteristic impish impulse. "It will probably be an extravaganza," she confided.

Behind her, she felt Michael tense. He was probably wondering what she was up to and whether or not it was covered in their comprehensive contract. The imp within her grew to a full-fledged devil. If Michael persisted in making her carry the bulk of this interview charade, then he would have to suffer the consequences.

She smiled sweetly at Faith. "Knowing Michael as I do, he'll insist on having the works—you know, thousands of guests, ice sculptures on the lawn, a multicolored striped tent, a full orchestra, a seven-course dinner. Maybe even hot-air-balloon rides."

"Naturally, you'll want the whole event videotaped," Ken interjected eagerly." I freelance on the side and I've done weddings, bar mitzvahs, reunions—you name it, I've recorded it. Can I leave my card with you?"

"Ken, you're not supposed to be drumming up business for yourself during an interview. It's unprofessional," Faith scolded, but Ken didn't care. He was reaching into his pocket, hoping to score what promised to be the video job of the year.

Julia stepped forward to accept the card, moving out of Michael's arms. "Any other questions, Faith?"

"Have you chosen an engagement ring yet?" Faith asked.

Michael suddenly came to life and reached into the pocket of his suit jacket to remove the ring box. He explained the legacy of the ruby ring, left to him by his grandmother to be given to his future bride.

"The ring had to be sized for Julia," he lied. "But it's ready for her to wear now."

Ken zoomed the lens in on a shot of Michael slipping the ruby ring onto Julia's finger.

After a few more minutes of small talk, Faith declared the interview at an end. The newswoman was downright friendly as she and Ken departed, lugging their equipment. Julia walked them to the elevator. Michael chose to remain inside the apartment, after bidding the pair a cool goodbye.

"This is off the record," Faith said to Julia as they waited for the elevator to arrive. "Strictly woman-to-woman. Are you going to live here after you and Mike are married?"

"I suppose so," Julia said. It hardly seemed worth the effort to fabricate a brand-new address for the newlyweds who would never be.

"Well, I recommend throwing out everything in that apartment and furnishing it from scratch," Faith said earnestly. "The decor is terrible, about the worst I've ever seen, and I've been in some pretty tacky places. And that birdcage in the dining room should be the first thing to go. I wouldn't even wait for the wedding to get rid of it!"

"I agree, but unfortunately, it's one of Michael's favorite things." Julia grinned wickedly, unable to resist her own private joke.

"I guess you're stuck with it then," Faith commiserated.

"It just goes to prove that having money is no guarantee against bad taste."

"How true," agreed Julia.

The elevator arrived, and the news team stepped inside the car. "The story will run tomorrow at five-thirty. Tell all your friends to watch," Faith called as the doors snapped shut.

The door to Michael's apartment swung open the moment the elevator left. Had he been standing there listening?

"The birdcage is one of my favorite things?" he exclaimed, thereby proving that he'd been eavesdropping. "That was a cheap shot, Julia."

"I couldn't resist." She slipped past him into the apartment. "And since you left me alone with her, you left yourself wide open for whatever cheap shot I could deliver."

"You delivered more cheap shots than an amusement-park shooting gallery. 'Knowing Michael as I do, he'll insist on having the works—thousands of guests, ice sculptures, a multicolored striped tent, hot-air-balloon rides!' I'm surprised you didn't say I'd want dancing elephants, too."

"I didn't think of that one." Julia tried and failed to suppress a laugh.

"It isn't funny, Julia." But Michael was smiling in spite of himself. "I wouldn't set foot in a hot-air balloon. As for the ice-sculptures—"

"I was going to add you preferred them in the shapes of Roman gods and goddesses, but I thought that would be overdoing it," Julia confided.

"To say the least! As it is, after tomorrow, I'll probably be hounded by ambitious ice sculptors and hot-air balloonists and tacky wedding consultants." He had a predatory and unmistakably sexual gleam in his eye as he reached out and grabbed her wrists. "And it'll be all your fault."

"But at least you'll no longer be eligible," Julia murmured. Her heart was beginning to race. Michael pulled her closer, his eyes fixed on her mouth. Her eyelids drooped; her voice grew huskier. "And the voice-mail system won't be jammed, because how many ice sculptors and hot-air balloonists and tacky wedding consultants can there be in Minneapolis and St. Paul?"

He slowly lowered his head to hers. "You are always so serious. I never knew you could be such a jokester."

"I never knew it, either. But the dynamics of the situation inspired me." Her eyes met his. He was going to kiss her, she knew, and she wanted him to.

"The dynamics of the situation inspire me, too," Michael said raspily. "To do this."

His mouth covered hers in blatant demand. Julia responded at once as desire, sharp and almost violent in its intensity, shot through her. He thrust his tongue deeply into her mouth and she welcomed the intimacy. It was as if Faith's interruption hadn't occurred, and they were picking up where they'd left off earlier in the kitchen, in the middle of that wild maelstrom of kisses.

He gathered her against his hard frame, and Julia clung to him, wrapping her arms around his neck and instinctively fitting her soft curves to the unyielding male planes of his body. The two of them seemed to fit together perfectly, she thought dizzily, complementary halves combining their strength and passion to form a binding, inseparable whole.

He kissed her harder and deeper, and she strained even closer, wanting more. Michael drank in her soft sweet moans and felt drunk with pleasure.

He could feel the tips of her breasts tightening into hard little buds, and the subtle, sensual pressure against his chest tantalized him. A shudder of desire racked him. He wanted to see her, to touch her and taste her....

With a low growl of passion, he slid his hand over her breast, cupping the softness. He rubbed his thumb over her nipple, circling it, teasing the beaded crest until she whimpered and pushed herself more fully against his palm. A river of intense pleasure flowed from her nipple to her loins, which were tight and aching and moist with yearning.

She felt his erection, hard and forceful against her. His hands and mouth grew more demanding. Julia sensed his loss of control and was shocked to realize that her own control was just as precarious. Abruptly, she pulled away from him. Her lack of restraint was as alarming as her swift, tumultuous arousal.

What was she doing? Was she crazy? Julia stared blindly at the floor, her breathing fast and shallow, her heart rate topping any chart. If she kept on letting him kiss her and touch her this way—and if she continued kissing and touching him—they would end up in bed! Even worse, part of her wanted nothing more than to forget everything but the passion of the moment and go to bed with him.

Fortunately, the more sensible, cautious part of herself prevailed. Julia thought of the title of the latest book she'd borrowed from the library: *The Twelve Most Stupid Things Women Can Do to Screw Up Their Lives*. Though she hadn't read it yet, she was certain that having an affair with one's boss must be close to the top of the list. Faking an engagement to him undoubtedly belonged there, too, although it probably was not a common-enough occurrence to rate inclusion.

She glanced down at the ruby ring on her finger, the symbol of their duplicity. Fooling Faith Carlisle and everyone in the Twin Cities about this faux relationship with Michael was one thing, but fooling herself was something else entirely. Sexually acting the part of his fiancée—with no witnesses around to put on the brakes—was dangerous and stupid, because she knew very well what Michael thought of her.

And if she were ever to forget, she had those encyclopedia-size legal contracts he'd had drawn up to remind her. He found her basically untrustworthy, greedy and out for as much as she could get. There were plenty of books on the market about men with pathological views of women, but Julia hadn't bothered to read them because she'd never felt the need. She was sure that she would never be one of those hapless *Women Who Love Men Who Won't or Can't Love Them Back*.

Her eyes flew to Michael. His face was tight and drawn, his blue eyes glittering, the pupils constricted to black pin-points. "Come here," he said, his voice a raspy growl.

The sexy masculine command nearly undid her. If she didn't get out of here fast, she would be right back in his arms and would end up committing a "stupid thing to screw up her life."

"I have to go home now," Julia cried, and she rushed into the living room to retrieve her purse from the sofa.

Michael followed her, driven by his own primitive male instincts. At that particular moment, he was not so far removed from some ancient Fortune ancestor who'd lived in a cave and resolutely pursued the fleeing female of his choice.

His body pulsed with ferocious urgency. This time it was no use trying to convince himself that he didn't want Julia. He watched her snatch her purse and start for the door, his eyes sweeping over her.

He could see the outline of her nipples under the soft stretchy fabric of her black jersey, and the sight stimulated a physical recollection of how they'd felt rubbing against him. He stared at her mouth, moist and swollen from their kisses, and once again he felt the sweetness of her lips, the provocative play of her tongue.

Oh, yes, he wanted her. The admission irritated him, but he did not believe in self-deception. Face the problem and find a solution was his credo. Wanting Julia Chandler was definitely a problem. However, at the moment the solution to it eluded him.

Julia was already out of the apartment and frantically pressing the elevator button. Without turning around, she knew Michael had joined her in the small vestibule.

"There is a code disengaging the security lock on the elevator," he said coolly. "The car won't come until I punch in the numbers."

"I would appreciate it very much if you'd do that right now." Julia kept her eyes affixed to the elevator door.

Michael didn't move. "Did you drive here?" he asked.

She nodded her head. Where was the panel with the security code? she wondered. She only saw one button to press, the conventional one to summon the car.

"And where did you park?"

"In the parking lot in the building." Julia shifted impatiently. "Michael, please call the elevator."

"What level?"

"Does it matter?" She turned to face him. Her nerves were on edge, and she temporarily forgot proper employee protocol. "Why are you quizzing me, Michael? I just want the elevator to come so I can get out of here!"

"I wasn't conducting an inquisition, I was merely making conversation." Michael stared at her, his eyes, his body burning as another unexpected, unwelcome riptide of lust dragged him under. The intensity stunned him, worried him, too. He wanted to cast his much-vaunted self-control to the wind and carry her back inside his apartment, directly to his bedroom.

Julia's mouth was dry and she swallowed hard. Her emotions were too volatile for her to stick around and chat. She wanted to cry, she wanted to hit him, but most of all, she wanted to be back in his arms. Too bad that what she wanted most was not in her best interests, which was to get away from him as quickly as possible.

"I think we should talk about what happened here tonight," Michael began, but Julia immediately cut him off.

"There is nothing to talk about. We did what we planned and I think we fooled Faith. Now, *please,* call the elevator."

Michael fumed. "What's your rush? You're being paid for your time." His tone was caustic, insultingly so.

"The meter stopped running the moment Faith left the

building," Julia retorted. "You might regard me as a bought-and-paid-for hooker, but I—"

"I never said that! I never even implied it!" Michael was surprised to hear shouting—and even more amazed to realize that he was the one doing it.

Julia had turned her back to him again and was standing stiffly, her posture ramrod straight, staring intently at the elevator as if it were an object of rare fascination for her.

"All right, since you're so desperate to leave, then go!" Michael strode inside his apartment, practically assaulting the numbered buttons on the security panel on the wall as he punched in the code.

Julia heard the elevator whir into action as Michael shut the door to his apartment with a bang. A moment after the car arrived, she noticed that she was still wearing the ruby ring. Her spirits sagging, she hit the button to the level where she'd parked.

Nice going, Julia, she lectured herself. *Not only have you infuriated your boss, you left with his grandmother's ring, which undoubtedly assures that you'll be mugged tonight.*

The doors swung open and she stepped out of the elevator, surveying the parking level filled with cars. She'd pulled her 1986, chocolate-brown Plymouth Horizon into a space designated for compacts between the wall and a column, about fifty feet from the elevators.

As she started toward her car, she heard footsteps in the nearby stairwell. Her heart jumped into her throat. She had been uneasy since she'd realized she was still wearing the ruby ring, but now terror gripped her. The door above the stairwell Exit sign was thrust open, and Julia began to run, a difficult feat in high heels.

"Julia, wait!"

She heard Michael's voice resounding through the deserted parking garage. Julia stopped in her tracks and whirled around to see him walking toward her. A great surge of relief collided with the rush of adrenaline coursing through her. She felt as if she'd been hit by an earthquake, she was so shaken.

"Oh, thank God, it's you!" She rushed toward Michael, pulling the ring off her finger. "I'm so glad you remembered the ring," she exclaimed breathlessly. "I forgot about it until I was on the elevator, and then I was sure it would be stolen."

She thrust the ring into his hand. Michael gripped her fingers with his, the ring trapped between them. "I'm not here to retrieve the ring," he rasped. "The panel above the elevator flashed the number of the floor you pressed and I came to escort you to your car."

"You didn't have to," she murmured uncertainly. "Although I'm glad you did, so I could give you back the—"

"It is customary for a gentleman to see a lady safely home," Michael interrupted. "Since you drove yourself here, the least I can do is to make sure you reach your car safely."

"Especially when I'm wearing your grandmother's antique heirloom," Julia said dryly. She smiled at him.

Her smile affected him in a way he did not want to acknowledge. "I'm tired of playing hot potato with this ring," he complained instead. "It's ridiculous the way we keep tossing it back and forth to each other. Just keep the damn thing on your finger, okay?"

She had started walking to her car and he walked beside her. In unspoken complicity, they held on to each other's fingers, both clutching the ring between them.

"Okay?" he repeated when she didn't answer.

"I can't take that chance. This ring is worth more than my car, Michael. I can't afford to be held financially responsible in case it gets lost or stolen and—" She broke off. "Here's my car."

Michael stared at the small, mud brown vehicle in front of him. It was clean, but in his view, old enough to qualify as an artifact, and a not-very-appealing one at that. Everyone in his circle bought a new car every year or two, perhaps keeping a vintage model as a collector's item, certainly not for everyday use. Julia's car definitely did not qualify for collector status.

"The ring is worth more than this car," he agreed bluntly. "I thought you were exaggerating. I hope you plan to use some of your bonus money to buy a new one."

A new car was a luxury Julia had never even considered. As long as her trusty little Horizon was running, she would keep it, and upon its demise she would visit a used-car lot to choose its successor.

"I'm using the bonus for my trip around the world." Julia was flippant. "The new car will have to wait until the next time I'm paid to play the role of some desperate eligible bachelor's fiancée."

"I suppose that is your not-very-subtle way of telling me to mind my own business and let you spend your money as you choose?"

"I thought I was being very subtle. I was trying to be." Removing her hand from his, she delved into her purse and pulled out her car keys. She flashed him a forgiving smile.

Michael's fingers closed over the ring, his eyes riveted upon her as she unlocked her car. Outside the office, Julia was a very different person from the compliant, eager-to-serve assistant who worked for him. As his employee, she followed his directions to the letter. Out in the world, she not only wouldn't follow his orders, she wouldn't even accept his advice.

But her smile was irresistible. Hard as he tried, he couldn't keep himself from smiling back. "So you think we successfully fooled Faith?" he asked, returning to a safer subject.

"I think we did. I guess we'll know tomorrow when we see the interview."

"If it's a cutesy puff piece, she bought our act. If it's a hatchet job, we failed." Michael ran his hand through his hair. "I'll give you a list of names to call tomorrow morning. Tell them to watch Channel 3 at five-thirty. My whole family will be on the list, and some friends, some colleagues. It'll save me from having to personally contact them.''

"It's a nontraditional way to announce an engagement.'' Julia shrugged. "But, of course, this is definitely a nontraditional engagement.''

"Definitely nontraditional,'' Michael agreed as he watched her slip behind the wheel.

If this was a traditional engagement, he wouldn't be standing here, watching her drive off in a car not much larger than a tuna can. If this was a traditional engagement, she would be wearing his grandmother's ruby ring instead of fretting over the possibility of having to reimburse him for it.

And most of all, if this was a traditional engagement, she would be spending the night in his bed. There was no way he would've allowed her to leave him—no way she would've wanted to leave him!—after the sexual heat they'd cooked up in the kitchen earlier tonight.

Michael successfully managed to suppress the sensual fires that kindled within him at the mere thought of making love to Julia. The farther away from her he was, the better his self-control. He noticed it had increased exponentially as she drove toward the exit ramp.

Everything was working according to plan, he reassured himself. Everything was proceeding exactly the way he wanted it to. He repeated that like a mantra as he returned alone to his penthouse apartment.

Eight

The next morning, Julia contacted every name on Michael's list. As instructed, she didn't tell anybody what they would be seeing and hearing. From the comments some people made, she knew they were assuming the news segment involved publicity for Fortune products.

Only Kristina and Sterling Foster knew the secret. Sterling was reticent, assuring Julia that he would watch the telecast. Kristina was exuberant, exclaiming that she wouldn't miss the historic broadcast for anything and that she intended to make copies of it.

Michael flew to Chicago for the day, so Julia saw him only briefly, when he stopped by the office to pick up some necessary files. He was accompanied by another Fortune executive and merely nodded to her, paying her no more attention than he did the desk or the halogen pole lamp.

Telling her roommates in person was as difficult as Julia had anticipated. Maybe even more so.

"You're engaged to your boss?" Jen was flabbergasted when Julia broke the news shortly before the five-thirty telecast. "But I've never heard you mention him, Julia. I didn't even know you were dating him!"

"I didn't know you were dating anybody," Debby added, looking astounded. "Talk about a top-secret romance!"

Julia smiled wanly. She hated deceiving the girls. It had been so much simpler lying to Faith Carlisle. Julia felt a glimmer of understanding for those politicians who could lie with such ease to the media.

And when she looked at Kia, she cringed. They'd lived together for the past two years, and she knew Kia didn't believe this sudden engagement fairy tale.

Julia was amazed, therefore, when Kia turned to Jen and Debby and said, "You two have only been around since August. You weren't here when Julia was heavily involved with Michael Fortune all last year. They broke up in the summer—around the Fourth of July, wasn't it, Julia?—because he didn't want to get married. Seems like he changed his mind."

Julia gulped, throwing Kia a grateful look. She decided that this was the tale she would tell her friends at work, along with Kristina's story about maintaining secrecy to guard their privacy. She wondered if they would believe it and couldn't blame them if they didn't.

"I wanted to keep our, um, relationship quiet because I wasn't sure how things would turn out this time," Julia murmured. At least she didn't have to *act* uneasy and uncomfortable—she genuinely was.

"Who can blame you? Once dumped, twice shy," Debby said with feeling.

"We're so happy for you, Julia!" cried Jen.

Kia's dark brown eyes met her roommate's. "Girlfriend, right now I can't find the words to express how I feel about all this...."

Julia knew she would find some words later, after Jen and Debby had left for the theater. And she did.

The two sat in the living room, sipping Frenchvanilla-flavored coffee from their Minnesota Vikings mugs.

"That was a nice story Faith Carlisle did on you and your *fiancé*," Kia said, accentuating the word. "I always thought the news was supposed to be factual, but hey, a little fiction can be fun. And you and Mike Fortune both did a brilliant job of acting the part of a newly engaged couple. When you leave the Fortune Corporation, don't bother with a career in psychology, Julia. Apply directly to UM's drama department—you could give the acting professors lessons in how to play a role.''

"Thanks for not cluing in Jen and Debby," Julia said quietly. "No one is supposed to know the engagement is bogus except Michael and his sister, who came up with the idea, and his attorney and me, of course."

"Well, you can trust me to keep my mouth shut, though I think you're crazy to get dragged into some rich people's scheme." Julia knew that Kia didn't have much use for the wealthy; she claimed they were as dysfunctional as the poor she served in her social-work career, but their money allowed them to buy their way out of trouble.

"What are they up to, some insurance scam or something?" Kia continued, her smooth brown forehead furrowed with disapproval.

Julia smiled ruefully. "Nothing illegal, Kia, I promise." She told Kia the whole story, beginning with the top-ten-most-eligible-bachelors-in-the-U.S.A. list to the calamities that had ensued at the company as a result of Michael's astronomical popularity. She did not leave out the extraordinary bonus she'd been offered or the air-tight contracts Sterling Foster had drawn up on Michael's demand.

"You shouldn't have signed those contracts, girl," Kia admonished. "Then you could've sued Mr. Bigshot Bachelor for breach of promise when he didn't marry you and won a big enough settlement to buy that rehab hospital that Joanna's in. But I suppose double-crossing those Fortunes could be hazardous to your health. One phone call and they could make you disappear forever," she added darkly.

"Kia, they're not mobsters!" Julia protested. "I agreed to Michael's terms. Nobody forced me into it. Now promise me you won't tell anybody that you know the engagement is fake."

"I promise, because I don't want you to have to pay back Mr. Millionaire with double-interest penalties or whatever.

But did you ever consider that this little game might backfire on you, Julia?'' Kia was suddenly very serious. ''I saw that TV clip of the two of you kissing, and I also saw the look in Michael Fortune's eyes when he was looking at you. He wants you, and rich guys like him are accustomed to taking what they want. You be careful, and don't be caught alone with him.''

Julia's heart began to thud in her chest. ''Oh Kia, Michael doesn't want—''

''Michael does want,'' Kia interrupted sternly. ''The camera never lies, girl. I know what I saw.''

Apparently, so did everybody else who'd watched the three-minute telecast. The way Faith had presented the story and the clips she'd shown of the newly engaged pair were both flattering and convincing—so convincing that everybody wanted to contact the happy couple.

Michael's office was flooded with calls the next day, beginning in the early morning. Fortunately, the number of callers didn't overwhelm the voice-mail system, but it seemed to Julia that everybody on Michael's list she had called yesterday called back today. They offered congratulations, best wishes, jokes, advice and admonishments for keeping the romance such a complete secret. Nobody questioned the validity of the engagement.

''Trying to get anything done today is futile,'' Michael complained, summoning Julia into his office shortly before noon. ''I can't get off the damn phone long enough to read a word. I've barely had enough time to glance at the computer screen.''

''I know.'' Julia studied him covertly. He did not look at all like the impassioned, demanding man whose kisses had knocked her senseless the other night. He looked harassed and annoyed. ''But today will probably be the worst of it,'' she said soothingly, wanting to ease his stress. ''After tomorrow, we'll be old news and it will be back to business as usual.''

"I hope you're right."

Though Michael tried to drag his eyes away, his gaze seemed to compulsively fix on her. She was wearing her hair down, the way he liked it. He was delighted that she'd abandoned the severe braid. He did not allow himself to reach out and snatch a dark, silky strand of her hair, but the urge to do so was both arousing and disturbing.

So were the memories of their kisses, which had been haunting him. He'd thought of Julia all yesterday afternoon during his meetings in Chicago, on the flights to and from the city. The steamy new images he'd conjured up as a supplement to what had actually occurred between them had kept him awake most of last night.

"Everybody I know in the company stopped by this morning to see the ring." Julia stared down at Kate Fortune's ruby ring on her finger. Michael had handed it to her this morning when she walked into the office. "It's weird pretending that we've had an ongoing secret romance. I can't tell if Lynn and Diana and Margaret—they're my closest friends here at work—believe me or not."

"They believe you," Michael assured her. "Because the only other explanation for this engagement announcement is that we're faking it."

Julia's lips twisted in a wry smile. "I guess that seems even more improbable than an ongoing secret romance."

"True. Only Kristina would dream up such a concept. I think it's her advertising mentality run amok."

Julia laughed. "It's a relief to be able to dispense with the fiancée facade for a while and talk honestly with someone. I don't know how spies and double agents do it—you know, living a lie day in and day out."

"I hope we'll always deal honestly with each other, Julia."

Standing a few feet away, Michael stared intently at her, noticing the small flecks of blue amidst the deep gray of her eyes. Her lips were pink and full and soft; he knew exactly how soft. He felt his loins tighten in anticipation of...

Of what could not be allowed to happen.

He cleared his throat. "I've, uh, never seen you wear that dress before. You always wear suits to the office—except for that dark gray dress of yours that looks just right for a funeral."

"You hate my clothes, you hate my French braid and you don't mind telling me so. Hmm, maybe we should rethink this honesty pact," Julia said dryly.

"Maybe I should say something positive," Michael suggested instead. "I like your dress."

"You do?" Julia smoothed her palms over the skirt of her black-and-yellow-striped dress, which was shorter and more fitted than the functional, practical suits she wore to the office. And far brighter than her funereal gray dress.

"I bought it on sale last year, but I wasn't sure if it was appropriate to wear to work. My roommates thought I should wear something different to the office today, that people would expect it after the broadcast last night."

She caught her lower lip between her teeth, staring at the wide stripes in the material. Suddenly, she was inexplicably nervous and couldn't seem to stop talking. "But I had second thoughts about this dress as soon as I brought it home. Does it make me look like a bee?"

"A bee?" Michael stared at the vivid stripes and suddenly laughed out loud. "Well, now that you mention it, the colors and the stripes do have a certain bumblebee-esque look to them."

"I knew it!" Julia was chagrined. "Never buy anything that's been marked down seventy-five percent. There's a reason why it's so cheap—nobody else wants it."

"Bee or not, I told you I like it." Michael moved closer and laid his hand on the slender hollow of her waist. "At least it fits." His hand glided over the curve of her hip. "It fits very well,'' he added, spanning his fingers over the firm flatness of her abdomen.

Julia's breath caught in her throat. Reflexively, her eyes flew to his face, and she saw the blue flames burning there. Before she could speak, move or even breathe, he'd curved his other hand around her neck and was drawing her to him....

''We'll give you two till the count of five to quit making out and put yourselves together, and then we're coming in!'' The jovial threat was issued by Nate Fortune, and from the sound of his voice, he was standing right outside the door, in Julia's office. ''One... Two...''

''Come on in, Dad,'' Michael called at once.

Julia quickly moved away from him to stand by the window and peer out at the bright October sunshine. Thirty floors below, traffic and pedestrians moved through the downtown area, looking like miniatures of the real thing. It was a long, long way to the ground. As Michael's office door opened and four Fortunes filed in, Julia wished for a parachute. If she'd had one, she would've bailed right out of the upcoming scene.

Nate and his wife, Barbara, entered the office, accompanied by Jake and his wife, Erica.

''Mike, honey, congratulations!'' Barbara wrapped her arms around her stepson and hugged him tightly. Nate attempted to shake his hand at the same time.

Erica moved toward Julia. ''Julia, darling, I am absolutely delighted with the news of your engagement.''

Julia managed a nervous smile. She was completely flummoxed. What did one say to the top corporate management and their wives when one was perpetrating a hoax on them?

''Julia is a wonderful girl! Mike is so lucky to have found such a beautiful, intelligent, dedicated, hardworking young lady!'' Jake boomed, a bit too heartily. ''The company is lucky to have her, too!''

His compliments were a bit too fulsome, as well. Julia knew he'd remembered calling her an idiotic sycophant and was trying to make amends. "Thank you, Mr. Fortune," she said politely.

"None of that 'Mr. Fortune' business!" Jake enveloped Julia in a bear hug. "From now on I'm Jake—or Uncle Jake, if you prefer."

Julia knew she could never call him either one. He would always be Mr. Fortune to her. And just when she thought things couldn't get any more awkward, Nate Fortune crossed the office to pry her loose from Jake's avuncular embrace.

"You've had her long enough, Jake." Nate's eyes held their usual competitive glitter as he literally pulled Julia away from his brother. For a moment, Julia felt like a bone caught between two rottweilers. Then Jake released her arm.

"Barbara and I want to congratulate our new little daughter-in-law," Nate said, dragging her over to where his wife and Michael stood together.

"Julia, dear, we're just thrilled that you and Mike are getting married!" Barbara exclaimed. "And we so enjoyed watching the announcement last night on Channel 3. You two were adorable together! It's plain to see that you are very much in love."

Julia and Michael dared to catch each other's eyes. Both had to look away to keep from laughing.

"It was excellent publicity for the company, Mike," Jake said approvingly. "I bet there'll be a rush on Fortune cosmetics—all those working gals out there buying them up, hoping to snare their boss, just like Julia did."

"Honestly, Jake, what an incredibly tactless, sexist thing to say!" Erica snapped. She turned to Julia and Michael with a bright, false smile, her green eyes flaming like emerald fire. "I hope you'll forgive Jake's—well, I'll be kind and call it his lack of diplomacy. Julia, we know that you did not *snare* Mike. Unlike my generation, a young woman today isn't under intense pressure to find a husband to define herself through marriage. My own daughters are proof that a—"

"No one *pressured* you into marriage, Erica," Jake interrupted sharply. "Truth be told, you were chomping at the bit to be Mrs. Jacob Fortune, and for years you were happy to be *defined* as such. But I suppose those facts have been discarded in your own personal revisionist history."

Erica's eyes narrowed to slits and she glared at her husband.

Julia's own eyes widened in horror. They were going to have a fight, and once again she was right on the battlefield when a Fortune war was being declared! Instinctively, she inched toward Michael. Either he sensed her distress or else he didn't want to witness a Jake-Erica blowout, either.

"As you know, I gave Julia the ring Grandmother left to me." His announcement, forceful and firm, immediately drew the attention of the two older couples. Michael took Julia's hand, raising it to show the ruby ring on her finger.

"Mother's ring," Jake said quietly, staring at it. "I remember her wearing it."

"I only wish she could be here to share our joy in your engagement," Nate added solemnly.

The tension was diffused. Both men were staring at the ring, consumed by memories of their lost mother. Erica and Barbara sadly, quietly looked on, caught up in their own memories.

Julia, feeling like a guilty fraud, sought to console them all. "I'll take very good care of the ring," she promised.

"We know you will, sweet." Michael frowned slightly as Julia carefully removed her hand from his. He'd been enjoying holding it. "Julia is so worried about something happening to the ring that she's afraid to keep it at her place at night," he explained to the others.

He managed to feign an indulgent chuckle, but her hang-up about the ring's safety was beginning to exasperate him. Maybe he should ask Sterling Foster to add a codicil to the

contract, legally exempting her from financial responsibility
for the ring?

The idea held little appeal. When he'd spoken to Sterling
yesterday, the attorney had been brusque to the point of rude-
ness, making cutting references to "litigious morons who are
governed by pettiness and paranoia." Michael had the sneaking suspicion that Foster might be referring to him.

"Every woman worries about her jewelry, Mike," Erica
explained patiently. "Do you have a security system, Julia?
Or perhaps a small safe disguised as something else? Either
are effective against potential jewel thieves."

"My roommates and I keep a baseball bat in the hall," said
Julia. When Erica looked alarmed, she added reassuringly,
"We've never had to use it, though."

All five Fortunes stared at her. Julia winced. She hadn't
realized her brand of home security would be such a total
conversation stopper. "As a precaution, I'm going to give
Michael the ring back every night. His apartment has state-
of-the-art security." She hoped to assure them that the heirloom's safety would not be dependent on the swing of a baseball bat.

"But what about you, honey?" Barbara looked worried.
"A baseball bat for protection? Oh my! We're far more concerned for your safety than with the ring."

"Barbara is right, Mike." Nate addressed his son. "As
your fiancée, Julia will need more protection than a baseball
bat can provide."

"Kidnapping is a very real threat, one the Fortune family
takes extremely seriously," Jake intoned grimly.

"Nobody is going to kidnap me!" Julia was aghast. What
had she set in motion by her offhand baseball-bat reference?
"My neighborhood is quite safe. I live near the West Bank
Campus, not far from—"

The two older couples all began to talk at once, voices

raised, arms gesticulating. It was as if she'd just announced that she resided in a den of murderous pirates.

"I can't believe a son of mine would be stupid enough to flaunt his fiancée on television, then leave her defenseless in a borderline neighborhood!" exclaimed Nate.

"Every thief, kidnapper and crackpot in Minneapolis and St. Paul probably has the girl's address circled and is plotting when and how to strike," Jake added, shooting Michael a baleful look.

"Julia, did you notice anyone following you when you drove to work this morning?" Nate interrogated, detective style.

"I don't drive to work, I take the bus, and no, nobody was following me," Julia replied breathlessly.

"What you mean is you weren't *aware* of anyone following you," Jake amended.

"The bus!" exclaimed Erica. "My God, *anybody* can ride a bus!"

Julia, who'd ridden buses all her life and had never once had a problem, realized that they were caught in the middle of a major culture clash. "I understand the need to be careful," she said, attempting to ease the strife. "My mom used to worry about serial killers, and she insisted that my sister and I memorize a list of FBI tips on how to avoid them. I'm really very safety conscious."

"That's well and good, but you require more intensive protection now," Nate said. "Everybody knows you're Mike Fortune's fiancée and that makes you a target, Julia."

"Julia, honey, why don't you move in with us until the wedding?" Smiling warmly, Barbara took Julia's hand in hers. "We have plenty of room, and I promise that we're easy to get along with. We'd love spending time getting to know our lovely new daughter-in-law-to-be."

"What a good idea!" Erica exclaimed.

"Oh, I simply couldn't!" Julia said at the same time. "I—

I...'' She felt an overwhelming urge to dash out of the office and keep on running, not stopping until she had reached—the Pacific Northwest, perhaps? Anywhere far, far from the Fortunes.

"You've scared her to death!" Michael scolded his relatives. Julia looked so young and so alarmed that he felt protective of her. "She probably wants to break the engagement right now."

Was that a hint? Julia wondered. She quickly seized upon it. "Yes, I do," she exclaimed, tugging the ring off her finger.

To her total consternation, everybody laughed.

"And she has a great sense of humor, too! You're one lucky devil, Mike." Jake slapped his nephew on the back.

"I certainly am," agreed Michael. "Julia loves to kid around." He slipped his arm around her waist, anchoring her to his side. "We enjoyed the joke, sweetheart. Now put the ring back on."

It was a Michael Fortune order. Here in the office, surrounded by Fortunes, Julia the faithful employee instantly and automatically complied with his command. She glanced down at the ruby ring. It might as well be the proverbial millstone around her neck, she thought glumly. The effect was the same.

"We don't want to frighten you, Julia. I don't believe that you're in imminent danger, but we do want to keep you safe," soothed Barbara.

"Perhaps we tend to get overwrought on the subject of kidnapping," Jake explained. "You see, our family has personally experienced that heinous crime. My younger sister Lindsay's twin was kidnapped as a newborn. The ransom was paid, but the child was never returned."

"A kidnapped baby?" Julia cried. "How terrible! I had no idea!"

"Jake and I were in our teens, but it's something we'll never forget," said Nate. "Our parents were never quite the same afterward."

"No wonder! It's every parent's nightmare to lose a child forever." Barbara slipped her arm through her husband's. "Mike, I know you think we're being intrusive and overanxious, but we're still coping with your grandmother's death, and we don't want any more tragic losses in this family."

"You must take steps to ensure your fiancée's safety, Mike," Jake interjected in his authoritative CEO tone. "But I can understand why you and Julia might not want her to move in with your folks. Who needs chaperones, hmm? I remember very well how it feels when you're young and in love...." His voice trailed off and he stared almost hungrily at his wife.

Erica did not meet his gaze.

"We're all adults, so I'll be blunt," Nate interjected. "Mike, have Julia move in with you right away."

"That would solve the security problem," agreed Barbara.

And create countless others! Julia stared imploringly at Michael, willing him to look at her. He seemed to deliberately avoid making eye contact with her.

"Maybe you're right," she heard him say. "Julia can move in with me."

"Have you lost your mind?" Julia cried.

It was not a question she would've dared to ask twenty-four hours earlier. But the customary calm reserve and control she exercised in Michael's presence had evaporated along with her usual tact. Their roles seemed to have taken a dramatic shift. Instead of cooperative, obedient assistant and authoritarian boss, they were now coconspirators on an equal footing.

And at the moment, she was an extremely agitated coconspirator, irate with her accomplice.

She paced the floor of his office, from his desk to the windows and back again. Perhaps the Fortunes' pacing habit was contagious and she'd caught it? "I am *not* moving in with you! Why did you ever tell your family that I would?"

"Because I know them." Michael sat at his desk, leaning back in his chair, his feet resting on the desktop. "I knew we'd never get them out of my office until I agreed to safeguard you. They left almost immediately afterward, you'll remember."

Julia remembered. "I hope they're not angry we turned down their invitation to lunch."

Michael hadn't merely declined the invitation, he'd adamantly refused it, stating that he and Julia had made prior arrangements. They hadn't, of course. "I sensed that you didn't care to join them in a celebratory meal."

Julia shuddered at the prospect. She'd had quite enough of the Fortunes for one day. "Now do we have to pretend I'm staying at your apartment?" she murmured anxiously. The web of deceit seemed to grow more tangled by the minute. "Oh, my mother was right! She always said that for every lie, you have to tell at least three more to cover it, so it's easier to tell the truth in the first place. Heaven only knows how many more lies this mock-engagement is going to require!"

"It's too bad the kidnapping issue arose." Michael drummed his fingers on the arm of his chair. "Who would've anticipated that?"

"I wish you had! Why did you have to tell them we're worried about keeping the ring safe and get them all stirred up?"

"I'm not worried about the safety of the ring and I never said I was," Michael countered indignantly. "It was you who brought up the baseball bat, which scared the hell out of all four of them."

"I told them we'd never had to use it."

"Not good enough, Julia. Uncle Jake was right when he said the family is nuts when it comes to the danger of kidnapping. And they do have a point, you know. As my fiancée, you are an attractive, available target.''

"I'm staying in my own apartment, Michael," Julia informed him sternly. "I am not going to be kidnapped. I'm not even your fiancée, remember?"

"But all those avaricious crazies out there don't know that, Julia. We did such a convincing job in the Faith Carlisle interview that my own family believes we're 'so adorable together. And so much in love.'" He gave a derisive hoot of laughter.

"It's not funny." Julia scowled at him. "I felt awful lying to your family. It didn't seem as bad when we were making up the story to discourage callers and help the company, and then it became a challenge to fool Faith Carlisle. But having to lie to my roommates, and now your folks..." She heaved a sigh. "I feel like a creep. What we're doing is dishonest and deceitful and—"

"I take it you don't subscribe to the ends-justify-the-means theory?"

Julia thought of the bonus payment she'd accepted for playing this role, the means of achieving her end—Joanna's care and ultimate recovery.

"I'm afraid that I do. There was a time when I was idealistic and didn't, though," she added gloomily.

"Same here. And then I turned eight years old and wised up."

"The sad thing is you're probably not exaggerating," Julia murmured. "It would be hard to be Nate and Sheila Fortune's son and not turn cynical at an early age."

"I prefer to call it practical. And speaking of good old Mom, she hasn't phoned in her opinion of last night's performance—which could mean that she is coming in to tell us in person."

"Oh, the day needs only that!" Julia groaned. "Coming face-to-face with Sheila Fortune and having her believe her precious son is engaged to me, a nonheiress in a heavily marked down bee dress."

"Not her precious son, her most-marketable son," Michael corrected with a laugh. "And you look great in that dress, sale rack or not. You remind me of an industrious little honeybee buzzing nonstop around the office."

Julia stopped pacing to stare at him. "You're certainly lighthearted, considering the circumstances—which are grave, by the way."

"Hardly that. You need to lighten up, Julia. Where's your sense of humor, which I bragged about to the family?"

"I've either lost it or your sense of humor is totally warped, because I find nothing funny about—oh!"

She gasped as he rose, his arm snaking out to grasp her wrist. Manacling it with his fingers, he gave her a sharp tug as he sank back into his chair. He was strong, his grip firm, and she was caught completely off guard. Julia landed directly in his lap.

Their faces were very close. Julia stared at the strong line of his jaw, his dark brows and thick black eyelashes. She saw the hungry gleam in his blue eyes, and her mouth went dry.

"You were saying?" His tone was mocking, but his voice was husky and deep and sent sensual shivers tingling through her. He spread his knees and placed his hands on her hips to situate her bottom more securely on his lap.

She felt a hard ridge growing and pressing against her. One of his arms tightened around her while he cupped her chin with his other hand. Her whole body began to throb as a turgid heat stole through her.

"Michael," she whimpered. It could have been a plea or a protest. Perhaps it was a combination of both. His thumb was caressing her bottom lip, and she quivered, the last ounce of rigidity draining from her body.

Sensing her acquiescence, he angled her head and lowered his mouth. The force of his lips opened hers and he thrust his tongue inside to claim her. His kiss was hot and urgent and she responded wildly, enticing him, wanting more. Needing more.

She clung to him, arching her back, her head falling against his shoulder, inviting greater access and intimacy. He accepted the unspoken sensual invitation by deepening the kiss and placing his hand firmly over her breast. Gently he palmed the rounded softness.

The sweet, fierce pleasure that streaked through her was so intense it bordered on pain. She wanted it to stop; she wanted it to go on forever. Julia moaned into his mouth as an aching tension began to swell hotly between her legs.

With a rough growl of passion, he quickly unfastened the big black buttons at the front of her dress and slipped his hand inside. His fingers dipped into the cup of her lacy black bra and stroked her taut, throbbing nipple.

Julia felt the effects of the caress everywhere. She clutched at him, feverishly kissing the hard, tanned column of his neck, wanting him with an intensity she had never before experienced.

A hot, sensual magic burned between them, eliminating all sense of time and place. When he shifted her position and pushed aside the bodice of her dress to kiss the upper swell of her breast, she clasped his head tightly, running her fingers through his thick hair, encouraging him.

Lost in a daze of desire, she didn't realize that he'd opened the front clasp of her bra until she felt his lips on her raised nipple. She breathed a husky cry of need as he circled the pink tip with his tongue, then drew her full nipple into the moist warmth of his mouth and sucked strongly. She twisted in his arms, offering herself up to him, demanding that he take her.

The empty ache within her was craving to be filled, and he needed to fill her. His manhood was pulsing wildly; his body radiated blazing sexual heat. He suckled her breast as his hand moved over her stomach and the curve of her hip to her thighs. Her skirt had ridden up and he pushed it higher, to her hips, and then raised his head to steal a glance at her legs. They were clad in sheer, smoky black stockings, and the sight made his sex thicken with lusty urgency.

He stared down at her, his gaze ravenous. Her breasts were round, firm and high; her thighs were shapely and parted for him as he glided his hand between them. Beneath her pant-yhose, she wore lacy, black bikini panties that matched her bra. Michael groaned with sensual appreciation. Who would've thought starchy little Julia would have a penchant for sexy lingerie? Now every time he saw her in one of those serviceable suits of hers, he would wonder what she was wearing under it.

His fingers slipped beneath the waistband of her panties and tangled gently in the soft tuft of hair at the apex of her thighs. She cried his name again and arched her hips, opening herself to him. She was hot and wet, and Michael smiled as he touched the swollen feminine folds, savoring the physical proof that she wanted him as much as he wanted her.

He wouldn't have to wonder about her lingerie; from now on she would let him see for himself. And after the visual treat, he would have the sublime pleasure of undressing her. He wanted to do that now. He wanted her naked and warm and open for him. He wanted to surge deeply inside her and…

His thoughts were suddenly as scrambled as a computer struck by lightning. And then he couldn't think at all, he could only moan with pleasure as he felt Julia's small hand pressed against the front of his trousers. Her slender fingers kneaded the long, pulsing length of him, conforming her palm to fit his shape, exploring him, driving him wild.

"I want you," he rasped, kissing her with a desperate urgency. "Please, baby, let me have you."

She squeezed him gently. Her head was spinning. She could hardly breathe. The way he was touching her, the way she was touching him, made her feel helpless and powerful at the same time. She was shocked by her boldness, equally shocked by her own sexual hunger, which inspired her to be bold.

"I want you, too," Julia heard herself whisper, and her words seemed to echo in the erotic haze enveloping them both.

Michael couldn't remember ever feeling such scorching-hot need. He brought his mouth down to hers and kissed her deeply, possessively, and she responded with an ardency that stoked the flames between them even higher.

The chair was becoming too confining. The leather couch in the far corner of the office beckoned invitingly, and Michael rose to his feet, lifting Julia in his arms. She draped her arms around him, hanging on tightly.

He carried her to the couch, and upon reaching their destination, paused for a moment as he held her above it. She lifted her head and gazed at him. Her eyes were dreamy, glazed with passion.

They were so engrossed in each other that neither noticed the door to Michael's office opening. Neither saw Kristina enter the office, but when she uttered an astonished, "Wow!" they both heard her loud and clear.

Still holding Julia in his arms, Michael whirled around to face his younger sister, who was standing on the threshold, her blue eyes round as saucers, her mouth agape.

Julia cringed, utterly mortified. "Michael, put me down."

Her voice was husky with unslaked desire, and the sound of it made him ache. His hands tightened around her. Even with his sister eyeballing them, he could not bring himself to release Julia. He held her high against his chest, his body trembling with frustration.

Kristina grinned. "Excuse me, I should have knocked. But I never dreamed that I'd catch the two of you about to do the wild thing, right here in the office."

"Shut up, Kristina," Michael ordered hoarsely. "And get out of here!"

Kristina had never been one to do as she was told unless it happened to coincide with what she wanted to do. This time it didn't. She closed the door behind her and sauntered toward them.

"You really ought to lock the door," she suggested. "Or have a guard posted at Julia's desk to screen intruders. You're lucky it was me who came through that door."

"I'm feeling many things at this moment, but lucky isn't one of them," Michael snapped.

Julia twisted and wriggled so vigorously in his arms that he almost dropped her. Reluctantly, he set her on her feet, and she fled to the privacy of his bathroom, adjacent to the office.

Michael sank down onto the couch, resting his elbows on his knees and holding his head in his hands. Within seconds, he'd plunged from rapture to turmoil, and his body was taking more time than his mind to adjust to the switch.

Kristina came over to sit down beside him. She fingered the small silver charm embossed in a heart that dangled from a chain around her neck. "I guess I really am a matchmaker," she said, clearly pleased with herself. "You and Julia are—"

"It was all part of the hoax, little sister. Julia and I heard you out there and arranged that scene for your benefit. We're testing our credibility as an engaged couple. We thought if we could fool you, we could fool anybody. Guess we pulled it off."

In the bathroom, Julia, who'd hastened to refasten her bra and button her dress, heard his sardonic explanation and wished it were true. But she hadn't been acting, and she knew Michael hadn't, either. Neither could fake the overwhelming physical proof of their desire. The explosion of passion had been very real, and if Kristina hadn't made her untimely appearance, they would be lying on that couch right now....

Julia shivered and blocked the provocative images that shimmered in her mind's eye. Quickly, she glanced in the mirror and attempted to comb her hair with her fingers, but she only succeeded in tousling it more. Her pupils were dilated, her mouth sensuously swollen, her lipstick completely rubbed off.

Michael watched the closed door of the bathroom where Julia had retreated. Kristina patted his arm consolingly. "You don't have to pretend with me, Mike. I think it's cool you're in love with Julia. And you're already engaged. What could be simpler?"

"Don't be ridiculous!" Michael sprang up as if he'd been ejected by a spring. "I'm not in love!"

The door opened and Julia emerged. He stared at her hungrily, the sight of her an instant stimulus. Her cheeks were still flushed, her mouth looked well kissed, and though her dress was proper and in place, he knew the sexy secrets concealed beneath it. The fire still kindling in his groin threatened to blaze into another full-fledged conflagration.

He was suddenly furiously, irrationally angry with himself for wanting her so much and with Julia for making him want her. *What could be simpler?* his sassy little sister had asked. He knew better. This was the most complicated, threatening trap he had ever encountered.

"I'm going to lunch," Julia said, and she was relieved that at least her voice sounded cool and calm. She felt anything but as she deliberately strolled across the office toward the door.

"You'd better go with her, Mike," Kristina advised.

"No!" Julia and Michael chorused in unison.

"I'm going shopping after I grab a quick sandwich," Julia lied.

She had no appetite for food and no desire to shop, but she had to get away from Michael. She felt as if she were on an emotional Ferris wheel, going up and over, round and round.

It was disorienting and she wanted off. "I'm taking a much-needed one-hour break from my fiancée duties," she added.

"Take two hours." Michael's voice was cold and caustic, his eyes glittering with barely suppressed rage. "We most definitely need a time-out from all this suffocating togetherness."

"Well, whether you go separately or together, I suggest you leave quickly, because your mother is in the building, Mike," Kristina said. "That's why I'm here—to sound the alarm. First Sheila stopped off in the legal department to torture Daddy, but luckily, he'd already left for lunch. Then I asked Caroline to talk to Sheila and keep her at bay while I ran up here to warn you two. Caroline's a real trooper, but how long can she hold off the Wicked Witch of the Midwest? You two had better scram, unless you want to play the role of loving couple for *her*."

"I'm already gone. Thanks, Kristina," Julia called gratefully, scurrying from the office.

She went immediately to the stairwell, knowing that Sheila Fortune would never dream of using the stairs. She boarded the elevator on the twenty-sixth floor and rode it to the lobby, undisturbed.

Michael wasn't as lucky. He was waiting for the elevator to arrive when the opposite car stopped to discharge its passengers, one of whom was Sheila Fortune. Today her turquoise suit matched her brilliant turquoise eyes.

"You're engaged to your assistant?" was Sheila's outraged greeting to her son. The one-sided conversation went downhill from there.

Nine

"Must be nice to be engaged to the boss," sang out Felicia, one of the receptionists, when Julia returned to the office later that afternoon.

Michael had said to take two hours and she'd done so, needing the time away from him to try to clear her muddled mind. She'd munched a grilled-cheese sandwich, not tasting it, then wandered through the shops in the downtown mall, looking at the merchandise without really seeing it.

Every time she thought of Michael, her body felt achy with desire. And frustration. And then confusion would kick in. She didn't understand what was happening to her. She'd worked for Michael for fourteen months without either of them ever touching each other, or wanting to. But since their phony engagement, since he'd kissed her for the first time, it seemed they couldn't be alone for very long without touching. Without kissing. And wanting more.

Julia sank into her desk chair, feeling her whole body flush with an unnerving combination of arousal and shame. Not only had she responded to Michael's amorous advances, she'd encouraged him. More than that, she had initiated some heavily amorous advances of her own!

What was going to happen now? she wondered. By his actions, Michael had made it quite clear that he was not averse to a little sex on the side while pretending to be her fiancé. And she'd given him every reason to believe that she wasn't averse to sex with him, either.

The insights left her badly shaken. This mock engagement

had the potential to mirror all of Michael's other temporary liaisons—a relationship limited to sex and occasional social outings for a limited time. And while that was fine for him, for her the consequences would be dire. If she gave in to her libidinous impulses and had a full-blown affair with Michael, how would she be able to continue working for him when the relationship ended?

That it would end, Julia had no doubt. She'd had fourteen months to learn that Michael had no intention of ever committing himself to one woman, and if she was foolish enough to delude herself that he might make an exception for her, all she had to do was review her copy of the engagement contract. The document had been created to deal with the inevitable end of their relationship.

She'd never been so mixed-up in her entire life. She thought she knew herself well enough to know that she could never make love with a man unless she was in love with him. Yet she'd been ready to mindlessly cast aside her values and her common sense to make love with Michael this morning.

That wasn't love, it was pure lust!

Julia groaned aloud and covered her face with her hands. She was in lust with Michael Fortune, and he was perfectly willing to accommodate her urges, for the time being at least. And if she were willing to go along with his it's-fun-while-it-lasts-but-when-I-say-it's-over, we're-through philosophy, they could have a sizzling, short-term affair.

If. A small word but a major obstacle. *If* she possessed the ability to live by the it's-fun-while-it-lasts policy, she wouldn't have remained a virgin for twenty-six years. But here she was, probably the oldest living virgin in the State of Minnesota, who certainly wasn't averse to having fun, but who also wanted something more. She wanted a relationship that would last.

Dolefully, Julia predicted what would happen if she were to give in to her sexual attraction to Michael. Though her hormones made her ready and willing for sex with him, her mind-set would make her fall in love with him first. And after they'd made love, she would find herself in the heartbreaking position of being deeply in love with a man who didn't love her. Julia knew it was a depressingly common situation. The self-help psychology section in the bookstores had shelves of books dealing with unrequited love and unmet needs, written and analyzed from both the masculine and feminine perspectives.

And she would be a textbook case, because whenever Michael decided the engagement charade had served his purposes, he would end it along with their sexual relationship. It wouldn't matter how she felt about him, she would be expected to carry on as usual, working for him. Julia imagined that grim scenario. Seeing him every day. Wanting him but not having him. Making dinner reservations for him and his newest lady friend. Ordering roses in Michael's name for her replacement.

How would she be able to stand it? Julia knew she couldn't. Furthermore, she didn't need her degree in psychology to know that the easiest way to cure emotional pain was to avoid the cause of it. Which would mean quitting her job to get away from Michael.

Viewed from that angle, the dilemma disappeared. Julia's confusion was banished, replaced by a clear vision of reality. She couldn't quit her job, not with Joanna depending on her. She wouldn't do anything to jeopardize her sister's welfare, and that meant hanging on to her reliable, well-paying job as Michael's assistant.

It also meant the end of these sexy little games she and Michael were playing. There would be no more exchanging long, lingering glances with him. No more touching, no more kissing, no more putting herself in temptation's way...

"How gracious of you to honor us with your presence." Michael's voice rang out, making her jump. She'd been so preoccupied she hadn't heard him come into her office, but he was walking toward her, looking displeased indeed.

Julia quickly rose to her feet, strategically positioning her chair between herself and Michael. "You said to take two hours for lunch," she reminded him.

"You know very well I didn't mean it. What was I supposed to say after you tossed off that insulting crack about needing a break from your fiancée duties?"

"You said you needed a break from our 'suffocating togetherness,'" Julia retorted. "Didn't you mean that, either?"

"What do you think?" he demanded huskily.

The way he was looking at her made her quiver with awareness. Sexual tension hung heavy and thick between them. Julia's color deepened. And she remembered her pledge to her sister. "What I think is that it—it would be a major mistake to pick up where we were when Kristina...discovered us," she said bravely.

"I assume you spent the past two hours convincing yourself of that?"

"Yes," Julia admitted.

Michael scowled. She was right, of course. After his mother's brief visit—unpleasant but thoroughly predictable—he'd spent the time apart from Julia trying to regain his equilibrium. He'd reminded himself of his long-standing policy: that sex and work were two entirely different spheres and should never converge. Having an affair with his assistant was the office equivalent of detonating a live grenade.

But somehow, hearing Julia declare herself off-limits to him called forth atavistic instincts he'd never dreamed he possessed. His ability to compartmentalize and rationalize promptly deserted him. He wanted to pick up Julia in his arms, carry her back into his office and lay her down on his couch; he wanted to hear the hungry, passionate little pleas that had fired his blood.

A pleasurable surge of warmth heated his body. Michael

fought against it, determined not to give in to the insidious temptation. He had never been at the mercy of his impulses. He controlled his urges, they did not control him!

"Well, I agree with you." His lips glided apart, exposing his teeth.

Julia guessed he was supposed to be smiling, but it was a rather scary facsimile of a smile.

"It would be stupid to make the mistake some of those Hollywood actors do and confuse the parts they are playing with their real lives," Michael continued. His shark's smile remained intact. "In other words, an on-location romance is not for us."

"And since we're on-location in an office of the Fortune Building, it should be easy to keep our heads. I mean, it's not like we're acting our roles in some romantic place like Paris or Tahiti." Julia clutched the back of her chair. The ruby ring sparkled in the sunlight streaming into the office.

"Precisely. It will be business as usual for us, except when we're in the presence of others. Then we'll launch into our engaged-couple act."

Julia nodded her agreement.

"Now let's try to salvage what's left of the afternoon. Give Steve Gelman in Washington a call and ask him if he has any better idea when the staff of the FDA will be able to meet with us to discuss the new package-labeling requirements. If he can give a definite date, put me through to schedule a meeting." Michael was all-business now, the exacting, focused employer she'd known for the past fourteen months.

She was relieved, Julia told herself. This was the way she wanted it, the way it had to be.

Michael headed back into his office, but paused in the doorway. "Oh, and Julia, make dinner reservations for us for tomorrow night. Kristina thinks we ought to be seen together as a follow-up to our announcement, and I'm inclined to agree with her."

"Any particular place?" Julia asked, her tone impersonal and efficient.

Michael felt a peculiar pang. When he looked at Julia, he saw not a trace of his smiling coconspirator, nor a vestige of the warm, passionate woman who had moaned softly in his arms, responding to him and generating a response within him the likes of which he'd never before experienced.

It was better this way, he insisted to himself. The boundaries between them must remain clearly defined.

"Wherever you'd like to go. It doesn't matter to me." He shrugged indifferently. "Feel free to arrange a first-class night on the town. You know, the usual. Spare no expense." He went into his office and closed the door behind him.

"A first-class night on the town. You know, the usual," Julia repeated under her breath. "Translation: being seen in all the right places with a Fortune is undoubtedly the thrill of a lifetime for a peon like you, though it's *the usual* for me."

She glared at her keyboard. The more she thought about it, the more irritated she became. "Spare no expense," she muttered aloud. "Translation: I'm sure that soaking me for a meal at the highest-priced restaurant in the city would be the highlight of your humble pauper's life, so go for it."

Indignation surged through her. Was that the way he saw her—as grasping and subservient? Eager to scramble for whatever crumbs a Fortune threw her way?

By the time Julia completed the call to the FDA—Steve Gelman was out of town; phone back next week—she had calmed down enough to grudgingly concede that Michael hadn't intentionally insulted her.

Obviously, he intended his fake engagement to follow the same boring, predictable pattern as his other courtships. Starting with a first-class night on the town, no expense spared.

He'd had hundreds—thousands?—of such nights. Julia hadn't had one, and what would be novel and memorable for her would be nothing out of the ordinary for him. Perhaps it was false pride, but she decided she couldn't stand the disparity.

"Wherever you'd like to go. It doesn't matter to me," Michael had said. Of course, he didn't expect to be taken literally. She was supposed to understand that she should want to accompany him to his usual high-class haunts. Maybe even be thrilled at the opportunity to do so.

Wherever you'd like to go. Julia decided that instead of arranging a first-class night on the town, she would feel free to arrange another type of evening altogether.

Michael arrived at the door of Julia's apartment the next evening promptly at seven. The weather was unseasonably warm, and college students strolled the sidewalks, talking and laughing and shouting to other students, who yelled back from windows in the aging houses and apartment buildings lining both sides of the street.

They seemed so young, so carefree, with nothing better to do than to go partying through the neighborhood. Michael viewed them as he might aliens from a distant planet. Even when he was a college student himself, he'd been serious and self-controlled. If he had ever caroused the streets with his peers, looking for fun, he had no recollection of it.

The apartment door opened, and a young black woman dressed in olive green leggings and a long, olive cotton shirt stood before him. "I recognize you from your TV appearance the other night. You're Mr. Money, Julia's boss."

"That would be Fortune," Michael corrected, flashing his friendliest smile. "Mike Fortune. And of course, I'm also Julia's fiancé."

"Yeah, right! That, too." Kia gave a scornful laugh. She didn't invite him in.

Michael shifted uncomfortably under her unblinking scrutiny. "I'm taking Julia to dinner," he said at last. "Will you tell her I'm here?"

"You're going dressed like that?" Kia asked incredulously.

Michael glanced down at his new midnight blue suit, which he was wearing for the first time tonight. He'd quickly showered, shaved and changed clothes in the half hour between leaving the office and arriving at Julia's door.

"That color and fabric should only be worn in a hermetically sealed room," Kia observed. She shrugged. "Well, it's your dry-cleaning bill. Julia, your gentleman caller is here."

Michael guessed her tone would be the same if she were announcing that a rabid bat had just flown through the door. He watched her leave the living room, then stepped inside and looked around. The furniture was sparse—an ancient sofa and three shabby, mismatched chairs of rummage-sale or attic-reject quality. Only the television set and VCR looked fairly new.

He concluded that the apartment and the neighborhood would be suitable—okay, maybe even fun—for money-strapped students, but why on earth did Julia live here? The salary she earned was enough to enable her to have a place of her own, away from the beer-swilling college crowd. Unless she liked the atmosphere?

It occurred to Michael how very little he actually knew about his assistant/fausse fiancée. Until tonight, he'd never even known Julia had a roommate. He had certainly never thought to ask why she lived where she did.

Julia entered the room, dressed in jeans and a short-sleeved, white, ribbed cotton sweater. Her brown hair hung loose and soft and shiny, and she smiled when she saw him.

His heart lurched queerly. It took a moment or two before he fully comprehended the extreme differences in their attire. By then, her roommate had joined them and pointed it out.

"Wearing a suit to the Artsfest." Kia shook her head. "Well, there's a first time for everything, I guess. And people like you Fortunes make your own rules. Always have, always will."

"I think there's been a misunderstanding," Michael said. He made an effort to keep his voice calm and agreeable, because he suspected that Julia's roommate was expecting him to rant and rave, venting his temper like a spoiled brat who hadn't gotten his own way.

People like you make your own rules. Always have, always will. Her words echoed unpleasantly in his ears. He wondered if Julia saw him that way—as a pampered rich man accustomed to doing and getting whatever he wanted. He was disturbed by the image. That was not who he was!

"You said you'd go wherever I wanted tonight," Julia said, her tone as amiable as his. "It's the Fall Artsfest in the neighborhood and that's where I want to go. Kia is coming with us. I told her you wouldn't mind."

"Of course not," Michael assured her, the soul of congeniality. "Although we've yet to be properly introduced."

Julia hastened to make the introductions. "Oh, and we don't have to worry about faking our engagement around Kia. She knows the truth."

Michael gave up any pretense of a smile. "Julia, we agreed not to tell anyone else about—"

"Your attorney and your sister know," Kia interjected sharply. "That's two on your side who know the truth. Wouldn't you agree that Julia is entitled to at least one person on her side who has all the facts?"

Michael saw the logic in the argument, but he didn't like it. Kia's talk about "sides" made it seem that he and Julia were on opposing ones. But they weren't—they were allies! And the fact that Julia felt the need to tell someone the truth about their engagement unsettled him. It seemed to prove that she didn't fully trust him. That bothered him.

"Don't worry, Kia is sworn to secrecy," Julia promised. "She is as trustworthy as Kristina and Sterling Foster, I assure you."

"I like to think I'm a lot more trustworthy than scheming

rich people who use their money to spread lies," Kia muttered.

"Kia, no lectures, please," Julia interjected. She turned to Michael, all smiles and sweetness. "Kia and I have agreed to disagree on the subject of our false engagement. Now, are you ready to go? You're in for a real treat, Michael. This is the second annual neighborhood Fall Artsfest, and it's twice as big as it was last year."

"I've never heard of it," Michael confessed. Even if he had, he would've never thought of going to it. "I suppose there are food stands along with the art?" he asked resignedly.

"Oh yes!" Julia exclaimed. "Jen and Debby, our other roommates, have already been there and said there are more food stands than artists this year!"

"Let me guess what they're offering," said Michael. "Funnel cakes with toppings, greasy fries with chili or cheese—a fat-on-fat extravaganza. Beverages that are all sugar and ice, and as a nod to the health conscious, vegetables. However, they're deep-fried and drowned in cheese sauce as thick as glue to offset any possible nutritional value."

"My mouth is watering already!" Julia exclaimed. "Let's go."

"You might have notified me as to the change in plans, Julia," Michael murmured as they approached the wide, closed-to-traffic blocks where the festival was being held.

They were on foot. He'd left his Corvette parked along the street in front of Julia's apartment building, where it drew admiring glances from the roving bands of students. Michael could only hope that they limited themselves to looking and not touching.

"But you never asked me where we were going," Julia replied sweetly. "If you had, I would have been glad to tell you."

"But not as glad as you are right now, enjoying the spectacle of me in my new suit at a food festival." Michael felt a smile tug the corners of his mouth. Julia had successfully tricked him, and while he was slightly irked, mostly he admired her for it. He was seldom surprised, but Julia had surprised him tonight in more ways than one.

"Correction, it's an art festival," Julia reminded him with a grin.

"Of course. One tends to forget the artists among all these calories, but just look at that stand featuring chainsaw sculptures. Now that's art for the ages!"

"They say art is in the eye of the beholder." Julia's smile widened. "Wouldn't that big chainsaw bird be an interesting addition to your dining room? You could hang it alongside your special birdcage."

"A low blow, bringing up that birdcage, Julia."

Kia moved ahead of them to join a group of friends. "See you later, Julia. Hope you enjoy your dinner, Michael," she called, snickering.

"Do you think she senses I hate festival-type food and hopes I choke on it?" Michael asked wryly.

"How can you hate it? It's delicious!" Julia headed toward a booth selling something called Chicken Divine on Pita, which consisted of browned chicken with liquid cheese, canned mushrooms, fried onions, lettuce, tomato and a runny, white sauce dressing.

"Even as a child, I refused to eat in amusement parks," Michael said, watching her bite into the overstuffed concoction. The dressing squirted out and trickled over her fingers. With a paper napkin—he'd grabbed a huge handful from the stand—he proceeded to mop the liquid from her hand. "I remember my father buying us kids lunch at a park on one of our Sunday visits with him. The sight of a corn dog on a stick made my hair stand on end. It still does."

"Poor Michael. I had no idea." Julia laughed.

"Didn't you?" He linked his fingers through the belt loops of her jeans and pulled her out of the way of a little boy brandishing an enormous puff of blue cotton candy as if it were a sword.

But even after the sticky danger was past, Michael didn't release his grip on her. Instead he tightened it, pulling her closer—so close that Julia could feel his body heat. Her shoulder brushed the muscular wall of his chest. She could smell his Fortune aftershave. Her senses swam.

Because her cotton sweater was not tucked into her jeans, his thumb slid easily beneath the material to stroke her midriff. Julia stood rooted to the spot. The rough pad of his thumb against her bare skin was tantalizing. She tried hard to remember all the reasons why she should keep Michael literally at arm's length, why letting him touch her was ill advised and irresponsible and downright stupid. But her body had its own sensual agenda and blocked all her well-reasoned objections.

Julia allowed herself to lean against him. She could feel his lips against her temple, his breath stirring her hair...stirring her. If she were to turn her head a fraction of an inch and tilt her chin, her lips would be within kissing range of his. And she wanted that, she admitted achingly. She wanted to kiss him. She remembered how exciting, how arousing it felt, his mouth covering hers, taking and giving an erotic pleasure so potent that just thinking about it made her shiver with need.

Michael was close enough to feel that sensual little shudder run through her. "Cold?" he murmured against her ear, his voice a deep, virile growl.

The question struck her as ridiculous and she gave a husky little laugh. "No," she whispered, "not cold at all."

"Hot?" he murmured. The sensuous little whimper that was her response made his heart surge wildly in his chest. She wasn't cold, she was as hot as he was, and their internal heat had nothing to do with the warm, Indian-summer temperature. He desperately wanted to leave the crowds and the atrocious food and the alleged art and be alone with her. His carefully crafted argument against blurring their real-life relationship with their faux relationship, his dedication to the separation of sex and work, all vanished in an instant. Just to be near her, to touch her…

"Julia," he began hoarsely.

But he didn't have the chance to finish whatever he'd been about to say. Because walking toward them was his younger cousin Rachel, Jake and Erica's daughter, Allison's identical twin.

"Mike?" Rachel's expression reflected both amusement and incredulity. "Is it really you or am I hallucinating?"

"I'm very real, Rocky," Michael said dryly, greeting her by her longtime nickname.

"You could very well be an imposter," Rocky teased. "Nobody who knows Mike Fortune would ever expect to see you at the West Bank Campus neighborhood Fall Artsfest. Not with all these stands selling the kind of festival and amusement-park cuisine you loathe."

"I thought you were in Wyoming, Rocky." Michael's fingers remained locked in Julia's belt loops, keeping her firmly in his grasp. "What a surprise to see you here."

"That was going to be my line." Rocky grinned at her cousin. "This is the last place I'd ever expect to find you, Mike. Surrounded by sausage sandwiches and kebobs cooked in smoke and grease. Not to mention the offending presence of candy apples and snow cones and fried ice cream." She turned her laughing eyes to Julia. "Did you talk him into coming here? Now I know he's truly, madly in love!"

"There are limits to my influence," Julia joked back. "He's here in body but definitely not in spirit. He has yet to touch a single morsel of food."

She'd never met Allison's twin, but she had heard a lot about Rocky through the very thorough, very efficient Fortune Corporation grapevine. Although Allie was the company's spokesperson "supermodel," her identical twin had chosen a very different career path. Rocky, an excellent pilot, had inherited her grandmother's airplanes and helicopter and had begun her own search-and-rescue and tracking service in Wyoming.

Julia studied the young woman. It was a fascinating paradox that Rocky's features were identical to Allie's, yet somehow she appeared quite different from her glamorous twin. Closer inspection revealed that Rocky downplayed her looks in every way possible. She had the same thick, wine red hair as her sister, but unlike Allie's gorgeous flowing mane, Rocky's hair was blunt cut in a practical chin-length bob. Her large, wide-set brown eyes were not emphasized and accentuated by the Fortune cosmetics that Allison so skillfully applied. In fact, Rocky was wearing no makeup at all. The twins' taste in clothes was just as dissimilar. Julia couldn't imagine the always elegant, stylish Allison ever being seen in the faded, no-name jeans and loose striped T-shirt her twin currently had on.

"I heard all about your engagement from the family but I haven't had a chance to congratulate you two," Rocky exclaimed. "Mike, I want you to introduce me to your fiancée right now!"

Michael quickly and matter-of-factly performed the introductions. "Julia, my cousin Rocky. Rocky, Julia."

"Allie told me you work for Mike. When did you start dating him? How did you ever manage to keep things secret from *everybody* until you decided to announce your engagement?" Rocky fired the questions at Julia, knowing her taciturn cousin well enough to be certain she wouldn't get any interesting romantic details from him.

Julia tried to remember what they'd told Faith Carlisle and couldn't. The TV interview seemed like a distant blur. "When did we start dating, Michael?" She turned to him, her gray eyes gleaming. "I can hardly remember when it all began. It seems like we've been together forever," she added with a sweet, girlish sigh.

"Nice save, darling," Michael murmured against her ear. "Julia and I have decided that it was love at first sight between us," he said to his cousin. "As for keeping our relationship a secret, it was easy. We were very, very discreet. Now I want to hear about you, Rocky. The last I heard you were tracking down lost hikers in the wilds of Wyoming. When did you get back to Minneapolis?"

"Yesterday," Rocky said. Her eyes were suddenly sad. "My sisters called and asked me to come home for a couple days so we could all talk to Mom and Dad about what's going on between them. A sort of group intervention, I guess. You know that they're…" she paused, her voice lowering "…not getting along very well. At breakfast this morning they were so cold to each other, like acquaintances who hardly knew each other and didn't like what they did know."

Julia shifted uneasily, feeling like an eavesdropper who shouldn't be privy to such personal family information. Rocky hadn't hesitated to confide in Michael in front of her because she considered her, as Michael's fiancée, to be almost one of the family. But Julia wasn't.

"It's too bad," Michael murmured. "I'd hate to see Jake and Erica split and end up hating each other like my parents. But I suppose it's to be expected. The only surprise is that they stayed together this long." He shook his head and heaved a disgusted sigh. "Marriage! What an appalling, unfathomable, unfeasible institution! And institution is certainly the correct term, because the unfortunate participants are usually ready to enter one after serving time as husband and wife."

Rocky eyed him strangely. "That's a terrible attitude for a newly engaged man to have, Mike." She looked at Julia, sympathy in her brown eyes. "And it must be difficult for Julia to hear you say such things."

Julia and Michael looked at each other. Damage control was definitely required, but neither was quite sure who should say what.

"He's just sounding off. He doesn't really mean it," Julia murmured.

At the same time Michael said, "Old habits die hard. I used to feel that way, but I've changed my mind, of course."

"Sometimes Michael spouts his antimarriage spiel by rote," Julia continued. "He manages to forget that his dad has been happily married to his stepmother for nearly a quarter century and that my mom and dad had a long, happy marriage, too."

Rocky raised her slanted brows. "I suggest you change that negative tape in your head before it does some real harm, Mike."

"I agree. We are what we think," Julia said earnestly. "It's a long-held psychological tenet."

"Well, I think I'm sick of being here," Michael interjected, with a most charming smile. "May I interest you two in leaving?"

"Sorry, I'm here with some friends and we're going to a movie after we eat," said Rocky. She looked her cousin up and down and grinned broadly. "You're certainly all decked out tonight, Mike. A dark suit is just the thing to wear to a—"

"I know, I know, I've already heard it." Michael held up his hands, as if to physically ward off whatever remark she was about to make.

"We were playing truth or dare and I dared him to wear a suit tonight," Julia improvised, laughing up at Michael. "I never thought he'd do it, but here he is."

"I told you I wouldn't back down from a dare, sweetheart." Michael played along with her ruse.

"Oh, Julia, dare him to eat the curly fries with cheese and gravy! Please!" Rocky begged, laughing. "Followed by that old ballpark fave, a corn dog on a stick!"

"She doesn't want to kill me, she merely wanted to teach me a lesson," Michael interjected. "Isn't that right, Julia?"

Julia looked up at him. His blue eyes were watching her intently. She lowered her gaze to follow the sensual lines of his well-shaped mouth. The hot memory of his kiss caused her mind to go blank.

"Well, you've made your point, Julia," Michael continued. Her eyes were cloudy and unfocused, her lips slightly parted. She looked the way she did when he was about to kiss her—sensuous and hungry, as eager for the taste of him as he was for her.

He took a deep breath. "When it comes to dinner reservations for us, I'll make them myself. No more ordering my assistant to do it."

"I think I've missed something in the translation, but it sounds like a plan to me," Rocky said cheerfully. "And since two's company and I'm beginning to feel like we're a crowd of three, I'll find my friends and hit the cheesecake booth. I heard the Mississippi Mud cheesecake squares are to die for."

"I would choose to die rather than eat something called Mississippi Mud from one of these stands," Michael countered. "It might actually be something dredged from the river. And let's not forget the omnipresent risk of food poisoning, which is rampant in—"

"This harangue is bringing back memories of that fun family vacation we all spent at Disneyworld when Allie and I were eight," Rocky interjected wryly. "Mike made us leave the park every night to have dinner at restaurants he deemed nutritionally sound. I still can't believe we all caved into him—he was only twelve!"

"Michael has a way of getting people to do what he wants," Julia agreed. An observation that served as a reminder to disengage herself from him, physically and emotionally. She did so, stepping out of touching distance and scanning the crowd for Kia.

She needed Kia, her anchor with reality, who didn't hesitate to point out that by agreeing to this fake engagement, Julia had made herself a pawn on the Fortune chessboard of life.

"My roommate is here somewhere, but I don't see her," Julia murmured.

"Maybe she's pigging out at the apple-dumpling stand," suggested Rocky. "I heard they're scrumptious. In fact, I think I'll go there instead of the cheesecake stand." She took Julia's hand in hers. "I'm so happy we met, Julia. You're just right for my cousin. Congratulations again, Mike." Standing on tiptoe, Rocky planted a quick kiss on her cousin's cheek. "I'm going back to Wyoming the day after tomorrow, but I'll be home for your engagement party. You know I wouldn't miss it for the world."

She rushed off, melting into the crowd, leaving Julia and Michael to stare at each other. For a moment, neither spoke a word.

And then they both chorused in perfect unison, "Engagement party?"

Ten

"It's like trying to cancel the Fourth of July or Thanksgiving," Michael complained as he paced the floor of his office. "I've never seen my stepmother and my aunt so determined. They are absolutely insistent on throwing this engagement party for us. All the arrangements are made and the acceptances are pouring in. The party is set for Friday night, the day before Halloween."

"Then I guess we'd better show up," Julia said wryly.

She was sitting at Michael's desk, her elbows propped on its gleaming surface. He'd been pacing since summoning her into his office, and Julia had sunk gratefully into his unoccupied chair. Her new shoes, sleek and narrow with very high heels, did not encourage the wearer to stand for very long. Julia wondered again why she'd let Kristina talk her into buying them, why she'd forsaken her comfortable pumps in favor of such frothy footwear. She decided that if Kristina ever tired of her advertising career, the younger Fortune could make a killing in the sister field of sales; she'd exhibited world-class salesmanship in pressuring Julia into buying these impractical but ultrasexy shoes.

It had been slightly over two weeks since Julia and Michael had announced their mock-engagement. At first, Julia hadn't realized that the position of Michael Fortune's fiancée would require a considerable image overhaul from her role as his assistant. But according to Kristina, a successful fiancée portrayal carried certain inescapable, decorative obligations.

"Julia, you need to wear something... How can I say this

without hurting your feelings? Okay, I'll be blunt: something less dowdy to the office," Kristina had announced on day five of the mock engagement, during one of her frequent visits to Michael's office.

"There's nothing wrong with my work clothes," Julia had stated, equally frank. Since the announcement, she'd unconsciously begun to respond to Kristina as more of a peer and less as a vaunted Fortune, family member of her employer.

Julia had already made one concession in her office appearance—she no longer wore her hair in the tight braid she now knew Michael loathed. But she wasn't about to waste her money on a new wardrobe of office clothes for her temporary role as a Fortune fiancée, and nobody was going to needle her into doing so.

"My suits are well made and in good condition," she added defensively.

Both Kristina and Michael eyed Julia's chronic beige suit and white blouse, then looked at each other.

"Julia, the suits you wear to the office would be perfectly fine if you were fifty," Kristina said, and then frowned. "No, I'm not doing justice to my mom and Aunt Erica, who are over fifty and wouldn't be caught dead in that suit of yours. It would be perfect if you were sixty-five and a nun."

Julia laughed. Kristina's tendency to exaggerate to make a point amused her. "Okay, I agree that my work clothes are bland and unexciting, but they're tasteful and appropriate for the office. Just ask Michael what he thinks of assistants who run around in spandex minis and halter tops. He's fired quite a few."

"I think Michael would love to see you running around in a spandex miniskirt and halter top," Kristina said slyly. "What guy wants his fiancée dressing like a sixty-five-year-old nun?"

"I'm not his fiancée," Julia stated calmly. "This engagement is only make-believe, remember?"

"Nevertheless, Kristina does have a point." Michael spoke up, surprising Julia. "There are only five people who know this engagement isn't real, so you ought to dress the part of my fiancée, Julia. And my fiancée would wear something, uh..." His voice trailed off, his face suddenly flushing.

"Something sexier!" Kristina crowed. "Who can blame Mike for wanting you to make the most of yourself, Julia? You have a pretty face and a great body, though you do your best to downplay both. But no more! Come on, we're going shopping."

"We're not!" Julia declared. "I don't need more clothes, I have a closetful."

"I think it's time to weed out that closet, Julia." Michael removed several credit cards from his wallet and handed them to his sister. "And to restock it. Kristina, take her shopping."

"An official executive order!" Kristina grabbed Julia's arm and propelled her out of the office. "When the vice president of Fortune speaks, we shop."

"This is a first. I've never seen you so willing to follow orders," Julia had mumbled, but she'd given in and shopped with Kristina.

As she sat in Michael's desk chair this afternoon, watching and listening to him vent his irritation about the proposed engagement party, Julia glanced down at her new two-piece, hunter green suit, which was one of the three most beautiful and expensive outfits she'd ever owned. The other two were also courtesy of Michael's credit cards and Kristina's tastes during that forced shopping expedition: a black-and-white houndstooth suit and a deep heather blue suit. All were similar styles, with fitted jackets and short straight skirts, the type of suits seen in catalogs worn by leggy models who'd never been near an office in their lives and never would be.

Though Kristina had insisted that she buy them—along with complementing shoes—Julia had feared the suits were unacceptable and unprofessional for a working woman. Especially a woman working for Michael Fortune, who had been quite vocal in protesting the inappropriate garb worn by his previous assistants.

But Michael had been all compliments and enthusiasm, even encouraging her to buy more! Julia had quickly declined the offer of yet another shopping spree. She was still trying to come to terms with the fact she had acquiesced to the first.

Clearly, Michael had different standards for his fiancée—even a fausse one—than for his employees. And he didn't mind paying to have those standards met.

He stopped pacing and turned to look at Julia, cozily ensconced in his chair. "You seem quite sanguine about this party," he said, his tone rather accusing.

"Probably because it's ten days away and doesn't seem real," Julia confessed. "I can't imagine myself at a party at the Fortune mansion. It falls into the realm of fantasy, like getting invited to a White House state dinner or something."

"The Fortune mansion," Michael repeated. "I never think of it in those terms."

"Everybody who's not a Fortune does," Julia assured him. "It's a Minneapolis frame of reference for size and luxury. People say things like, 'Well, this house is nice, but compared to the Fortune mansion, it's a shack.' I've heard about the Fortune mansion for years. Part of me is actually looking forward to seeing it," she admitted sheepishly.

"You could've already seen it. I've asked you out to the house to go boating the past two weekends and both times you refused." Michael frowned, still displeased by her refusals. Julia had stated very firmly that she could not play the role of his fiancée on Saturdays or Sundays, and nothing could sway her from that decision.

Even Barbara and Erica, determined to host that infernal engagement party, had bowed to Julia concerning the date. They'd wanted to schedule the event on Halloween, which fell on a Saturday. When Julia had said that any Saturday was unacceptable, she'd had such a look of steely determination on her face and such a note of resolve in her voice that his stepmother and aunt, accustomed to dealing with the strong willed and knowing when to negotiate a point, had immediately chosen Friday night for the party instead.

Michael found it telling that although he'd griped continually about the party, the two social mavens had completely ignored *his* resolve and steely determination not to have the party at all.

"We understand that you're introverted, Mike, but this party is a must," his aunt had said, dismissing his protests as if he were a grumpy eighth-grader.

"We want everybody, including Julia, to know that she is fully accepted by the family and that all the Fortunes are delighted by your engagement," his stepmother declared. "It's especially important that we step in and fill the void because the poor girl is an orphan with no family to plan any wedding festivities. Sterling told us about the tragic loss of her parents."

Sterling hadn't told them anything else about Julia, but the orphan information had galvanized the family. The imagery of Little Orphan Julia with the kindly Fortunes becoming her surrogate family clearly appealed to them all...with the obvious exception of his mother, of course. Sheila was still bemoaning Michael's lost chances to snag an heiress. Never mind that the daughter of a sinfully rich billionaire had failed to appear; Sheila was convinced she was out there somewhere, ready and willing to share the wealth.

"I'm not free on Saturdays or Sundays, Michael." Julia cut into his reverie with the same answer she had given when he'd extended his boating invitations.

"Why not?" Michael pressed.

"I'm not free to tell you," Julia replied flatly.

Frustration gripped him. What was so sacrosanct about her Saturdays and Sundays that nothing could induce her to give them up? What did she do, where did she go and why did she classify such facts as privileged information? Which he was not privileged to know!

Michael didn't bother to ask himself why he was so determined to spend Saturdays or Sundays with his fausse fiancée or why he wanted to be taken into her confidence. *Those* were questions best ignored.

So he held on to his irritation and his frustration and reluctantly imagined what Julia did on her tightly guarded weekends. Was she seeing another man, a boyfriend who was also in on their secret? A man whose position in her life was authentic and not a fakery, who did not have to pay her for her time and her company?

Those thoughts were so unpleasant that Michael promptly blocked them. He refused to ruminate about her and some phantom.

He jammed his hands into the pockets of his trousers and stared broodingly at Julia, who was seated so comfortably in his chair. She was wearing one of her new suits, the dark green one that lent an arresting green cast to her eyes.

That suit showcased more than her eyes, Michael conceded grimly, his body tightening. Her new clothes displayed her figure most delectably. Her breasts were firm and rounded under the fitted jacket, and he remembered all too well how they had looked and felt and tasted during those brief moments of ecstasy right here in his office.

The memory heated his blood, and his mind started to grow fuzzy. He felt sweat bead on his forehead, though the office was cool and the fall temperature outside even cooler. Michael began to pace again. He knew he would be spending time in the pool swimming laps today—and then running a few miles on the river trail to work off his pent-up, ever increasing sexual energy.

Julia appeared composed and calm, displaying none of his passion-hungry urgency, he thought resentfully. Clearly, she was not burning with the need to touch him—or to be touched by him. His fevered thoughts swung to the last time he had touched her, on that evening they'd gone to the neighborhood Artsfest. He had linked his fingers through the belt loops of her jeans and pulled her against him, and the memory of the natural way she'd cuddled up to him sent a fiery ache streaking through him.

Julia had kept herself out of his reach since that evening. Anytime he came close, she backed away. Her movements were slow and subtle, yet she carefully managed to distance herself wherever they happened to be and no matter whom they were with. The fact that they'd spent a number of evenings together made the situation worse, because the more he was in her company, the more he *needed* to touch her. But was unable to.

He'd made dinner reservations on five weekday nights at five of the top restaurants in the Twin Cities area. Julia had seemed to enjoy herself on those evenings, and he'd been surprised by how very much he had enjoyed being with her. She was good company, an intelligent conversationalist, lively, animated and fun, quite different from her quiet, efficient office persona.

But the dinners were strictly platonic. There was no hand holding, no legs touching provocatively under the table, no gazing soulfully into each other's eyes. Nothing to fuel his hopes for a more intimate interlude later on. All five evenings, he'd dropped Julia off at her apartment after dinner, and they'd parted without even a peck on the cheek.

Their lunches together were equally sterile. They talked business like colleagues and conversed like good friends, but there was absolutely nothing loverlike between them.

Which was only logical and right, because they weren't lovers and they weren't going to become lovers. Michael reminded himself of that fact several times a day. And then he told himself how glad he was that Julia was being so sensible about this engagement, which, after all, had been designed for his own convenience. Nothing could be more inconvenient than a fausse fiancée who wanted to take the relationship further, who wouldn't mind blurring the lines between fantasy and reality.

What a mess that would be when it ended! The agreement Sterling had drawn up probably could be invalidated if he and Julia went to bed together. But he had no worries along those lines, thanks to Julia.

"I'm going to the gym," Michael announced tersely, and he rushed off as though the hounds of hell were barking at his heels.

Julia stared thoughtfully at the door that he'd failed to close after bolting out of the office. She rose slowly from his chair and headed back to her own office. As much as Michael hated the idea of an engagement party, and though she couldn't fathom herself as an invited guest to the Fortune mansion, she enjoyed their daily talks about the upcoming event.

She liked being with Michael for any reason, Julia silently admitted. She liked it too much. So much that she didn't trust herself even to stand too close to him. She'd logged too many daydreams and sleepless nights reliving each time he had touched her, and an equal number of hours longing to create new memories.

Julia thought of their dinner dates, the reservations made by Michael himself for the purpose of being seen together in the Twin Cities area. To him it was simply part of their agreement, but for her having Michael at his most charming, seated across the table in an atmosphere of candlelight, fine wine and delicious food, was escalating temptation to the breaking point.

She had to be stronger, Julia told herself. She had to ignore the sparks of desire that shot through her every time Michael was near. She had to remember that the chemistry and camaraderie between them was as ephemeral as a dream. She was lucky that her weekend visits to Joanna rendered her un-available for Saturday and Sunday charades, granting her a full forty-eight hours to restore her willpower to resist him.

Julia knew she was in trouble when she'd been sorely tempted to accept Michael's invitations to go boating the past two weekends. Until then, she had never dreamed of canceling a visit with Joanna, but for the past two weekends she had struggled with her decision…boating with Michael or the hos-pital with Joanna? Her temptation struck Julia as a very dan-gerous sign. A warning to be heeded.

Michael was spending time with her to support the illusion of their bogus engagement. She'd agreed to the arrangement because it was beneficial for Joanna. Those were the cold, hard, unromantic facts she must never forget, not even if she wanted to.

And she wanted to. Desperately.

Feeling dismal, Julia went back to her own office and lost herself in reviewing the quarterly customer-satisfaction sur-vey. Replies revealed that both regular and occasional users of Fortune products were satisfied with their purchases and planned to repeat their choices.

Julia tried to be glad that somebody somewhere felt they'd made the right decision about something.

The Fortune mansion was ablaze with lights on the night before Halloween, as a continuous stream of guests arrived to celebrate the engagement of Michael Fortune and Julia Chandler. A band played in an enormous room that had been cleared for dancing, and some of the guests took to the floor, while others wandered through the spacious downstairs rooms, talking, drinking and eating.

Michael kept his arm firmly around Julia's waist as he guided her through the crowd, introducing her to people whose names she'd heard and seen in print but had never expected to meet. She was too awed to be scared. The whole situation—the engagement to the Fortune scion, the party in their honor at the famed mansion, the celebrated guest list—didn't seem real.

Once again she was an actress playing the role of Michael's fiancée, this time in a full-costume drama—or was this a farce? Whichever, Jen's acting tip, "The actor leaves her own self behind and becomes the character," resonated in Julia's head.

It seemed to grow easier, playing the same character to a familiar audience, Julia decided. She greeted her Fortune hosts—Jake and Erica, Nate and Barbara—with the confidence and warmth a real fiancée of Michael's would possess. They actually seemed to like her, and Julia felt another guilty pang for deceiving them. She had begun to view them as people rather than demigods and found herself hoping they would never learn of her and Michael's conspiracy after the prearranged breakup. Far better to let the older Fortunes believe she'd been dumped by Michael instead of finding out they'd been duped by the two of them.

For Michael the party was all too real, a repeat of countless social occasions he'd attended—and come to loathe—through the years. Though he performed introductions and made small talk with seasoned grace, in between his acts of charm he shared his real feelings with Julia.

"I hate parties, especially mammoth ones like this. I hate the meaningless chatter and the inane jokes inevitable to socializing." He scowled at the uniformed waitresses who moved unobtrusively among the guests, passing out elaborate hors d'oeuvres. A sumptuous buffet was being readied in the dining room for later in the evening.

"I would rather be eating shish kebabs and cotton candy at that neighborhood festival than be here," he announced, refusing a miniature asparagus tart from one of the circulating waitresses's trays. He did not turn down the glass of champagne that a waiter offered him, however.

Julia watched him down it in a few gulps and set the empty goblet on another passing tray. It was not Michael's first glass of the night. She wasn't quite sure if it was his third or fourth, but decided that his mind must've been affected by the champagne if he wished himself to be surrounded by outdoor stands of festival food.

"I think you're forgetting exactly how much you hated the Artsfest, Michael," she reminded him.

"At least the festival had chainsaw sculpting." Michael flashed her a droll smile. "Find me anything here to compare to *that*."

"Well, you might take this place for granted, but I feel like I'm on a movie set."

"The Grand Family Mansion, Scene I, Take I."

Michael found the comparison amusing, but Julia was serious. This was not real life as she knew it. He had given her a tour of the place before the guests began to arrive.

The exterior was impressive and classic, a huge, white, colonial-style house with verandas and French doors and a meticulously tended expanse of lawns and gardens. Tennis courts were in the back of the house, as well as a beautifully landscaped, kidney-shaped pool. The clear blue waters of Lake Travis shimmered beyond, and the estate's outbuildings, plus a dock and a boathouse, were located on the shore.

Julia had been amazed at the extent of the Fortune fleet: two motorboats, a thirty-foot sailboat and various rowboats and canoes. She'd thought she saw a Jet Ski tucked inside the boathouse, too. Once again she'd regretted her lost opportunity to spend a Saturday on Lake Travis with Michael, and once again she'd reminded herself how important her weekend visits were both to Joanna and herself.

Inside, the mansion was filled with antiques that even to Julia's untutored eye looked priceless. There were museum-quality Persian rugs and original Impressionist paintings, and all sorts of "special interest" rooms including a large library, a billiard room, a music room and a cheerful sunroom filled with thriving plants. In the private areas of the house, the decor was still luxurious, yet well suited for comfort.

Julia counted at least ten bedrooms, including an amazingly large and well-appointed master-bedroom suite. She thought of the three-bedroom, split-level house she'd grown up in, now owned by another busy young suburban family. The square footage of that entire house wouldn't come close to filling the Fortunes' first floor. As for her current abode, the whole apartment seemed smaller than the palatial master bathroom!

Once again she was struck by the ridiculous pretense of this false engagement. She and Michael weren't merely from different social classes, they were from different worlds. They might as well have been from different planets, so disparate were their origins. How could anybody possibly believe that he would ever become engaged to her for real? All the facts revealed how absurd a Michael Fortune–Julia Chandler engagement really was, but the facts kept being ignored, over and over again.

When Erica and Barbara had asked her for the names of people she would like to invite to the party, Julia gave them none, offering no explanations. The true one, of course, was that she didn't want to entangle anyone else in this charade. And Kia herself had opted out, saying she "flatly refused to take part in a celebration of a wealth-related fraud."

Yet no one questioned Julia's lack of guests, no one questioned the validity of the engagement they were celebrating tonight. People smiled and wished them well. Some of the men actually congratulated Michael on his "good fortune," delighting in the pun. Julia's mind was truly boggled.

She sipped the second glass of champagne Michael handed her. She rarely drank the stuff, and the few times she had, she'd found the taste unpleasantly bitter. Not this, though. The pale, bubbly liquid was mellow and light and glided smoothly down her throat.

"My face feels ready to crack from all this smiling," Michael growled as they made a gracious departure from yet another cluster of guests. "And if somebody makes another Cinderella analogy, I won't be responsible for my actions. You aren't a downtrodden waif who needed magical intervention by some fairy godmother."

"Everybody has been very kind. But when it comes to fairy tales, *Alice in Wonderland* is probably closer to the mark."

"This particular scene would be the Mad Hatter's tea party," muttered Michael.

"And maybe there is a little of the Cinderella story thrown in," Julia said lightly. "I know you'll rebel at being cast as a fairy godmother, but your credit card is the magic wand that conjured up this dress."

She glanced down at the short, sexy, yet elegant ruby red dress she was wearing. Both Michael and Kristina had been adamant that her little black dress, the trusty garment that had served her so well during college and since, would definitely not do for tonight's illustrious party. Michael insisted that providing a dress for Julia was his responsibility, even going so far as to threaten to bring Sterling to the office to draw up another contract specifying an engagement-party gown as part of their deal. Julia, remembering how long and boring a Michael-specified contract could be, allowed him to buy it.

"You look spectacular in that dress," Michael said huskily, his eyes straying to Julia, as they'd been doing all evening. Kristina's plan had been to focus attention on Kate's ring, enhancing it by duplicating the ruby color with the dress, thus keeping the memory of their grandmother front and center on this special night.

But for Michael, the ruby color did not call forth thoughts of his grandmother. His mind was too filled with thoughts of Julia. Admiring, lascivious, obsessive thoughts of Julia. She was dazzling in that dress, possessing a sexual elegance that left him reeling. He'd proudly accepted all the congratulations from the admiring men present; he'd also wanted to sock a few of them for openly slavering over Julia.

"There's your aunt Rebecca," Julia said, gripping his forearm. She was glad to see a familiar face, someone she wouldn't have to be introduced to. "She's over there, see?"

Heat rolled over Michael in waves. This was the first time Julia had touched him in weeks, and the feel of her fingers brought forth a sensual memory of that incredible time she'd closed them over a far-more-intimate part of his body. Desire and need coiled explosively in his belly. At this moment, he didn't feel up to making conversation with his favorite aunt. He wanted to converse privately with Julia. And he wanted their private conversation to lead to a great deal more....

But Julia had already made eye contact with Rebecca, and his aunt was smiling and moving toward them. Accompanying her was a tall, muscular man Michael recognized as Gabriel Devereax, a private investigator whom Rebecca had hired to investigate Kate's plane crash. Michael assumed that Devereax was also probing into the suspicious fire and break-in at the lab. The investigator looked like he'd seen a lot of the hard side of life, but had yet to be caught unaware by anything or anybody.

"Julia," Rebecca exclaimed warmly, taking her hands. "You look beautiful to—"

"Please, no Cinderella references, Rebecca," Michael warned. "We've heard enough of them tonight."

"I wouldn't dream of it," Rebecca promised. "I think your story is closer to Beauty and the Beast, anyway."

Rebecca introduced Gabe to Julia, taking great care to explain that he was a private investigator and not her date for the evening.

"I see." Julia was puzzled. "Are you here tonight on a case, Mr. Devereax?"

Devereax shrugged. "Not really."

He was a man of few words, and he didn't expend any on the allegedly engaged couple. After exchanging a few more pleasantries with Rebecca, Julia and Michael slowly drifted away.

"This night isn't as bad as I thought it would be. I remember one really bad date I had when the guy wouldn't speak or even make eye contact." Julia laughed reminiscently. "He mumbled hello when he arrived at the door and didn't say another word for the rest of the evening. I had to do the talking for both of us, and you know I'm hardly a terrific conversationalist myself."

"No, I didn't know that. You've always managed to hold up your end of the conversation with me." Michael drained his glass.

"Oh well, that's different," Julia said. She finished her own glass of champagne. "You're my boss. And it's not like we're actually dating, so there isn't that—well, you know—that pressure."

"The guys you date pressure you for sex?" The thought outraged him. And her admission that she considered him her safely neutered boss and nothing more was additional fuel to his internal fire.

"No!" Julia's cheeks turned the shade of her dress, ring and shoes. "I didn't mean to imply that. I meant the social pressure, you know, to keep the conversation going and to—"

"Michael, when do you intend to introduce me to your little bride-to-be?" The shrill, unmistakable voice of Sheila Fortune sounded behind them.

"Uh-oh!" Michael muttered in a low voice. "Speaking of social pressure, get ready for a megadose of it."

The Fortunes hadn't been thrilled with the prospect of inviting Sheila to the engagement party, but at Michael's insistence bowed to convention and extended an invitation to the mother of the groom-to-be. Though he was aware of Sheila's propensity to stir things up, he recognized his duty as a son not to snub her publicly.

He and Julia turned around and faced her as a unit, smiles pasted bravely on their faces. "You already know Julia, Mother," Michael said through his teeth. "You've met her a number of times when you've come to my office."

"That girl in your office was a plain little mouse," Sheila said, eyeing Julia from head to toe. "She blended into your boring corporate wallpaper. I could never remember what she looked like, so I don't remember meeting her."

Sheila Fortune continued to scrutinize Julia with her startling eyes. They were accented by her brilliant aqua dress, which was undoubtedly expensive—all those beads and sequins added up, Julia knew. Yet Sheila's gown was a little too loud and a little too tacky, especially in comparison to the understated good taste of Barbara and Erica and the other women at the party. Sheila's gaudy jewelry and brassy hair did not lend a much needed touch of class, either. She'd had so many nips, tucks and various additions to her body that she had a fake, stretched look to her, and her brittle air was discomfiting.

But the woman was Michael's mother, and Julia had been raised to be polite. "Hello, Mrs. Fortune," she said, maintaining her smile. She knew that Sheila insisted on that appellation despite her divorce nearly a quarter century ago. "I'm Julia Chandler."

Sheila tossed her head, and her long, dangling diamond earrings battered against her neck. "Are you pregnant?" she asked bluntly.

"Mother!" Michael gasped. "Of all the—"

"No, I'm not," Julia said quickly.

"You don't have to lie to me. I'm not Erica or Barbara, who pretend to be so sweet and sincere and who act as if that thought had never crossed their minds. Ha! It's crossed everybody's minds, but I'm the only one honest enough to ask.

Why else would Michael be marrying his secretary or whatever you are? I am not being malicious, I'm merely curious to know when the baby is due. I can't believe I'm going to be a *grandmother. Again!*'' Sheila added morosely.

"I'm not going to have a baby. We've never even gone to bed together," Julia blurted out, and then clasped her hands to her flaming cheeks in horrified embarrassment.

"So that's your strategy? Playing hard to get? Holding out for a *wedding* ring?" Sheila's eyes narrowed. "You're far more clever than I thought, Julie. That prim getup of yours was just a disguise, hmm? An effective tactic, for sure. Watching a woman change from a shy little mouse to a hot little tease is intriguing, especially to a jaded man like Michael. Oh, I can guess exactly how you played it, opening a few buttons to show some cleavage, hiking up your skirt to show some leg and then—''

"Mother, stop this at once!" Michael ordered sternly. "And my fiancée's name is Julia, not Julie."

"I have no intention of stopping until I have my say. As a mother, I'm entitled." Sheila glared at her son. "So proper little Julie dangled the bait and you went for it hook, line and sinker? Oh, Michael! Though when she's not playing the office frump, she is an attractive girl, I'll give her that," Sheila said grudgingly. "That dress she's wearing must have set you back plenty, Mike. Oh, I know you bought it for her. That bratty Kristina told Jane all about the shopping trips with Julie and how you paid for everything. Frankly, I'm astonished. I remember you swore off buying gifts for women after that tramp Delilah made such a fool of you."

"That was a long time ago, Mother, and certainly has nothing to do with the current situation," Michael said defensively.

"Perhaps, perhaps not." Sheila shrugged, then gave Julia a hard stare. "You've managed to ingratiate yourself with the whole family, haven't you, Julie? And even though you're wearing Mike's grandmother's ruby ring, you still haven't come across in the bedroom." She gave a shrill laugh. "I'm sure you won't until you get that wedding band securely on your finger. Oh, I know all about your kind, with the so-sweet facade and the calculating mind of a divorce attorney. If you didn't have your hooks in my son, I'd actually admire you, Julie. I'd ask you to pass along some tactical advice to my daughter, Jane, who is clueless when it comes to managing men."

Julia said nothing. She felt clueless when it came to managing Sheila Fortune.

"Mother, you've completely misinterpreted everything," Michael said tightly. "I want you to apologize to *Julia* and—"

"Apologize to her for what?" Sheila raised her voice. "I've been complimenting the girl. She's certainly displayed far more cunning and guile than you have, Michael."

"Aunt Sheila! It's so good to see you!" Rocky Fortune rushed over to the trio and threw her arms around Sheila, taking care not to touch her hair or makeup. "You look gorgeous tonight—as usual, of course."

Over her aunt's shoulder, Rocky winked conspiratorially at Michael and Julia. She'd noticed the increasingly tense encounter and had appointed herself as intercessor.

"Aunt Sheila, that color is perfect on you!" Rocky exclaimed with credible enthusiasm. "Nobody can wear shades of blue the way you do."

Sheila preened. "Blue is my best color," she agreed. "And you look just precious yourself tonight, darling. So girlish and natural. I've seen your twin sister, and that dress of hers is way too trendy and glamorous for a family party. But dear little Rocky, you look just right. I bet you bought your dress off the rack in one of those mall stores, didn't you? Probably on sale, too. You're so practical! How I admire that because my preferences and tastes simply cannot be economized."

"Thank you, Aunt Sheila," Rocky said angelically. "Now, I want to hear all about what you've been doing. I've hardly seen you since I moved to Wyoming."

"Wyoming," Sheila repeated with a martyred sigh. "You're living there now, too, aren't you, dear? I just don't understand the appeal of that place. Kyle moved there, and it's as if he dropped off the face of the earth. I am quite upset that he couldn't be bothered to fly back to Minnesota for his own brother's engagement party and—"

"Kyle is especially busy with the ranch right now, Mother," Michael interrupted. "He called to explain and I understand."

"Well, I don't." Sheila pouted. "And I notice that stepbrother of yours isn't here to celebrate with you tonight. Couldn't he bring himself to leave his ranch in Wyoming, either?" She glanced at Julia. "Did you know Michael has a stepbrother named Grant McClure? He is Barbara's son by her first husband."

Julia nodded her head uneasily. "Yes, I knew that." She also knew that Sheila was taking aim and was about to fire.

"Well, I wonder if you know that when Grant was just a small child, he *chose* to live in Wyoming with his father?" Sheila's eyes flashed. "Yes, he deliberately decided *not* to come to Minnesota to live with his mother and Nate. Isn't it sad when a child chooses not to live with his own mother, Julie? I simply can't envision it myself. My children lived with me, of course. And though Barbara is always insisting that she and Grant are so close, the truth is, he chose to grow up with his father in Wyoming."

"Wyoming is a beautiful state, Aunt Sheila," Rocky interjected. "I hope you'll come out for a visit sometime and stay with me." She turned to Michael and Julia. "Why don't you two go and mingle with the crowd while Aunt Sheila and I catch up?"

Sheila was ready and eager to yield to Rocky's attentive interest. Michael quickly pulled Julia away from the pair.

"Rocky is definitely in the right business. She is gifted when it comes to finding people who need to be rescued," he murmured, glancing over his shoulder to see his cousin listening patiently as his mother chattered on.

"Whether it's the wilds of Wyoming or the Fortune mansion in Minneapolis, Rocky comes through," Julia agreed. She was deeply appreciative of being saved from that mortifying conversation with Sheila Fortune. "Your mother seems to like Rocky," she added. That came as something of a surprise; she didn't think Sheila liked anybody.

"Rocky has always been friendly, and Mother has never found reason to envy her. As a child Rocky was an independent, adventurous tomboy, and now she flies planes. It's her twin, Allie, who really bugs my mother. Allie's always drawn a lot of male attention, and then she went on to become a successful model. An unforgivable sin in Sheila Fortune's eyes."

Julia thought of Snow White, the wicked queen and her magic mirror, and the basic psychology underlying that tale. "Some women view other females as competition, no matter what their age."

"Do you?" Michael asked abruptly.

His question startled Julia. "Why, no."

"So you're not the competitive or the jealous type? If another woman draped herself around me, you wouldn't care?"

Julia blinked owlishly. Her conversations with Michael, though brief and disjointed due to constant interruptions tonight, definitely had taken an odd turn. "I wouldn't have the right to care," she reminded him. "But if a woman draped herself around you this evening, it would look awfully strange to the guests, considering this is supposed to be our engagement party."

Her attempt to lighten his sudden dark mood proved futile.

Michael frowned and looked away from her. Confused, Julia wondered what to say next. She hoped he wasn't one of those personalities who turned mute and brooding after a few drinks…or even worse, into a snarling, contentious boor.

"Hi, you two!" Kristina joined them, looking gorgeous in a stylish, sexy dress of ecru silk. "I noticed that you escaped unscathed from Sheila, thanks to our own brave, Rocky. Was Sheila positively horrible to you, Julia?"

"Actually, she was complimentary." Julia glanced from Kristina, whom she was delighted to see, over to Michael, who was still scowling. She tried again to make him smile. "Sheila said I have more cunning and guile than Michael does."

Michael didn't laugh, but Kristina did. "The high priestess of manipulation praised your cunning and guile? You should be very proud, Julia!"

Kristina noticed Michael's lack of response. "What's with you, Mike?" she demanded. "You should be elated that our hoax is working so well. You've fooled everybody at this party, and that is no small thing. Instead you look as surly as a—"

"I hate the music the band is playing, okay?" Michael interrupted testily. "I've heard car alarms that sound better. Who hired that band, anyway? Do you realize they've played the "Electric Slide" twice in the same hour? I mean, come on! That's torture!"

Kristina eyed him strangely. "Good grief, you sound like Granddaddy ranting and raving about the decline of pop music." She turned to Julia. "Our Grandfather Ben used to say there hasn't been a good song written since Jerome Kern."

"Well, I'm beginning to believe the old man had a point," growled Michael.

"Michael really isn't an "Electric Slide" type of person," Julia explained.

"Well sure, but he doesn't have to go nuclear over it,"

said Kristina. She threw up her hands in an exaggerated gesture of concession. "Okay, big brother, tonight your wish is
my command. I'll go have a talk with the band right now."

With Kristina gone, Julia and Michael stood side by side
in silence. She cast a sidelong glance at him. He was staring
into space, his expression remote and unreadable. Julia was
certain that his bad mood could not be solely attributed to
having listened to the "Electric Slide" twice in one hour. She
shifted from one foot to the other and chewed her lower lip,
searching for something to say.

"You look like you're on one of those really bad dates you
were telling me about earlier." Michael's tone was mocking.
"Is the social pressure getting to you? Aren't I doing my part
to keep the conversation flowing smoothly?"

"It's a conversation I'm having trouble following. I think
you're angry with me, but I'm not sure why."

He didn't have a chance to reply. From the other room, a
voice boomed over the microphone. "I've just been told that
our groom-to-be has some special requests. So, from Mike to
Julia…"

The band launched into the lush, romantic Jerome Kern
standard, "All The Things You Are." Amidst teasing and
affectionate oohs and ahhs, Julia and Michael were ordered
to go into the other room and dance.

"I'm going to kill Kristina for this," Michael rasped under
his breath.

"It could be worse," Julia reminded him. "What if she'd
requested the "Electric Slide" again? Or even worse, the
Limbo?"

Michael made a sound that was half laugh and half groan.
Leading Julia to the middle of the dance floor, he pulled her
into his arms.

Eleven

"At last they're playing some real music. Jerome Kern. One of Ben's favorites." Sterling Foster stood on the veranda and peered through a window at the young couple dancing inside. He was hidden from view by the shrubbery and plants lining the side of the house.

With him stood Kate Fortune, who unknown to her family, was very much alive. Kate had survived the crash in the rain forest, and on Sterling's advice had decided to "stay dead" for a time. The crash incident had all the telltale signs of sabotage, and both Kate and Sterling believed that until more facts were uncovered, she was safer "dead" than alive.

"They're such a darling couple, aren't they, Sterling?" Kate stared wistfully at her grandson and his fausse fiancée. "I've never seen Mike look at a woman in that particular way. He has fallen in love, Sterling. It's so obvious that he is crazy about Julia, and I couldn't be more pleased. She is such a sweet, lovely girl."

"Unfortunately, your grandson is a blockhead," Sterling declared flatly.

"That was uncalled for, Sterling," Kate scolded. "Mike is extremely bright and he—"

"Oh, he's a business whiz, I'll grant you that, but when it comes to women, he can't tell the difference between the dross and the gold. Not to mention the gold diggers. I know you have high hopes for him and Julia as a couple, but you'll have to prepare yourself for disappointment, Kate, because I don't think it's going to happen. Not with that contract looming between them.''

Kate sighed. ''From what you've told me, I'd have to agree the contract Mike made you draw up was, well, insulting, perhaps—''

''Not perhaps, Kate. It was grievously insulting. I'm ashamed to have been a part of it. If you had read it…well, I'm glad you didn't. That wretched contract reeks of his distrust and cynicism, and if I were Julia I would've told Master Michael to take a long walk off a short pier, then would have quit on the spot rather than sign such an odious document. But of course she didn't have that option, because she is taking care of her poor little sister.''

''You told me you went out to the rehabilitation hospital to check things out,'' Kate reminded him. ''Don't you mean you went to see if her story checked out? Honestly, Sterling, and you accuse Mike of being distrustful and cynical!''

''As an attorney, it's my job to be thorough,'' Sterling said in self-defense. ''I did go to the rehab hospital, and everything Julia said is true. The little sister broke almost every bone in her body in the car accident, including her head in a couple places. She is solely dependent on Julia, who has moved heaven and earth to get the kid the best possible care. The hospital staff can't say enough good things about Julia's devotion to young Joanna. Almost every penny she earns, including the bonus, has gone to pay the kid's medical bills, which are astronomical.''

''Those poor girls. To be so young and have experienced such tragedy,'' Kate murmured softly.

''Julia has triumphed over the tragedy in her life,'' Sterling proclaimed. ''As her attorney—pro bono, of course—I've never felt more proud of a client.''

''Julia is dedicated and loyal and strong and loving.'' Kate smiled. ''The perfect young woman for my grandson.''

''The girl is an angel, and Mike has treated her as if she

were a sleazy combination of his mother and Delilah De-Silva.'' Sterling was offended on behalf of his new, favorite client. ''Maybe Mike will eventually realize Julia's true worth. Maybe he'll even admit that he loves her, but it won't matter. It'll be too little, too late. Along with all those other fine qualities you mentioned, Julia also has a strong sense of pride and self-worth that won't allow her to be treated badly by anybody, even if his name happens to be Fortune.''

''What if she loves him, Sterling?''

''Sometimes love isn't enough, Kate. I agree Julia could be the best thing that ever happened to Mike, but he's behaved like such a suspicious misogynist that I don't think she will be able to—''

''You're certainly down on poor Michael.'' Kate frowned. ''I happen to believe that in spite of the damage caused him by his parents' bitter divorce and Sheila's incessant conniving that my dear Mike has enough love to give and is—''

''You've been reading too many novels and watching too many sentimental old movies in your hours alone, Kate.'' It was Sterling's turn to interrupt. ''Michael is an angry, bitter young man, and it is unlikely he will be redeemed by true love.''

''I'm not listening to another negative word, Sterling.'' Kate folded her arms in front of her chest and stared straight ahead, through the window at Michael and Julia.

They were dancing very, very close together, and Kate watched with delight as Julia slowly slid her arms around Michael's neck, bringing their bodies into even more intimate proximity.

''Before long, this engagement is going to be a real one and Mike will order you to tear up that dreadful contract. I'm certain of it,'' Kate added in a determined tone that Sterling knew well from their long years of professional and personal friendship.

''Nothing would please me more. But—''

"No buts. The two of them will... Uh-oh!" Kate quickly ducked down. "I think Michael saw me."

"What?" Sterling squawked. "Good Lord, Kate, I warned you not to come here tonight, that the chance of someone seeing you was too much of a risk to take, but would you listen to me? No! You insisted on coming anyway and now—"

"Hush, Sterling. And calm down. You're starting to turn purple and it doesn't become you."

"We've got to get you out of here right now, Kate!" Sterling took both her arms and propelled her away from the windows. They snaked through the shrubbery, taking care to keep out of sight of the windows.

"Sneaking around, peeking in windows! I feel like I'm trapped in one of those cheesy Monica Malone films she made in the waning years of her career," Sterling complained. "I don't know how I let you talk me into doing such—"

"Please! No Monica Malone references, not even disparaging ones," Kate ordered. "I don't want to hear that woman's name. And I'm glad I came tonight. It was worth the risk, Sterling. I just hope I'm wrong about Michael catching a glimpse of me. If he did, heaven only knows what he must be thinking...."

Inside the ballroom, Michael drew back with a visible start and then went utterly still. Other couples kept on dancing to the string of slow, romantic Jerome Kern melodies. Until a moment ago, Michael and Julia had been dancing, too—clinging together, moving slowly in a dreamy, sensual daze.

Until he'd seen his grandmother's face at the window!

"Michael, what's wrong?" Julia asked huskily. Her arms were around his neck; she'd put them there at his request. They had been dancing in formal ballroom style when Michael had yanked her closer and locked his arms around her.

"Put your arms around me," he'd whispered, and she had immediately obeyed, nestling closer to him.

Their bodies fit together in an elemental way that electrified them both. Julia was achingly aware of every breath he took because her own breathing had become shaky and shallow. Her breasts were taut and tingling and crushed against his chest; their thighs brushed provocatively as they moved to the music. She felt the evidence of his desire thick and hard against her, and she was unable to keep herself from subtly rubbing against him.

Michael inhaled sharply and buried his lips in the curve of her neck. This was what he'd been wanting, what he'd been needing for weeks. To hold her in his arms. To be close to her and feel her softness, her warmth. Silently, he gave thanks for the memory of his grandfather, whose musical tastes had inspired the request for songs enabling him to hold Julia close. The moment Michael had taken her into his arms, the suspicion and anger his mother's negative remarks had engendered instantly dissolved.

Playing hard to get…holding out for a wedding ring…a hot little tease. His mother's take on Julia had infuriated him at first and then begun to eat at him. He thought of Julia's passionate responses to him at the beginning of their fake engagement. He'd made no secret of how much he wanted her, but then she had pulled back. Playing hard to get? A very effective tactic, because he'd been unable to stop thinking about her, to stop wanting her. Holding out for a very real wedding and ring? Was that Julia's plan? Had he actually fallen for the wiles of a hot little tease?

That prim getup was just a disguise…. The new clothes Julia wore—granted, they'd been bought at his own insistence—revealed a sexy, pretty woman, and the contrast between his assistant then and now continued to floor him. Because she had been in deliberate disguise as a shy little mouse in order to intrigue him? If that was her goal, she'd been wildly successful!

He'd been pondering those disturbing perspectives when

Kristina had joined them and questioned his foul mood. He'd needed an excuse—he could hardly confess to questioning his own gullibility, could he?—and the annoying music had been the first thing that came to mind. Besides, he really did hate the "Electric Slide."

But when the band had launched into "All The Things You Are," and he and Julia had begun to dance together, all his doubts and suspicions had melted. He was tired of fighting, tired of wanting her and not having her. Being close to her was paradoxically soothing and exciting, stimulating and re-laxing...and totally addictive.

And then he had seen his grandmother at the window, look-ing in, watching Julia and him dancing.

"Michael, are you all right?" Julia drew back a little and gazed up at him. They were conspicuously still in the middle of a crowd of dancing couples.

"Do I look like I've seen a ghost?" He ran his hand through his hair and then shook his head. "I must've had more to drink than I thought."

"You've had several glasses of champagne and you drank them awfully fast," Julia murmured. "Are you feeling sick?"

"Not sick. Crazy is probably closer to the mark." He gulped. "I thought I saw my grandmother looking in the win-dow."

At least Julia didn't stare at him as if he'd lost his mind. "You're still grieving over the loss of your grandmother, and the band is playing music that reminds you of your grand-parents," she said quietly. "And you did have all that cham-pagne."

"I'm not drunk," he protested, then his shoulders slumped in defeat. "Maybe I am. I guess I have to be...." He stared at the window where he'd seen his grandmother, and of course, she was not there.

A tidal wave of grief crashed over him. His grandmother had been smiling, watching him and Julia, looking very

pleased. He thought about how it would've been if Grandmother Kate really were alive and attending this party. She'd
been so energetic and exuberant; she would've been dancing
to the Jerome Kern melodies and probably taken a turn at the
"Electric Slide" with the younger set as well. How he missed
her. Her vitality and her wisdom, too.

Julia slid her arms from his neck and folded them in front
of her as she stared assessingly at Michael. "I think you
should have something to eat. And some strong black coffee,
too."

"Not now." He shook his head. He was too shaken and
off-balance to think of such mundane things as food and coffee. "I can't be here any longer, Julia. I need some peace and
quiet. There are too many people, too much noise." He felt
suddenly overwhelmed by it all. "Let's get out of here."
Grabbing her hand, he headed out of the room.

She thought they were going outside on the veranda. The
chill in the late-autumn night air would certainly clear a fuzzy
head. Instead, Michael made another couple of turns, leading
her to the grand staircase.

He started up the stairs and then stumbled slightly. Julia
instinctively moved closer and slipped her arm around him to
support him.

He draped his own arm around her shoulders, leaning
heavily against her. "I wish it were true, Julia. I wish I really
had seen my grandmother at that window."

Julia saw the pain in his blue eyes and her heart ached for
him. She knew all too well how it felt to long for a lost loved
one. "Maybe you did," she said softly. "Maybe she really is
here in spirit and you picked up on it somehow. Clairvoyance
is—"

"If my grandmother decided to appear as a ghost, you can
bet she wouldn't limit herself to being an apparition at the
window. Knowing Grandmother, she'd do something spectacularly otherwordly—plates flying through the air or some-

thing. She had a great sense of humor.'' Michael smiled, the good memories filling him.

They reached the top of the stairway and walked along the long, lighted corridor. "Do you know where you're going?" Julia asked as they passed room after room.

"I used to think I did. I thought I knew exactly how—"

"I meant right now," she interrupted, hoping to divert him from a tipsy discourse on some esoteric philosophy of life. "Do you know which room you want?"

"The room I always use when I stay—and here it is.'' He led her into a rather small bedroom, decorated in pale shades of blue, gray and yellow.

Julia crossed the room to switch on the light on the bedside table. While she was doing that, Michael pulled the door closed behind him. And locked it. "You know, seeing Grandmother tonight—or thinking I saw her," he amended quickly, "made me remember something else. One of the most important things about her, something that she tried to instill in each and every one of us."

"And what was that?" Julia asked gently.

"The way she made things happen. When she wanted something, Grandmother went for it. She didn't let herself stew in a cauldron of doubts and negativity. If she were here tonight, she would take me aside and say, 'Mike, you know what you want, now get it!'"

"I don't think she would have any complaints about you, Michael," Julia assured him. "You've followed her example and are a first-rate executive. Ask anybody in the industry and they'll say you're—"

"I know this will come as a surprise to you, but I'm not talking about business." Michael sat down on the bed and kicked off his shoes. "I wasn't even thinking about it."

Julia nodded, but she was eyeing the phone on the nightstand. All that champagne had made Michael quite chatty, but he really ought to go to bed and sleep it off. "While you're lying down, I'll call a taxi to take me home. I'll slip out front and wait for it. There are so many people here tonight, I don't think anyone will even notice that we left the party."

"I consider an event where my presence is entirely superfluous to be a waste of my time." Michael shrugged out of his jacket and pulled off his tie.

"I know. And you'll take a business meeting over a party any day of the week."

His socks and belt were the next to go. He tossed them to the floor along with his previously discarded jacket and tie. "You know me so well."

Julia quickly reached for the phone. "Do I have to get an outside line, like in a hotel or—oh!"

Michael took the receiver out of her hand and replaced it firmly in its cradle. "Don't go, Julia," he said huskily.

Her eyes widened. He was unbuttoning his snowy white shirt. She ran her tongue over her lips. "Michael, I really don't think—"

"Good. Because I'm sick of thinking, I'm tired of thinking, I'm going crazy from too much thinking." He caught both her hands and pulled her to stand between his thighs. "Let's make a deal. No more thinking."

"A deal? Should we call Sterling to draw up the papers and make it legally official?" She tried to keep her tone bright and breezy, but her heart was racing. Michael slowly closed his legs, effectively trapping her between them.

"Forget Sterling. Forget everything and everybody but the two of us."

She felt the heat of his thighs pressing against her, and a tremor shot through her body. With one deft tug, he toppled her onto his knee, then quickly wrapped his arms around her. Julia struggled a little. Not enough to break free; certainly not enough to persuade him that she wanted to be free. She conceded to herself that she'd made such a paltry token effort because she didn't want Michael to let her go.

"Please, Julia." He settled her more fully against him and nuzzled her neck.

She knew what he wanted. Julia gazed at him, drawn by the power and the yearning in his deep blue eyes. The problem was, she wanted the same thing he did and she didn't know what to do about it. "You're not drunk," she murmured, stalling for time. "You're not going to pass out."

"Is that what you told yourself on the way up here? That you were aiding a helpless, drunken idiot?" His lips brushed against hers. "Noble, loyal little Julia."

He bent his head and kissed her with a thoroughness that took her breath away. Reflexively, Julia splayed her fingers against his chest. His bare chest. She felt the warmth of his skin and the wiry, soft mat of dark hair beneath her hands. Her fingertips found his flat male nipples and traced them. A wild, sensuous curiosity swept through her. She wanted to explore every one of his fascinating male features.

Michael groaned and kissed her again, a wondrous kiss of sweet, searing passion. His hands moved over her back in slow, arousing strokes. Julia had an audacious desire to feel him caress her bare skin. As if mentally in synch with her needs, he opened her dress, pushing it off her shoulders. He kissed the hollow of her neck, following the delicate line of her collarbone, then lowered his mouth to the curve of her breast.

She made a small sound in the back of her throat as he kissed her through the thin material of her ruby red bra. And then he dispensed with that particular garment, and the tip of his tongue touched her nipple, circling it until she was moaning with unbridled pleasure.

The next time she opened her eyes, they were lying on the bed, both practically undressed. She was wearing only red bikini panties and sheer, thigh-high stockings; he had on a pair of blue boxer shorts. Her head was spinning with a fierce, dizzying excitement. She'd been so caught up in the hot plea-

sure of their kissing and caressing that she could barely remember them shedding most of their clothes. It all seemed so
natural and so right. Being here with Michael, kissing him,
touching him, lying down with him...

"You are so beautiful," he said, staring at her torso, his
eyes burning with hot urgency. He cupped her breasts with
his hands, watching, tantalized, as the milky white softness
filled his palms. He flicked his thumbs over the rosy little
beads of her nipples.

Julia uttered a breathless moan and arched against him. She
moved her hands over his bare back and shoulders, learning
the texture of his muscles, the heat of his skin. Boldly, she
trailed her fingertips from his chest to his flat belly, following
the path of dark hair that arrowed lower.

Michael felt her gently brush him through the cotton, and
he drew in a sharp, shallow breath as his already tentative
control began to unravel. He didn't bother to try to summon
it back. His emotions took over and threw off the constraints
imposed by his mind. He felt as if liquid fire was racing
through his body. They were together at last. Finally, he was
seeing her, touching her, the way he'd been wanting to see
her and touch her for what seemed to be a lifetime....

His hand glided slowly, purposefully over her stomach. He
explored the indentation of her navel with his thumb, while
his fingertips rested just beneath the lace trim of her panties.
Julia held her breath. She desperately wanted him to move
his hand lower and touch her intimately. She wanted it with
an urgency that shocked her.

"You carried the monochrome concept right down to your
skin," he said huskily, toying with the edge of her panties.
"Everything matches the ring."

"I bought the lingerie myself." Julia blushed hotly, certain
that her whole body was ruby red. Truly, she'd carried mon-
ochromatic to new levels. "It's bad enough that you bought

me the suits and the dress, but I didn't think it was p-proper
for you to pay for—''

"I want to buy you things," he said, and realized that he
meant it. "I want you to have nice things. I want to give you
anything you want." Another surprising insight. Usually he
was wary of being "suckered" and limited his gifts to the
perfunctory candy and flowers.

"Oh, Michael." Her eyes filled with emotional tears. "All
I want is you."

Because she was in love with him, Julia admitted to herself.
She wished she could tell him so. She wanted to. But knowing
Michael as well as she did, she knew he wouldn't want the
words. They would be too much, too soon. He would feel
burdened by words of love, trapped by them. So she would
show him. Actions always spoke louder than words anyway,
or so the old adage claimed. She reached up to kiss him, and
all the love that she didn't dare to confess flowed from her,
heightening her passion.

His big, warm hand slid inside her panties. She shivered as
his fingers stroked the downy thatch of hair before moving
lower and deeper. Julia was embarrassed by the wetness he
found there. She twisted against his hand as he gently separated the swollen feminine folds to find her most secret and
sensitive places. The erotic way he rubbed her, the exquisite
pressure he applied soon had her moaning. The pleasure was
excruciating and intense.

"Michael, please!" she whimpered. She didn't know if she
was pleading with him to stop this exciting, devilish torment
or begging him not to.

He took her lips again, thrusting his tongue into her mouth
as his long, strong fingers entered the heart of her femininity.
The possessive dual invasion was shattering. Tension and heat
radiated from the primal core of her to every nerve in her
body. Julia had never felt like this before. A torrid storm of
tempestuous forces was gathering deep within her and she

writhed helplessly under the sensual onslaught. She ached, she shuddered as shards of throbbing, shimmering pleasure stabbed through her.

And then suddenly a hot burst of liquid lightning unleashed the storm within her. Julia felt herself implode with a pleasure so enthralling that she could do nothing but cling to Michael as waves of rapture pulsed through her.

Michael held her tightly, cradling her possessively in his arms. He kissed her temple, her cheek, her neck as she lay quivering in his embrace. The pleasure went on and on, like a spark to a fuse triggering a continuous chain reaction. Finally, she lay limp and weak against him. Her eyes drifted closed and then fluttered open to meet his piercing blue ones.

Julia's breath caught in her throat. He'd been watching her! She had always been so reserved and inhibited, she would never have dreamed she was capable of such a wild, unabandoned response—and Michael had observed the entire phenomenon.

"Oh, my." She turned her head, averting her eyes from his. "That's never happened to me before. I—I don't know what to say."

"You don't have to say anything, sweetheart. And you don't have to be shy with me." He hugged her tighter. He felt on top of the world, a powerful and possessive male whose woman had sweetly surrendered to him, a man who had brought his woman to a voluptuous satisfaction. He caught her chin and lifted her flushed face to his, looking into her wide, soft eyes.

"You were beautiful to watch, my baby. So passionate and sexy." He moved his hand slowly along the length of her body in an ardent caress.

She felt him carefully remove her panties, then her stockings, one by one. Though she didn't know how she could possibly be embarrassed after climaxing again and again as he watched her, Julia felt exposed and vulnerable as she lay nude under his gaze.

Michael's body was pounding with desire. "I can't wait any longer, sweetheart," he rasped. Still, he managed to wait long enough to sheath himself with the condom he removed from the drawer of the nightstand.

Julia watched him covertly, too intrigued by his bold male virility to look away, though shyness and doubt began to creep through her. Should she mention to Michael that he would be her first lover? She was certainly not his first. His every action revealed his experience, even the practicality of keeping a handy supply of condoms in the bedroom he visited!

Julia made her decision as she opened her arms to Michael, giving him loving access to her body. She loved him, and tonight she wasn't sensible and prosaic Julia Chandler, she was the heroine in a modern fairy tale who had finally been given the chance to express her love to the out-of-reach hero. Would Rapunzel have refused to lower her braid for the prince?

As for the physical details, she'd taken gymnastics and ridden horses as a young girl; she'd used tampons for years. Chances were great that there was no longer a physical barrier to proclaim her lack of experience.

"I don't want to wait any longer, either, Michael," Julia whispered. She smoothed her hands over the broad, warm expanse of his back. "Now, please."

She didn't have to ask twice. Michael slowly began to fill her, pushing into her, cupping her hips to lift her body to meet his strong, steady thrusts. Julia breathed deeply, forcing herself to relax. The intimacy was shattering, so physical, so elemental, so unlike anything else she had ever experienced. She couldn't imagine this mating, this giving of herself, with anyone else but Michael, the man she loved.

And though she didn't think it possible that he could arouse her desire to that earlier, feverish level, she was wrong. His slow, deep strokes rekindled the glowing embers of her passion; his urgent need sent her soaring higher and higher. Michael set the rhythm and the pace as waves of pleasure surged through her. An internal explosion rocked her, even deeper and stronger than before, and Julia clung to him and gasped his name.

Together they scaled the searing heights of passion and reached the rapturous summit, before finally floating into a quiet, private world where they rested in the blissful peace of completion.

Afterward, they lay in each other's arms. Michael's breathing was slow and heavy, and Julia knew he'd fallen asleep. She didn't mind. She didn't feel the need for conversation. A tiny smile curved her lips. She liked holding him while her mind drifted languorously, her body warm and slack and satiated.

Tonight was special and required no painstaking analysis, no thought-by-thought replays. Tonight she and Michael were lovers, and Julia knew that no matter what happened, she could never regret what she'd done. What she and Michael had shared.

Closing her eyes, Julia savored the feel of his body next to her and the knowledge of her deep, secret love for him.

Moments later she, too, was sound asleep.

Twelve

The phone rang as Julia was pouring steaming-hot tomato soup from the small saucepan into her bowl.

"That'll be for you, Julia," Kia predicted. "Michael Fortune has been calling every two hours since ten o'clock this morning. And no, I didn't tell him where you were." Kia spoke a few words into the receiver, then nodded her head and handed the phone to Julia.

Julia's pulses raced. She'd been wanting to talk to Michael, to see him all day. But she wasn't sure what kind of a reception she was going to get from him....

She'd awakened this morning around six, and for a few frantic seconds had been shocked to find herself naked in bed with Michael at the Fortune mansion. And then marvelous, sensuous memories of the night before had flooded her body and she'd wanted nothing more than to wake Michael and make love with him all over again.

But she couldn't. Today was Saturday. She had to go back to her apartment, shower and change and drive to the rehab hospital to spend the day with Joanna. There was a Halloween party planned, with activities, games and refreshments, and Joanna was looking forward to it. Julia couldn't disappoint her by not showing up.

Though her body protested, it was mind over matter as Julia slipped from the bed and quickly dressed. The big house seemed eerily quiet and still as she crept downstairs and called a taxi....

Now it was nearly 9:00 p.m. and she was back in her apartment after her day-long visit with Joanna. And Michael was on the phone. Julia murmured a shaky hello.

Even across the telephone line, the sound of her voice affected Michael viscerally. From the moment he'd awakened this morning, to find himself alone in bed, he could think of nothing else but Julia. The hours passed, and she continued to be inaccessible as he called her apartment, again and again.

All day long his emotions had been running the gamut— from concern to frustration to anger and back to worry. Now that he finally had her on the phone, he had to stop himself from shouting a hundred questions at her. After all, if she was playing a game, he could be a player, too, and a good one.

''I wondered if you'd like to go out for a drink?'' he asked with a casual air completely at odds with the tension that gripped his body. Of course, Julia couldn't see that; she couldn't know. He was grateful.

''Tonight?'' Her heart pounded in anticipation.

''In fifteen minutes.''

Julia glanced down at her worn jeans and baggy sweatshirt. She was wearing no makeup and her hair was pulled into a high ponytail, a good style to help out with Joanna's therapy exercises and activities, but hardly alluring to Michael Fortune. ''Could you make it twenty?''

He wanted to make it ten! ''I'll be over in half an hour,'' he said instead, with calculated nonchalance. He didn't want her to think he was pathetically, pantingly eager to see her. If she could disappear for a whole day without a word of explanation, then he would take his cue from her and play it equally cool.

Half an hour later, Michael was knocking at her apartment door. Julia had changed into a short skirt and a long sweater. Her curling iron had given a little style to her hair.

When she saw Michael, she wanted to hurl herself into his arms and cling to him. But he appeared too detached for such an emotional greeting, so Julia merely smiled and said hello in her efficient-assistant voice.

They exchanged civil banalities as he drove through the rain-slicked streets of Minneapolis. "Where are we going for a drink?" Julia asked, after they had thoroughly exhausted the subject of the weather.

"To my place." Michael's fingers tightened on the steering wheel. "Any objections?"

Julia swallowed. "I—I have to be back by ten o'clock tomorrow morning," she whispered. Sunday visiting hours at the hospital were from noon till six, and Joanna always wanted Julia there despite their long Saturday visits together.

Michael reached over and covered her knee with his hand. "You'll make it back in time, I promise."

Julia waited for him to ask why she had to be back at that particular time and where she'd been all day. She had already decided that if he asked her, she would tell him. Joanna was such a huge part of her life, and for Michael to have no knowledge of her younger sister severely limited their relationship.

But Michael asked no questions, so Julia volunteered no information. It struck her as unseemly to suddenly pour out the story of her sister's accident, unsolicited. From what Julia had gleaned, Michael's mother had always used her kids to serve her own ends. Julia refused to resort to such tactics. She would never use Joanna, not even to further her relationship with Michael. Especially not for that.

They arrived at the penthouse, and Michael actually went through the motions of pouring each of them a glass of wine. She took a sip, but he put his glass, untouched, on the coffee table and stared broodingly at her.

"The wine was just an excuse," he said huskily. "I've been wanting to be with you since I woke up this morning. Now that you're here..." His voice trailed off.

Julia set her glass down and stood up. "Now that I'm here…" she repeated, her eyes glowing. "What?"

They looked at each other for a long, silent moment. And then, simultaneously, they lunged at each other and kissed and kissed until they both were breathless. They stroked and caressed urgently, hungrily, fueling the fires of passion to a blazing high.

The first time, they didn't make it to the bedroom. Hastily discarding some essential garments, they sank onto the sofa. Not much foreplay was necessary. They'd been thinking about each other, wanting each other for hours, so their bodies were already primed and ready for the wild, hot consummation of their mutual desire.

Michael positioned himself between her thighs, and Julia opened herself to him, arching her hips and wrapping her legs around him. He groaned with pleasure as he thrust into her taut, moist heat. She moved with him and for him, matching his rhythm, as they whirled together into a consuming maelstrom of passion.

The shimmering, shuddering pleasure grew and built to a shattering intensity. And then the sweet hot flames engulfed them both. They burst into a tumultuous climax that left them blissfully drained and sated. Their bodies still joined, Michael collapsed against her, burying his face in her shoulder. Julia hugged him tightly. Anxiety and tension and frustration were a dim, unpleasant memory that neither felt the need to recall.

"Nothing else matters but right here and now," Michael murmured, nuzzling her. "The bogus engagement, the company, my family—none of that has anything to do with you and me when we're alone together."

Julia stroked the back of his neck and stirred lazily beneath him. "Yes," she agreed dreamily.

She was willing to consign reality to some nether zone in order to claim some precious time alone with Michael. A time out of time where everything that separated them could be ignored and where nothing else mattered but the two of them.

They spent the rest of the night in their own private universe, so absorbed in each other that their reentry into the real world the next morning was harder than either had anticipated.

They were both silent as Michael drove Julia to her apartment the next morning, to make it back by ten. He kept stealing glances at her, wondering how she planned to spend the day, wishing she would be spending it with him. But he asked no questions. He was already getting in too deep with Julia. To demand to know her whereabouts at any given moment would be akin to a drowning victim throwing away a life jacket. Julia expected him to ask questions. She wanted him to, so she could move ahead to the next level of her game plan. Oh, he knew all about female manipulations and wasn't about to be trapped by them!

Julia stared through the rain-streaked windshield, the glowing contentment she'd felt upon awakening slowly dissipating as the time for her separation from Michael grew near. If only he would ask her some questions, demand some answers. She wanted to tell him all about Joanna. After last night's closeness, keeping anything from him seemed unnatural.

But Michael didn't ask, because he didn't particularly care where she was or what she did when she wasn't with him, Julia reminded herself. They had sexualized their relationship, but their mock-engagement remained exactly that—a fake. She would be the biggest fool in the world to think that Michael had fallen in love with her simply because they'd gone to bed together. Mixed-up women who confused sex with love were practically a staple in behavioral-psychology studies, and Julia resolved not to be one of that hapless number.

She loved Michael, but she knew he didn't love her, and she didn't dare allow herself to imagine otherwise. Pretending that he was in love with her was far more dangerous than pretending to be engaged to him, for it involved deluding herself. Julia had never been into self-deception, and she wasn't about to indulge in it now. But whoever had coined the old adage "the truth hurts" knew exactly how she was feeling.

The moment Michael braked in front of her apartment building, she hopped out of the car and rushed away, blinking back a rush of scalding tears.

That evening, Jen and Debby took over the living room with some of their fellow drama students for a mime workshop. Julia and Kia retreated to their bedroom with books, Kia to study, Julia to read.

A knock sounded on the bedroom door shortly after nine. "I hope we're not expected to watch another one of those kids do an impression of drying her hair with a hair dryer on fire," Kia muttered, for the last knock had been a summons to do just that.

"At least that one was original," Julia replied. "If we have to sit through another tug-of-war with an invisible rope, I—"

"The girls told me you were up here." Michael's voice startled them both. He'd entered the room without waiting to be granted admittance.

"Do you exalted members of the elite class always barge into a place like you own it?" Kia demanded. "This is our bedroom, and we might not have been decent, you know."

"Sorry," Michael murmured, somewhat penitently. His eyes were fixed on Julia, who was stretched out on her bed in royal blue sweats, reading a book. He crossed the room and picked it up, reading the title aloud. "*I Hate You, Don't Leave Me: Understanding the Borderline Personality Disorder.* A real page-turner, huh?"

Julia smiled up at him. "Actually, it is."

She was thrilled to see Michael. And by the way he was looking at her, she knew he was glad to see her, even if he wasn't about to admit it outright. He didn't have to. He was here, wasn't he?

"Why don't you get some things together and spend the
night at my place? We can go to the office together tomorrow
morning." Michael had lowered his voice, glancing uneasily
at Kia. Julia's roommate always looked as if she'd like to
brain him, and knowing that she had full knowledge of their
bogus engagement was particularly unsettling.

"All right." Julia put aside her book and began to pack.
Kia didn't say a word, but she watched with her eyebrows
arched in disapproval.

Neither Julia nor Michael cared. They were entering their
own private world again, where there were no such things as
disapproval, interference, schemes or fakery. There was just
the two of them, wanting each other.

That weekend set the pattern for the upcoming ones. Julia
spent her Saturdays and Sundays visiting Joanna at the rehab
hospital, and Michael asked no questions regarding her whereabouts during that time. But every Saturday and Sunday night
he would arrive at her apartment and take her to his place.
Sticking to her vow, Julia offered no information about her
hours away from him. It remained an unspoken subject between them, with both too stubborn and too proud to break
the silence.

But that was the only tension between them. As the days
drifted into weeks and their false engagement continued, Julia
and Michael discovered other dimensions to their relationship.
In addition to their smooth working arrangement and fiery
passion, they were comfortable and compatible together, out
of the office and out of bed.

They spent almost every evening together, sometimes going
out to dinner or to the movies or to a play or concert. They
worked out together, using the exercise equipment Michael
bought to convert a spare bedroom into an at-home gym. They
tried to run along the river trail a few nights a week, though
the increasingly winterlike November weather often precluded

running. Occasionally, they socialized with other Fortunes or business associates.

Both Julia and Michael preferred their quiet evenings in Michael's apartment, where they read or talked or played. Neither were avid TV viewers, but there were certain shows they tried not to miss. They seemed to laugh a lot when they were together. The same things struck them as silly or funny, and they had a lot of inside jokes, known only to the two of them.

The nights they spent together had a honeymoonlike aura. No pair of newlyweds could have been as attentive and absorbed in each other, as passionate and hungry for each other, as Michael and his fausse fiancée.

Sometimes people asked about their wedding plans. Julia would invariably answer cheerfully, "We don't have any. Right now we're just enjoying being engaged." But she never felt very cheery afterward, because such questions drove home what she did her best to forget most of the time: that she was playing a part in a charade. The life she was leading with Michael was wonderful, loving and exciting, but it was based on a lie.

Michael never responded to wedding inquiries, but nobody seemed to mind. It was permissible, maybe even expected, for a man to be clueless about wedding plans. Michael didn't waste any time worrying about charades. He was too happy and too content with Julia. There was nothing in his considerable experience to compare with what he shared with her.

Rather than diminishing from constant exposure, his attraction to Julia had strengthened and deepened. Their lovemaking seemed to grow more profound and more satisfying each time, and he found he wanted her more than ever. The restless boredom that had doomed his other relationships never surfaced; he found Julia endlessly interesting, even fascinating. If he wasn't pleased by her long Saturday and Sunday afternoons away from him, he pushed those thoughts aside. She was with him on weekend nights, and every other night during the week.

But although he accepted her weekend afternoons away from him, he was not about to grant her any more unexplained absences. When he invited her to spend Thanksgiving with his family for the traditional Fortune holiday feast, and Julia refused, Michael was not inclined to be understanding.

"What do you mean, you can't have Thanksgiving dinner with us?" He frowned at her, both amazed and annoyed by her refusal. He wasn't used to Julia saying no to him.

"I've already promised to spend Thanksgiving with my sister," Julia said.

The hospital served Thanksgiving dinner with all the trimmings for patients like Joanna who could not go home on pass. Julia had no intention of letting her younger sister spend the holiday alone.

She watched as Michael strode to stand before the wide window in his office. He jammed his hands into his pockets and stared outside, his back to her. Her stomach was beginning to churn. She didn't want to argue with him. The past weeks they'd been together had been blissfully free of dissension. She found herself hoping he would invite her sister to spend Thanksgiving with the Fortunes. Joanna wouldn't be able to manage such an outing yet, but the subject of her sister would be out in the open and Julia could finally tell him all about her.

"Your sister!" Michael gave a disdainful sniff. "You never see her, you never even mention her, but now I'm supposed to believe that you *must* spend Thanksgiving with her?"

Julia stiffened. "Just because I've never mentioned my sister to you doesn't mean I'm not in contact with her."

She talked to Joanna on the phone every night, though Michael obviously was unaware of that. It wasn't that she kept her phone calls a secret; he just never asked who she was talking to.

Because he wasn't interested, of course. Sometimes—most of the time lately, it seemed—she managed to forget the true nature of their relationship. Now reality came roaring back at her. She worked for Michael Fortune and slept with him, but that was the total extent of their involvement. Julia issued herself a much-needed, if cruel reminder: they were not engaged, he was not in love with her and he never would be.

"Everybody in the family will expect you to spend Thanksgiving with me," Michael said curtly. "I don't feel like making up explanations for your absence. Just tell your sister you have other plans."

Any inclination Julia might've had to tell Michael about Joanna, or to invite him to join them for the holiday, was quashed by his surliness and her own crushing acknowledgment that nothing between them had changed since they'd begun this stupid mock-engagement. Yet everything had changed, for her, anyway.

"*You* can tell your family that *I* have other plans." Julia blinked back a sudden rush of tears. She would never let him see her cry! "It's probably about time we laid some groundwork for our breakup." Hurt made her lash out at him. "Your family ought to have some hint that there are problems between us, so that when we end this phony engagement it won't come as a total shock to them. We've managed to fool everybody so far, and it would be a shame to botch the last act."

"Yeah, a real shame." Michael gazed at the pedestrians on the sidewalk below without really seeing them.

Our breakup. The words echoed in his head. Until now, he hadn't given a thought to breaking their bogus engagement, and he realized with a shock how much he hated the idea. That worried him. Greatly. It occurred to him that Julia had backed him neatly into a metaphorical corner. He'd become accustomed to having her around; he was almost dangerously addicted to making love to her. Now she was threatening to withdraw from him. He had no doubts that once their mock-engagement was ended, their very real sexual relationship would be over, as well. And he didn't want that. Julia had to know it and was going to use his need for her to her own advantage.

He turned to stare at her, but he couldn't read her. Her expression was as inscrutable as—well, as one of his own. One thing was clear to him, however: he had been outmaneuvered by her. Well, he'd been warned—by his own mother, no less—that Julia possessed more cunning and guile than he did. He wondered if she'd planned her strategy far in advance, figuring she could get him hooked on her, then reel him in.

But all was not lost, he assured himself. He still had a few moves of his own. "You're right about hinting at some problems between us." He was proud of his tone, so cool and indifferent. He sounded as if he didn't care at all. Michael firmly tamped down the wave of pain cresting deep within him. "Spend Thanksgiving wherever you want, and I'll try to act peeved about your absence at the family dinner. Let the folks know that there is trouble in paradise." He smiled coldly.

Try to act peeved. His phrasing didn't go unnoticed by Julia. In truth, he didn't really care where she spent Thanksgiving. Why, he'd never even asked her sister's name or age! Julia was more certain than ever that keeping Joanna's circumstances from him had been the right thing to do.

When Michael announced that he was leaving the office that evening, Julia told him that she wouldn't be going to his place with him, that she wanted to go to her own apartment. It would be the first time in weeks they hadn't gone home together.

Michael's lips tightened into a thin, straight line. "Fine. You can sulk all the way to your apartment," he said tersely.

"If you want to come over later, give me a call and I'll pick you up."

Julia decided she would hand a pyromaniac a lighted match before she called Michael Fortune to come take her to his bed. She lifted her chin and held her head high, not bothering to dignify his remark with a response. Michael stared at her for a few tense moments, then stomped out of the office.

The bus ride to her apartment seemed much worse than she remembered. It was hot and crowded, and the continual stops and starts due to the heavy traffic soon had her gulping with nausea. She'd gotten spoiled, being chauffeured to and from work in Michael's car, Julia realized. But she felt queasy the rest of the evening, and when she woke up early the next morning, she barely made it into the bathroom before she was miserably, wretchedly sick.

Feeling too weak to move, Julia sat down on the floor and laid her head against the edge of the bathtub. Kia came in a few minutes later. "You don't look so good, honey. You're as green as the paint on the wall." She knelt down beside Julia and laid her hand against her clammy cheek.

"I feel terrible." Julia groaned. "Maybe I was poisoned by bus fumes yesterday."

Kia stared at her, long and hard. "I haven't seen much of you the past couple months, but your face looks different. There is a certain cast.... I've seen similar changes in other women's faces. The mask of pregnancy, according to folk wisdom, which always seems to contain a kernel of truth." Kia took a deep breath. "Julia, are you pregnant?"

Julia sat straight up, so quickly that the room seemed to spin and she felt like she was going to be sick all over again. She sank back against the wall. "Of course not, Kia. I... we...he...always used something."

"What did you use, honey? Foam, which isn't one-hundred-percent effective in preventing pregnancy? Condoms, which aren't one-hundred-percent effective, either? A contra-ceptive sponge, which isn't—''

''The first two.'' Julia felt too nauseated to be embarrassed.

''I'll tell you what I tell my clients who find themselves carrying an unexpected baby—that those methods have a cer-tain percentage of failure. I won't subject you to my condom-spillage statistics, which also apply. But exactly when was your last period, Julia? Have you been keeping track?''

Julia gulped, feeling like an impulsive teenager, the usual recipient of Kia's birth-control-failure information. ''I haven't had a period since the beginning of October. I didn't really question it. In fact, after I started to—to stay at Michael's place, I was glad because I thought it would be awkward... I never dreamed I might be... We always used something....''

''The only absolutely infallible method against pregnancy is abstinence or sterilization, Julia. Even the pill has a small failure rate.''

Julia closed her eyes as another wave of nausea rolled over her. ''Kia, I can't be pregnant. It must be the flu. Doesn't the flu have a sudden onset like this?''

Kia nodded her head. ''Time will tell, honey. Meanwhile, let me help you back into bed, and I'll get you a few saltine crackers to chew on. They're easy on the stomach.''

A little later, Julia phoned the office to call in sick. She felt exhausted, and though she was still a little queasy, those crackers Kia brought her definitely helped. Neither mentioned that if she'd had a bona fide case of the flu, she probably would've thrown up the crackers. But both of them thought it.

Michael drove to Julia's apartment after work. The day had been an utter waste of time. He'd been useless at the office because he couldn't stop thinking about Julia. Was she really sick? And if not, was this another tactic to manipulate him?

Had Julia been lying in bed, looking as wan as she had at dawn, he might've tempered his approach to her. But when he arrived, she was standing in front of her apartment building with Jen and Debby and some of their friends.

A thrill went through him at the sight of her. This was the longest time they'd spent apart since they had first made love, and he'd missed her terribly, all last night and through the endless hours at the office today. His eyes feasted hungrily on her. She was laughing and animated and looked incredibly beautiful. It took all Michael's willpower not to run to her, scoop her up in his arms and take her away with him.

But the nasty voice of mistrust beat out his initial impulse. *She sure as hell didn't look sick!* He slowed his car to a stop and stared at the group of young women for several long, furious seconds before stepping on the accelerator and zooming away.

"Hey, was that Michael?" Debby asked, squinting after the flash of red.

Julia's heart jumped into her throat. "I don't know, I didn't see." If it had been Michael, his speedy departure didn't bode well for her.

Neither did her bout of nausea the next morning. Julia managed to drag herself to work, but the bus ride made her so sick she threw up twice in the rest room before Michael arrived at the office.

He glanced at her as he passed her desk. She was wearing her beige suit, one of her old ones, one that he hated. He was convinced that she'd deliberately chosen it to punish him. But he paused on the threshold of his own office. "You don't look too well," he said bluntly. "You're pale and you have dark circles under your eyes."

He felt a pang of guilt. She really did look sick this morning. "Do you think you should be here? Do you want me to...take you home?"

Julie shook her head gingerly, because too much motion sent her precarious equilibrium spinning. "I'll be fine. I don't want to miss another day of work."

"You do have sick leave, you know." He willed her to look at him, but she kept her eyes glued to her computer screen. "Julia, if you're sick, you shouldn't be here. You could be infecting everybody else."

"Don't worry, I'm not infectious." She wished it was that simple. Kia was buying her a pregnancy-testing kit at the drugstore today. Julia simply couldn't bring herself to do it, though Kia insisted she had to find out for sure, to consider her options.

"Well, what's the matter with you?" Michael pressed. He acknowledged that he hadn't exactly sounded humane and tried to do better. "Food poisoning?" he asked on a more kindly note.

Julia gave a short laugh. She only wished! She made no further response and refrained from even glancing in Michael's direction.

Frustration roiled within him. His temper was frayed, his nerves on edge. Two nights without Julia in his bed and he was ready to turn into a snapping, snarling beast. Which she probably knew very well! Was this all a well-orchestrated plan to convert their false engagement into a real one? *Holding out for a wedding ring?* Michael stormed into his office.

Jake Fortune dropped in later that day. He asked Julia to come into Michael's office because he had "some sad news to tell them." She felt awkward being privy to confidential family information and tried to excuse herself, but both Jake and Michael insisted that she join them.

"Erica and I have separated," Jake blurted out. "We tried to stay together till at least after Thanksgiving, but—well, we just couldn't do it. Things haven't been good between the two of us for some time." He heaved a deep sigh. "Finally, the strain of trying to keep up a pretense got to be too much."

Julia knew all too well how difficult pretenses could be to maintain. "I'm so sorry," she murmured softly.

"You're separating?" Michael felt as if he'd been dealt a

body blow. Until he heard his uncle's announcement, he hadn't realized how much he had expected the couple to stay together, despite his cynical gibes to the contrary. He hadn't realized how very much he'd *counted* on them staying together.

Michael cleared his throat. "Uncle Jake, breaking up seems like an awfully drastic step to take. Isn't there some way you two could make it work? I mean, you and Erica have been married for thirty-some years! You have five kids, and grandchildren, too."

"Yes, well…" Jake shrugged. "We tried to work things out, but…" He extended his hands, palms upward, in a gesture of futility. "Don't let our troubles influence you two and your future plans. Just because Erica and I aren't—" he swallowed hard "—going to be together doesn't mean that marriage—"

"Jake, you don't have to give us the old hurrah-for-marriage pep talk," Michael interrupted. A bitter anger ripped through him. Really, what was the point? These days, nobody loved anybody forever. He felt oddly cheated and totally enraged. "I may as well be honest with you. Julia and I have been having second thoughts about this engagement of ours."

"Oh, surely not!" Jake sounded genuinely saddened. "You two seem so right for each other. Mike, I've never seen you happier or more at peace since you and Julia—"

"A pretense," Michael said. "You and Erica aren't the only ones who've been living behind one. And you're right, the strain does get to be too much."

Throughout the day, other members of the Fortune family visited Michael's office, presumably to commiserate over the Jake-Erica breakup. Julia remained at her desk and didn't join in those discussions, but she was certain that Michael mentioned "problems" between them and expressed doubts about continuing the engagement. The pitying glances given to her by departing family members said it all. They believed she was about to be dumped by Michael.

Julia was sure of it. He was on the verge of ending the mock-engagement, just as she was on the verge of finding out if she was suffering from a stomach virus or carrying his child.

Later that day, the home pregnancy test delivered the definitive answer. Julia and Kia stared at the telltale dot that had changed color.

"It's positive. That means...I'm pregnant." Even as she stared at the test results and spoke the words, Julia could hardly believe it. She was pregnant? *She was pregnant!* She burst into tears. "Oh, my God, Kia, what am I going to do?"

Thirteen

Kia suggested telling Michael the news immediately. "Putting it off isn't going to make telling him any easier," she warned.

Julia knew she was right. Every morning she arrived at the office determined to give Michael the small speech she'd rehearsed in her head, over and over, until it was as ingrained as a childhood prayer.

But he was so remote, so cold toward her. Under those conditions, how could she possibly tell him she was pregnant? She hadn't been able to tell him about Joanna when they'd been close—when they had been lovers! And since Julia was used to coping alone, the deeply established pattern was not easily discarded.

Thanksgiving Day came and went. Julia spent it with Joanna at the hospital, Michael with the Fortunes.

"Everybody wondered where you were this weekend," he remarked coolly the following Monday morning at the office. It was the first of December, the day marked by snow flurries. Julia's stomach was still lurching from the tortuous effects of the bus ride to work.

"Kyle and his family were here in Minneapolis, and Grant flew in, too," Michael continued. "They wanted to meet my fiancée and found it very strange that we were spending the entire holiday weekend apart. I called you, but there was no answer at your apartment," he added, his tone accusatory.

"I wasn't there."

Her answer, devoid of either apology or information, fueled

Michael's already simmering temper. "Obviously. Where the hell were you, Julia?"

Her head jerked up and she stared at him, her gray eyes wide. She'd become painfully accustomed to his curt coldness, so his sudden heated anger was jarring. "I was out."

"Out," he repeated, seething. "You were out? Is that all you're going to say?"

A grim little smile twisted her lips. "Believe me, you don't want to hear what I else I could say...." She stopped herself before she let anything slip. Telling Michael about her pregnancy when he was in this mood would be dumb, indeed. "I have a lot to do this morning, Michael. If you'll excuse me, I'd like to forgo the interrogation and start working."

"You're telling me, *your boss,* to get lost because you have work to do?" Michael was flabbergasted by her audacity.

His burning blue gaze traveled over her, taking in her drab gray dress and her hair, tightly braided in that style she knew he hated. It was all part of her plot, he decided feverishly. To let him stew for a long weekend not knowing where she was, to refuse to wear the clothes he'd bought for her, to treat him more coolly than she treated Denny, the lascivious mailroom clerk. Oh, she thought she really had him now! Michael realized. She was undoubtedly waiting for him to crack, to tell her he couldn't stand this distance between them any longer and that he wanted their relationship to go back to the way it had been before... Before what? Why were they at war with each other? How had they come to this?

"Why have we suddenly become enemies?" he blurted out. His mind was reeling and he could feel his iron control beginning to slip. Probably she'd planned for that, too! But he couldn't stop himself from asking, "This...fight we've been having, the way it's escalated. What was it originally about, anyway?"

He couldn't remember? Julia's hands clenched into fists. She would never forget how quickly and callously he'd turned on her, changing everything. Leaving her to face the terrifying possibility of pregnancy alone. "The week before Thanksgiving I told you I had plans to spend the holiday with my sister." Her voice was icy. "You've been hateful to me ever since."

"I have not! You've been colder than a—a witch's teat!" Michael surprised himself by resurrecting an old saying of his grandfather's. He hadn't even realized it was stored in his head.

"Well, if I've been cold it's because—" She clamped her teeth together abruptly. She knew she was precariously near to blurting out the results of that pregnancy test.

"Because what?" Michael goaded. "Because your little plan didn't go according to projection? Because I countered your moves with my own and you—"

"I don't know what you're talking about," Julia interjected crossly. "Now, if you don't mind, I'd really like to get started on my work."

"I do mind, and since you're my employee, I'll decide the agenda. Why don't you just admit it, Julia? I know, you see. I figured it out."

Julia felt the color drain from her face. "You know?" she gasped. "But...how?"

"I'm an experienced man, Julia. Give me a little credit."

Her throat felt so dry, it hurt to swallow. "Are you angry?" she whispered.

"Yes, I'm angry. Of course, I'm angry! I don't like being manipulated. All my life I've watched my mother scheme and maneuver to get what she wanted, and I promised myself that I would never be stupid enough to—"

"I didn't plan it, you know!" Pain and fear and anger surged through Julia, so intermingled she couldn't possibly separate one from the other.

Both of them began to speak at the same time, their voices rising with emotion.

"Of course you did. From the moment you decided to turn our fake engagement into a real one, you've carefully plotted every move to make it happen," said Michael.

"A woman doesn't get pregnant by herself! It happened even though we both thought we'd taken precautions. I accept my share of the responsibility, but I won't take all the blame," cried Julia.

Julia and Michael stared at each other as a heavy silence descended in the wake of their mutual outbursts.

Michael grasped the edge of her desk for some much-needed support. "You're—you're pregnant?" Her revelation almost knocked him off his feet, literally. He gaped at her, truly staggered.

"You—you said you knew."

"I was talking about what I thought was your plan to trap me. Your clever little tactics to make me want you so much that I would decide to make our engagement a real one."

"Clever tactics? You can't really believe that I've been following some kind of master chart with a game plan all mapped out to—"

"Oh, you're way beyond that, honey. To stack the odds in your favor, you decided to take out an insurance policy in case your manipulative little ploys didn't work. You resorted to the oldest female trick in the book to nab me. You made sure you got yourself knocked up!"

Julia could hardly breathe. "You're accusing me of deliberately getting pregnant to *nab* you?" A hazy red mist seemed to float before her eyes. For the first time ever, she understood the phenomenon of "seeing red." "How do you think I accomplished that, Michael? Did I prick your condoms with pins to lessen their effectiveness? Maybe I used foam with a ten-year-old expiration date to be sure of maximum failure? You were there every time we made love, so how did I manage to get myself *knocked up,* with you as the innocent victim?"

"You just offered some valid suggestions." Michael pinned her with a stare as frigid as dry ice. "And maybe I wasn't there the time you got knocked up, Julia. You go running off every weekend—and who do you run to? A secret lover? Maybe *he* is father of the brat you're trying to fob off as mine."

As soon as he spoke the words, he knew he'd gone too far. For a few awful seconds, the ugly accusation seemed to hang in the air between them before crashing down with full hurtful force.

Julia gave a sick, silent scream. Pulling the ruby ring off her finger, she laid it down on her desktop, restraining the primal urge to fling it at his head. The ring had belonged to Kate Fortune, and she deserved better than to have her heirloom bashed around. Part of Julia's thinking was clear and rational, the other part decimated by the force of her pain and rage.

"If you think I'm capable of doing such a thing, if you think I'm that dishonest and despicable, then you've never really known me at all. And I don't know you, either. I don't *want* to know you." Snatching her purse, she ran from the office.

Michael waited, floundering in a morass of anger and confusion. A deep dawning dread possessed him, and suddenly he grabbed his grandmother's ring and tore out into the corridor.

But his temporary delay had enabled Julia to board the elevator before he could reach it. "Julia, wait!" he shouted, but the doors snapped shut and the car began its descent, leaving him behind. He stood there, aware of the curious stares of the people passing by.

Slowly, Michael turned and walked back to his office. Julia was entitled to be angry with him, he allowed. And he was willing to grant her a little time to cool down. He would call her tonight.... On second thought, maybe he would go over to her apartment, just in case she wouldn't accept his call.

He would admit to her that he had overreacted upon hearing her shocking news. His accusations echoed spitefully in his head. Julia running off every weekend to meet a secret lover? Why had he said that? Thinking rationally, he was certain she would never practice such deception. But in that one searing flash of jealous fury, he hadn't been rational at all and he had lashed out at her....

Michael almost groaned aloud when Sterling Foster walked into his office a short while later. "Julia wasn't at her desk, so I let myself in," the attorney said, staring pointedly at Michael. "Word has it that you two quarreled and she left the office, while you created a big scene at the elevators."

"A big scene?" Michael snorted. "Well, that's gossip for you. I called her name. Once. Hardly what I would call a big scene."

"What was the fight about?"

Michael frowned. "Sterling, it's personal, okay? A private matter between Julia and myself."

"Word has it that she wasn't wearing the engagement ring."

"Damn! Don't people have enough to do around here without spending untold hours spying and speculating about things that don't concern them?" Michael jumped to his feet and began to pace.

"So it's true." Sterling looked glum. "It's over between you two."

"No, it's not over, Sterling. It's not over!" Michael's voice raised to a shout before he lowered it. Looking somewhat sheepish, he forced himself to sit down and assume at least an outward appearance of calm. "Is that why you're here, Sterling? To check out the latest Fortune gossip?"

"Hardly." Sterling leaned forward, his eyes intense. "I have some news, which is puzzling at best and disturbing at worst. You're aware that since the announcement of Jake and Erica's split, the company stock has fallen to an all-time low. There has been too much bad publicity for Fortune over the past months, too much instability. Investors don't like it.''

Michael's thoughts were riveted on Julia. In his mind's eye, he saw the expression on her face when he'd accused her of running off to a secret lover—and trying to pass off another man's child as his. He winced. That had been a low blow, unjustified and unfair. Maybe he'd better bring a dozen red roses with him when he went to Julia's apartment tonight.

"What do you make of it, Mike?" Sterling asked.

Michael looked blank, then flushed crimson. "Uh, would you mind repeating that last part, Sterling?"

"You didn't hear a word I said, did you?" Sterling studied him. "All shook up over your fight with Julia? Good! You ought to be. If you lose her—"

"I'm not going to lose her, Sterling." Despite Michael's firm avowal, anxiety flooded him. *Julia was pregnant!* And he had been somewhat cavalier upon hearing the news. He buried his head in his hands. Somewhat cavalier? He'd been downright rotten about it!

"I certainly hope you won't lose her, Mike. Anyway, as I said before, the company has become aware that Monica Malone is buying up shares of the stock. Snapping them up, actually. Jake and Nate and I can't figure out why. Do you have any ideas?"

"Monica Malone?" Michael repeated. She was the aging—and ageless—movie star who'd been the first Hollywood celebrity to endorse Fortune Cosmetics all those years ago. Everybody acknowledged that her endorsement had helped the company acquire its initial success. "She's always owned a few shares."

"A few token shares. But suddenly she doesn't seem satisfied with that." Sterling heaved a sigh. "It's troublesome."

Michael's head was already too filled with trouble to take

on any more. For the first time in his life he couldn't concentrate on business; his personal needs came first and foremost. And what he needed most was Julia's forgiveness—and her love. He would make their mock-engagement a real one and then arrange a quick, quiet wedding. There was no time to lose. Julia was going to have his baby!

Michael stood up. "Sterling, I hate to cut this short, but I'm on my way out of here. Thanks for the update on Monica Malone. I'll follow the developments closely."

"Meanwhile, you're going after Julia." Sterling smiled in satisfaction. "Grovel if you have to, Mike. Just don't let her get away."

Michael smiled wolfishly. "I have no intention of letting her go anywhere without me."

He stopped at a florist and bought a dozen long-stemmed, red roses before proceeding to Julia's apartment. At first he failed to notice that her little, mud brown compact car was not parked in front of the building. It wasn't until he'd pounded on her door for a while that he admitted to himself she wasn't there. She'd driven off, but where, he didn't have a clue....

Julia was driving to the hospital, although Joanna wasn't expecting her. But Julia needed to be with her sister; she hadn't felt so alone and bereft since the death of their mother three long, lonely years ago.

Abruptly, Julia's hurt was replaced by rage. Michael thought she had a secret lover. He'd actually accused her of plotting to saddle him with another man's child! He'd made it clear that he considered her little more than a tramp. Michael despised her! Julia swallowed a sob as pain lacerated her. She'd been experiencing these careening cycles of emotional turbulence since she'd run out of the Fortune Building.

Snow flurries pelted her windshield and the wind picked up, but Julia drove on. What was she going to do with a baby that Michael didn't even believe was his? She could only imagine the scope of the DNA testing he would require to prove paternity. And even with the baby's paternity no longer in question, the poor child would remain unwanted and unloved by its grudging father. Hot tears filled her eyes.

Kia had listed plenty of options she could consider—one of the advantages of having a social worker as a roommate. But for Julia, there was just one option: to have and keep her child. Her feelings grew stronger with every moment, surpassing even the strength of her anger and hurt. This baby was more than Michael Fortune's unwanted mistake; it was hers, too. A part of her. The baby was a Chandler, a direct link to her beloved parents.

A sudden glowing peace enveloped her. The Chandler family was being perpetuated. Her mother and father and the wonderful power of their love would continue to live on through their first grandchild. Joanna would be an aunt; she would have a role in a family beyond injured little sister. Julia smiled through her tears. Joanna was crazy about babies. She would be thrilled with her new niece or nephew.

And Julia vowed that she herself would be twice as thrilled with her son or daughter, to make up for Michael's lack of enthusiasm. She would be a good mother because she'd been raised herself by the best mother in the world. Helping her child to be a loving, happy, productive person would be her tribute to her own mom and dad.

A momentary twinge of fear gripped her. How was she going to support a child? Julia quickly, firmly pushed the worry aside. She would manage to do it and do it well, just as she had in providing for Joanna.

She drove through the gates of the rehabilitation hospital, a newfound sense of strength and determination filling her.

Michael was sitting in the front seat of his car when Kia finally arrived at the apartment building later that afternoon.

He raced out to greet her. "Julia's not here. Do you have any idea where she might be?"

Kia eyed him coolly. "What's going on, Mr. Moneybags? As if I can't guess."

He swallowed. "You know," he said quietly. "About the—the baby."

"And you just found out and were a total bastard about it, weren't you?" Kia nailed him with a glare. "Poor Julia. She didn't need that. And she surely doesn't deserve the likes of you!"

Michael said nothing. He deserved Kia's tongue-lashing, and worse. And the worst was yet to come when Kia proceeded to reveal the mystery surrounding Julia's weekend destination. Kia angrily told him all about Joanna and her critical injures, about the girl's long, slow rehabilitation, the exorbitant costs all borne by Julia.

"Joanna is the only reason why Julia agreed to your stupid bogus engagement scheme. That bonus you paid her helped considerably, although your insinuations that she was greedy, grasping and a body for hire ruined most of the relief she might've felt."

"Why didn't she tell me?" Michael was aghast.

"Why didn't you ask?" Kia countered. "Why didn't you make it easy for her to confide in you?"

Why hadn't he? Because he'd thought she was playing a game and he'd wanted to outmaneuver her. And he had accused Julia of being manipulative! *He* was the one who'd dreamed up strategies and tactics and countermoves like a possessed conspiracy buff.

"Kia, I've made a total mess of everything," he rasped unsteadily.

"You certainly have. You're a spoiled, self-centered, too-rich idiot." Kia wasn't about to cut him any slack. But she allowed him to come inside the apartment, where they found the note Julia had left. "She's at the rehab hospital, visiting

Joanna," Kia announced. "Are you going to go out there and find Julia or go back to your cushy apartment and sulk about how unfairly the world is treating you?"

"No more sulking, no more games," Michael vowed. "I'm going to find Julia."

"It's not going to be easy, you know," Kia called after him as he headed toward his car. "You won't be able to wave your checkbook and buy your way out of trouble." She sounded pleased at the thought.

Over an hour later—the roads were slippery from the snow and traffic was accordingly slow—Michael arrived at the rehabilitation hospital. A clerk at the information desk directed him to Joanna Chandler's room.

His heart seemed to have lodged permanently in his throat and his pulses were hammering in his ears as he approached the room. Which was empty!

"Joanna is in the auditorium, practicing for the holiday choral program," a nurse told him, directing him to yet another wing.

Julia sat in the darkness of the auditorium, watching Joanna and some other young patients on the stage. Today was the first day of practice for the annual holiday program, and Joanna had volunteered to play the bells. Julia watched her sister lift each different colored bell on cue and give it a shake. The girl's movements were slow and painstaking, but she managed to choose the right one each time and ring it at the appropriate moment.

Julia's eyes filled with tears as she watched the rehearsal. The bell ringing constituted a tremendous advance for Joanna; this time last year she would've been unable to perform such a task. But unbidden came the image of her little sister before the accident, when Joanna, seated at the piano, had effortlessly played a large repertoire of Christmas carols.

Michael stood in the back, but he made no move to approach Julia. He knew the timing was wrong, so he kept hidden, observing.

By the time Julia said good-night to Joanna, the snow had begun to fall more heavily. The lights in the parking lot illuminated the thick flakes as she trudged wearily toward her car. The hours with Joanna had provided a respite from her Fortune problems, but now they hit her with full force. What was she going to do? She didn't even know if she had a job to go to tomorrow. Her earlier optimism seemed juvenile and misplaced. How could she support Joanna and a baby when—

"Julia!"

The sound of her name stopped her in her tracks. She recognized Michael's voice, and for a moment she wondered if, on top of everything else, she was now prone to auditory hallucinations.

"Julia, wait."

She turned slowly to see Michael hurrying toward her amidst a swirl of snowflakes. A complex mixture of love and rage hit her with disorienting force. She wanted to run as much as she wanted to smack him; she wanted to throw herself into his arms and plead with him to love her as much as she loved him. Being Julia, she did not act on impulse. She stood still and waited for him to catch up to her.

"Sweetheart, I—" Michael began.

"Sweetheart? You must have me confused with someone else. I'm colder than a witch's teat, remember? I'm an immoral schemer who tried to pawn off my secret lover's brat on poor innocent you."

Michael had the grace to look deeply ashamed. "Julia, I want to tell you how sorry I am."

"Save it, Michael. I don't want to hear it." She turned and started toward her car.

He walked alongside her. "I don't expect you to forgive me easily, Julia. The things I said to you were reprehensible.

You're a saint and I deserve to be shot for casting aspersions on your character.''

"You're really going the distance with this, aren't you? Michael Fortune on a guilt trip is a rare sight to behold.'' Julia rolled her eyes. "I know what you're doing, you know. I've watched you at work. Right now you're applying all the hyberbole and salesmanship you normally use to woo a potential client to the fold.''

"It's not hyperbole. I love you, Julia. I know it took me too long to realize it and admit it, but it's true. I love you and I want to marry you, darling. I have my grandmother's ring right here and I want to put it back on your finger. As of this moment, our engagement is real.'' He lowered his voice. "As real as our baby.''

He was saying all the right words, but they had no discernible effect on Julia. She heaved a sigh. "I don't want the ring, Michael. I don't want to be engaged to you anymore, not for pretend or for real.''

"Then we won't be engaged, we'll get married. Tonight. We'll fly to Vegas and—''

"Get married in one of those tacky, all-night chapels by an Elvis-impersonator preacher? No thank you.''

"All right, then we'll take out a marriage license here in Minneapolis, and after the waiting period, we'll have the most tasteful wedding ceremony that Barbara and Erica can plan.''

"Never. I know the way you feel about marriage. To you, it's an institution with all the freedom and appeal of prison.''

"You're wrong, Julia. That is, I was wrong—about marriage and about a lot of other things. Please let—''

"You don't expect any marriage to last. You would rather die than get married. Does any of that sound familiar?'' Julia interjected. They had reached her car, and she fumbled in her purse for her keys. "A marriage between us wouldn't stand a chance, so why bother? I'm sick of charades and I refuse to participate in another one, especially a bogus happy marriage.''

"There would be nothing bogus about our marriage, Julia. We're going to be very happy and our marriage is going to last forever. Don't think about the past week or so—that's an unfortunate aberration and won't ever recur. Just think back to the way it's been between us during most of our engagement and how much—''

"*Fake* engagement," Julia amended. "And I'm remembering some things that you seem to have conveniently forgotten. The fact that you distrust me completely, for example."

"No, I don't! I admit that I...said some things—''

"Even if I forgive you for the things you said, which I probably will at some point, you'll distrust my motives for forgiving you. Who wants to live in that kind of poisonous atmosphere? Not me, not even for all the Fortune money you'll accuse me of marrying you for. And then there's the baby. I know you view it as yet another child brought into the world for all the wrong reasons, and I'm well aware of your views on shotgun weddings. You would absolutely hate being a forced participant in one, and if I marry you, you'll hate me for making you—oh damn!''

She was so upset that she dropped her keys in the snow. Michael stooped to pick them up and then slipped them into his pocket. "We're driving home in my car. I'll send someone out here tomorrow to bring your car back into town."

"I'll drive myself home tonight. Give me my keys, Michael!"

"Not a chance, honey. Now will you walk to my car or shall I carry you?"

She was not going to give in so easily. Julia lunged at him, trying to slip her hand into the pocket of his overcoat and retrieve her keys. Michael reacted instantly, wrapping his arms around her and holding her tightly against him.

"Let me go!" Julia demanded, struggling in his grasp.

"No, never. I can't." He buried his face in the crook of her neck and inhaled the sweet, familiar scent of her. "I love you, Julia. I know I can be a jerk. I know I get carried away by my distrust and my cynicism. That's why I need you so much. With you, everything is different. Everything is better. I'd never been in love until I fell in love with you. I'll never stop loving you, Julia."

"You couldn't have loved me when you accused me of—"

"Loving is new to me, Julia, and I couldn't trust what I didn't fully understand."

"But now you've seen the light and you believe we can live happily ever after?" She gave a cold, derisive laugh that cut him deeply.

"Don't let my cynical attitude infect you, Julia. I know I hurt you badly, but don't let me warp your ideals. I want you to give me the lecture about long happy marriages, like your parents had and like my dad and Barbara have."

Julia blinked back a flood of hot, emotional tears. "Stop trying to manipulate me, Michael. It's not fair, dragging my parents into this after I've just been with Joanna."

"I know, baby. But I'll use every bit of ammunition I can come up with to win you over. Julia, you're willing to..." He paused, remembering a certain book title. "To understand the borderline personality. Just give me the same chance. I'm not borderline, but I need you desperately. Don't give up on me and shut me out."

She drew back a little and tilted her head to look him in the eye. "You really are pulling out all the stops, Michael."

"Honey, I haven't even begun yet."

They gazed at each other for a long time, the snow swirling around them. "Let me drive you home, Julia."

His face was set in the stubborn, unyielding expression that meant he wasn't about to give an inch, not even if they had to stand outside in a blizzard for hours. Julia was getting cold and wet, and fatigue seeped through her. She knew she didn't possess the will or the endurance to stand out here for another minute.

"As usual, I'm giving in to you," she complained, but she allowed him to guide her toward his car. "God forbid that Michael Fortune wouldn't get his own way."

"God forbid," Michael agreed. He took heart in her crankiness. At least that hurt, haunted look was slowly draining from her face.

They drove in silence. Julia leaned her head against the headrest and closed her eyes. "I feel as if this day has been a hundred hours long," she murmured at last.

"You can go to bed as soon as we get home," Michael said solicitously.

"I'm going to my own bed in my own apartment," she announced.

"No, darling. You're not."

"Michael, I demand—"

"You said you would probably forgive me at some point," he interrupted, distracting her. "And that I would distrust your motives. What would be your motives in forgiving me, Julia?"

She folded her arms and frowned. "Never mind."

"You'll forgive me because you love me?"

"Even if I did, you wouldn't believe it." She glared across the car at him. "You don't believe in love any more than you believe in marriage, as I recall. Love is simply a word you throw around for effect, and you've done a lot of that tonight. Now take me home, Michael. I don't want anything from you. Well, except maybe a good reference when I'm job hunting."

Michael actually laughed. "Sorry, sweetie. You won't be working for anybody but me. You won't be dating anybody but me, you won't be engaged or married to anybody but me. And we are getting married as soon as possible and we're going to have the most well-loved, well-adjusted kids who ever graced the planet.''

"Stop it, Michael." Julia began to cry. "I can't fight you when you're being nice to me."

"I want to spend the rest of my life being nice to you, Julia." He reached over and took her hand. "I'm so sorry I hurt you, my love."

"You accused me of having a secret lover. And I've never had any other lover but you!" She pulled a rather ragged tissue from her purse and blew her nose daintily. "You didn't know that, did you, Michael? I was a virgin the first time we made love. But I'm sure you don't believe me. Looks like I'm up to my old, manipulative tricks again, doesn't it?"

"I believe you," he said quietly. "But I wish you would've told me sooner."

She smiled slightly. "I was afraid you'd be paralyzed with horror. I knew that getting involved with the oldest virgin in Minneapolis didn't top your list of things to do."

"Getting involved with you was the best thing I've ever done, Julia. And I intend to stay deeply involved with you for the rest of our lives."

By the time they reached Michael's apartment building, the snow was falling fast and furiously. "Snowed in or not, we're taking the day off tomorrow," Michael remarked as he and Julia stepped off the elevator. "And we're spending it in bed. Together."

He waited expectantly for Julia to protest. She didn't say a word.

"Am I being subjected to the silent treatment now?" he asked; leading her inside the penthouse.

"I've been thinking." Julia gazed longingly at him. "About everything you said."

"I meant every word of it, Julia. Are you going to let yourself believe me?" He pulled her into his arms. "I'm never going to stop proving how much I love you." His mouth caressed hers, then he kissed her with a deep, lingering tenderness.

"I love you, Michael," she breathed when he lifted his mouth to kiss the soft, scented hollow of her throat. "I've loved you for a long time, but I never thought you would love me, too."

"Darling, how could I not? You're everything I've ever wanted, everything I've ever needed. I adore you…though it did take me a lamentably long time to finally come to grips with it."

"Lamentably long," she agreed, cuddling closer.

He swept her up in his arms and strode quickly to the bedroom, where he laid her gently down on his big bed. "First, I have a call to make," he said suddenly, reaching for the phone.

Julia propped herself up on one elbow, watching him.

"Sterling, this is Mike Fortune. I want you to tear up that phony-engagement contract immediately. From this moment on, it's officially null and void. And I'd like you to know that Julia and I will be applying for a marriage license this week." He leaned over and kissed the top of Julia's head. "No, there will *not* be a prenuptial agreement, Sterling. There is no need because this is one marriage that is going to last."

He hung up and gathered Julia into a warm embrace.

"No prenuptial agreement?" She pulled back to stare at him nervously. "Michael, you'll regret it, I know you will. I—I can't marry you without one. Call Sterling back and tell him that I insist we have one."

"Afraid I might lay claim to that swamp brown wreck you call a car?" Michael pushed her down onto the mattress. "Sorry, baby. No prenup. You'll just have to have the same faith in our marriage as I do."

She linked her arms around his neck. "Michael, I don't want anything to come between us. I don't want there to be any suspicions about motives and money and—and when your mother demands to know about our iron-clad prenuptial agreement, I don't want to be around if there isn't one.''

''Knowing Mother, she'll stand in awe of your masterful cunning and guile. Be prepared to receive more Sheila Fortune–style compliments, *Julie*.''

''Only you would find that funny.'' Julia's hands glided over the smooth skin of his back. A river of warmth flowed through her. She was so in love with him, and the power of her love allowed her to forgive him, sooner rather than later. Michael had taken the first steps in abandoning his cynical attitude of distrust, and she had no doubt that he would continue to make the necessary adjustments. He loved her and he always would.

''Sterling extended his congratulations to both of us.'' Michael smiled into her eyes. ''He said he was glad I hadn't turned out to be such an officious pinhead, after all.''

Laughing together, loving each other, Julia and Michael began a passionate celebration on the first night of their very real engagement.

Epilogue

"She actually did it. She married him without a prenuptial agreement." Sterling Foster filled Kate's wineglass and then his own, and they raised their crystal goblets in a silent toast to the newlyweds. "Quite a twist there. Julia insisted on the prenup right up to the last minute, while Michael remained adamantly opposed to having one. Who'd have thought it? After that atrocious bogus-engagement contract he—"

"Michael is in love and that changes everything," Kate interrupted. "And let's forget all about that atrocious contract. Michael and Julia have." She sighed mistily. "I'm so happy for them, Sterling. I wish I could have been at their wedding."

"It was strictly a private affair, just the two of them, two witnesses and a preacher. They wanted it that way."

"I really can't blame them. We can only guess what mischief Sheila might have caused if Barbara and Nate tried to throw a big wedding for them. Still, the magic inspired by a lovely romantic wedding might've helped Jake and Erica rethink this awful separation of theirs."

"Wedding magic? Not for Jake and Erica, not at this point in time." Sterling grimaced. "Maybe black magic would work. Jake and Erica are both acting so unlike themselves, it's as if they've been possessed."

"Talking about demonic possession and black magic brings Monica Malone to mind. I'm quite concerned that she is buying up all those shares in the company, Sterling."

"There are too many things that aren't adding up, Kate. Which is why you have to stay deceased for a while longer."

"I shall hate to miss Christmas with the family," Kate said regretfully.

"We'll have to arrange a secret visit for you." Sterling smiled. "If Santa Claus can sneak in and out of houses, Kate Fortune certainly can. I don't know if everybody will be home for the holiday, though. Rocky seemed fairly certain that she would be staying in Wyoming. She is very busy with her search-and-rescue enterprise. Leaving her the planes and helicopter was right on the mark, Kate."

"Rocky has inherited my spirit of adventure." Kate looked quite pleased. "And I do know my family, Sterling. Each gift I willed was right on the mark. That ruby ring for Michael was a brilliant stroke, was it not?"

"A brilliant stroke," Sterling agreed. "And since you're fishing for compliments—not very subtly, I might add—may I congratulate you on your foresight and brilliance, for possibly the hundredth time?"

"You certainly may," agreed Kate.

They shared a hearty conspiratorial laugh as they replenished their wineglasses and proceeded to offer toasts to all the Fortune children.

*   *   *   *   *

FORTUNE'S CHILDREN

continues with

THE WOLF AND THE DOVE

by Linda Turner

available this month

Here's an exciting preview....

The Wolf and the Dove

A muscle clenching in his square jaw, Dr. Luke Greywolf watched his young patient limp away.

"You're doing all you can," his nurse said behind him. "You're already helping people more than you can afford to. Half the patients you see never carry through on their promise to pay and you just let it go. That's no way to run a business."

"It's not enough, Mary," he told her flatly. There was no way he was going to hound people who could barely put groceries on the table for the money for shots for their kids. "Who's next?"

"Jane Birdsong," she said, ticking them off on her fingers. "Then old man Thompson, Abigail Wilson and Rachel Fortune."

Reaching for the Birdsong chart, Luke threw her a sharp glance of surprise. "Fortune? As in one of old lady Kate's brood?"

"The one and only. If I remember correctly, this one belongs to Jake…one of the twins, I think."

"And she's here to see *me?*"

Chuckling at his suspicious tone, she nodded. "So she says. Word must have gotten out about what a good doctor you are. Want me to show her in?"

Curious, Luke nodded. "Room three," he began, only to stop short, scowling. What the hell was he doing? He had sick patients in the waiting room, poor people who would wait without complaint for as long as it took to see him. Rachel

Fortune couldn't just waltz in like she owned the place and cut to the head of the line because he couldn't imagine what she wanted with him and her family had more money than God.

"Forget that," he growled. "She can wait her turn just like everyone else."

"You're the boss," Mary said with a shrug.

Luke pushed the door to the room in and found Rachel studying the diploma framed on the far wall. Determined to keep this short and sweet, he said, "Ms. Fortune? I understand you wanted to talk to me—"

That was as far as he got. She turned then, a smile of welcome flirting with the edges of her mouth, and he felt the impact clear across the room. Stopping dead in his tracks, he would have sworn she knocked him out of his shoes. *This* was Rachel Fortune?

He'd expected her to be attractive. With good bone structure and skin, any woman could be reasonably pretty.

Pretty, however, didn't even begin to describe the woman before him. With her sculptured cheeks, slanting brows and large dark brown eyes, she could have stopped traffic in any city in the world, but here in Clear Springs she was as breathtaking and unexpected as a rose in the snow. And he couldn't stop staring. Tall and slim, she was dressed for business, but the effect was ruined by the way the fit of her black skirt emphasized her slender waist and the impossibly long length of her legs. And then there was her hair. Wine red, it fell in a soft, sweeping curve to her angled jaw, just begging for a man's touch.

He'd always been a sucker for red hair.

The thought slipped up on him like a craving in the night, easing into his blood in a sudden flash of heat that caught him totally off guard. Stunned, he stiffened, guilt and resentment twisting in his gut. He hadn't looked twice at a woman in the two years since Jan had died, and he didn't plan to start now with someone like Lady Fortune here, who had the world at her feet. He only had to see the amusement glinting in those big brown eyes of hers to know that not only was she aware of the effect she had on men, she expected it. If that was what she was here for, she'd made a wasted trip.

"I'm Doctor Greywolf," he said coolly. "What can I do for you, Ms. Fortune?"

Caught in his intense, dark brown eyes, Rocky hesitated, her smile wavering, her heart suddenly jumping crazily in her breast. Okay, she acknowledged, he was a good-looking man if you liked the stony type. She didn't. She liked a man who laughed easily, at himself and the world. That in no way, shape or form appeared to describe Luke Greywolf.

There was no glint of humor in his nearly black eyes, no smile to relieve the lean, chiseled features of his square face. Tall and broad-shouldered in a white lab coat, his straight, inky-black hair cut conservatively short, he stood like a pine in the forest, his proud Shoshone heritage stamped all over him. It was there in the width of his brow, the granite-hard set of his jaw, his blade of a nose. And it was there in his eyes. Never taking his gaze from her, he watched her like a wary hawk that just dared her to make a wrong move.

It wasn't, Rocky decided, swallowing to ease the sudden dryness in her throat, a look she particularly cared for. Her nerve endings bristling, she reminded herself that she didn't have to like the man to do business with him, then gave him a smile that had, in the past, left more than one unsuspecting male panting. "Please...call me Rocky."

And the battle was begun.

SILHOUETTE *Romance*®

Escape to a place where a kiss is still a kiss...

Feel the breathless connection...

*Fall in love as though it were
the very first time...*

Experience the power of love!

Come to where favorite authors—such as

Diana Palmer, Stella Bagwell, Marie Ferrarella

*and many more—deliver modern fairy tale
romances and genuine emotion,
time after time after time....*

*Silhouette Romance—
from today to forever.*

Silhouette®

Live the possibilities

Harlequin Historicals®
Historical Romantic Adventure!

*From rugged lawmen and
valiant knights to defiant heiresses
and spirited frontierswomen,
Harlequin Historicals will
capture your imagination with
their dramatic scope, passion
and adventure.*

*Harlequin Historicals . . .
they're too good to miss!*

HARLEQUIN®
INTRIGUE®

WE'LL LEAVE YOU BREATHLESS!

If you've been looking for thrilling tales of
contemporary passion and sensuous love stories
with taut, edge-of-the-seat suspense—then
you'll love Harlequin Intrigue!

Every month, you'll meet six new heroes
who are guaranteed to make your spine tingle
and your pulse pound. With them you'll enter
into the exciting world of Harlequin Intrigue—
where your life is on the line
and so is your heart!

THAT'S INTRIGUE—
ROMANTIC SUSPENSE
AT ITS BEST!

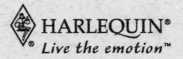

® HARLEQUIN®
Live the emotion™

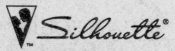